MAGICK RISING

THE MŌSA CHRONICLES

BOOK 2

THE GREAT LANDS OF
TRANSEA

GRIMERG RISE

SANCTUM

THE
VENTANE
WOODS

HOUSE OF
DO'RAMOS

KINGGUARD'S REEF

GALAMEDA
BRIDGE

MENELIK
ATHENAEUM

HOUSE OF
PORTE

MŌSA

IRIS
EXPANSE

THE
SANCTUARY

THE SIRENA SEA

THE KENALI
GARDENS

HOUSE OF
ALACOR

SUNDOM

THE DARK
WILDS

HOUSE OF
AVIREL

AZURE COVE

THE AZURE
MARKET

High Queen Sole Porte

MAGICK
RISING

THE MŌSA CHRONICLES

Book 2

Text and artwork copyright © 2024 Ligia Cushman
All rights reserved. No part of this book may be reproduced in any form or by any electronic or mechanical means, including information storage and retrieval systems, without permission in writing from the publisher, except by reviewers, who may quote brief passages in a review.

Published in the United States.

Visit me on the Web!
www.lnguzman.com

ISBN 979-8-9869869-8-2
Printed in the United States of America

AUTHOR'S NOTE

This book contains elements of ableism, abusive relationships, alcoholism, bullying, bodies/corpses, child abuse, classism, death/dying, death of a parent, death of a sibling, drinking (recreational), emotional abuse, forced captivity, graphic sex, murder, attempted murder, PTSD (panic attacks by the main character), racism (multiple discussions throughout the book), racist microaggressions, serious injury, sexism, sexual abuse, sexual content, slurs, smoking, swearing, torture, violent death of parents, warfare, and weapons.

To all the brown girls who were told they weren't enough, who were made to feel small. This book is dedicated to you. May you discover the power in vulnerability, embrace your fierceness, and never shrink yourself again.

Prince Rivian Alacor

PROLOGUE

"Whatever you're going to ask, the answer is no!" Lygia said to her youngest and most compulsive daughter. Her words were a firm warning to the young princess, leaving no room for negotiation. She knew her child well and knew her tendency to be impulsive, but this was not a decision that could be swayed.

Lola sat on her mother's knee, her eyes filled with fierce determination. "Mami," Lola demanded. "You see, I must go. Darius and the other boys told me I was too small to join them on the fishing trip. But everyone knows I'm a better fisherman than he is." She had to prove to them that she was just as capable as they were. Lygia could see the fire in her daughter's eyes. She knew that Lola was a force to be reckoned with and that she would do whatever it took.

Smiling at her brave little girl, Lygia took the time to rebraid Lola's long tousled braid, a gesture of affection and care. "You are right." Lola's bright eyes opened wide in surprise as she looked up at her mother, "You are a better fisherman than Darius and…he is right. You are still not old enough to join the hunt."

Lola's face fell as she understood the reality of her

situation. Being the youngest of the Porte girls came with its own set of challenges and limitations. Angry tears flowed down her warm brown face as she exclaimed, "It's not fair! I can do what they can do."

Lygia stroked Lola's hair as she spoke, trying to calm her daughter's frustration. "Just because you can do something, doesn't mean it's the right thing to do. Sometimes, the bravest thing to do is to step back and wait for the right moment. You are not ready to join the fishing trip yet, and that is okay. You have time to grow and learn. And when the time comes, you will be able to show Darius and the other boys that you are a better fisherman than they are." Lola sniffled and nodded, understanding the wisdom in her mother's words. She knew that her time would come, but it didn't make it any less frustrating.

Lygia held Lola close as she whispered words of comfort to her. "Oh my darling girl, I fear you are just like your Mami. Being brave and fearless can cost you." Lygia wanted to protect her daughter from the dangers that came with courage. She lifted Lola's tear-soaked chin and looked into her chestnut eyes. "Your time will come sooner than you think," she said. "Why don't we have a piece of marbled moss pie in the kitchen? Let's take a break and enjoy something sweet together." The offer of dessert helped to distract Lola from her disappointment and soothe her anger. They walked to the kitchen, hand in hand, to enjoy a slice of pie before the rest of the family returned home.

As they sat in the kitchen, devouring their slices of pie, Lola couldn't help but think about her future. She had always dreamed of becoming a Misa warrior just like her mother, but she knew that it was a difficult and dangerous path. She had seen her mother's scars, and she knew that the life of a warrior was not one of comfort and ease. But Lola was determined to prove herself, to show that she was just as capable as any of the boys in her village. She would not be held back by her age or her size. She would do whatever it took to become a Misa, even if it meant putting her own life at risk.

ACT I

Princess Lola Porte

CHAPTER 1

Lost memories,
dark secrets

In the shadowy embrace of the winter woods, her voice
pierced the stillness in a frosty breath of revelation.

Lola's voice trembled as she whispered, her palms
clammy with nerves. "I think my name is Lola," she confessed, the sound of her own name sparking a flicker of
recognition within her. With growing excitement, she continued, "Yes, yes, my name is Princess Lola Sirena Porte,
third daughter of Porte House."

The gorgeous man's eyebrows furrowed in disbelief.
"Are you joking, my lady?" he asked, his tone laced with
incredulity.

Confusion etched across her features, Lola shook her
head. "I'm sorry. What do you mean, am I joking?"

His gaze softened as he observed her earnest expression. Closing the gap between them, he reached out to
gently grasp her trembling hands. "Princess, it's just that

you were believed to be dead for over three years. Ever since the Darkness. Where have you been all this time?"

The weight of his words hung heavy in the air, the gravity of her absence casting a shadow over the moment. Lola's heart raced as she struggled to comprehend the magnitude of what he was telling her, the pieces of her shattered memory slowly beginning to fall into place.

"What Darkness?" She wondered.

Had she ever seen a man this tall? She couldn't remember, but it wouldn't surprise her if she hadn't. His captivating eyes were pools of gold and honey. They scared her and, at the same time, let her know she was safe with him. He smelled of chocolate, cinnamon, and pine.

"You're not serious…" he said.

"About what?" Lola asked apprehensively.

"About the *Darkness*? I fear you may not be well."

Not wanting to tell him about her newfound magick, she disclosed her second secret.

She was lost.

"I…I am not sure how I got here," she whispered.

Meanwhile, Lola's attention shifted to her own appearance. She began brushing the dirt from her dark trousers, realizing for the first time the state of her attire. These were not her clothes. The trousers hung loosely on her frame— far from a deliberate fashion choice. Their ill fit only added to her discomfort. To compound matters, a white tunic and a worn-out cape overwhelmed her petite figure.

Kind of him to call her a lady when she looked ghastly. She felt ghastly.

Lola's voice trembled with a mix of confusion and accusation.

"Where are we?"

Her gaze fixated on the tall figure before her, his incredible dimples captivating her attention. With a hint of apprehension, she raised her hand, its emerald glow casting an otherworldly hue, as if it possessed an energy of its own. She pointed directly at him.

"Did you have something to do with this?"

Her suspicion-laced words left them with a lingering tension in the air.

"You are in the Ventane Woods, Princess Lola. And no, I did not."

Bewildered and concerned, he said, "My name is Kingsley Do'Ramos. But you can call me King. All my friends do."

"Friends? We just met; how can we be friends?" she asked as he stared at her full lips.

"Of course we are friends? My dear snowdrop, I just saved you from being eaten alive by the bears in these woods. So I can assure you I am no stranger. Besides, I believe a beautiful woman should flirt with a King at least once in their lifetime, don't you think?" he asked with an adorable, crooked smile.

King couldn't understand why he was flirting with her. She was distressed, but he couldn't resist.

Her copper skin was like a windfall autumn leaf. Her green eyes smoldered and a queenly figure showcased her curly hair as it plunged over her shoulders in waves of midnight black. Her pouty lips, fuck…they looked soft as suede. But it was her smile that electrified him.

CHAPTER 2

The veil lifted

"What did you mean about me being dead? I'm standing right here," Lola said to King. She looked down at herself and, for the first time, noticed the attire that fell over her small physique: incredibly loose-fit black trousers covered in mud, a dusty white tunic, and an old cape. One thing was certain; these were not her clothes.

"Where are we?" she asked fearfully.

"You are in the Ventane Woods, Princess Lola."

She began recognizing it from her many trips with her family. How had she gotten here?

She remembered the pink fireflies glowing at their campsite as a child. The memories flooded in, seizing her breath and taking her back to laughing out loud with her older sisters, Sole and Luna, and their mother braiding her hair for hours while Lola squirmed. "You will love them when they are done," her mother would tell her. She was always right. Here in this forest is where she learned to fish with her father, King Axel. "You will thank me one day; this is a survival skill you may need in the future," he would tell her. When she was young, she never understood why the princess of Mōsa would need survival skills, but everything changed in the Ventane Woods. This was her favorite place in Transea. Now, it would be the place of her rebirth.

As if pulled out of a trance, Lola looked up into the amber eyes of the stranger and said with flashing eyes, "Where are they?"

"Whom do you speak of, Princess Lola?" King whispered.

"My family," she said, her voice cracking from lack of use. "Where are they? They must be worried. I must get to Mōsa at once."

"Princess Lola, please sit and I will do my best to answer all of your questions. I can't very well have my very first tesoro fainting on me." Guiding Lola to a large fallen oak tree, King saw how she appeared regal. *A queen on her throne*, he thought. *Holy mother, she is fucking beautiful.* Her dark glowing skin and raven coils fell like the waves of the Sirena sea upon her shoulders. But it was her vivid emerald eyes, their lashes gently kissing her cheeks with every blink, that enamored him. *Concentrate*, he thought. *She needs help, not an asshole.*

"Princess," he whispered as he held her hand. "Five years ago, the Darkness consumed all of Mōsa and killed many of your people, many of mine. Your parents, King and Queen Porte, and your sister Luna are gone. Many of the Misa warriors were consumed by the Darkness. It left only twelve alive in its wake.

She heard what he said, but she knew he was wrong.

"You must be mistaken. The Misa are the strongest, bravest regiment in all of Transea. You have been given misinformation, sir."

"Forgive me princess," he whispered, eyes cast down.

"You are wrong!"

"They are all gone."

"What do you mean, they are all gone?! I must get there at once. I must see for myself." But before she could take one step toward Mōsa, Lola's weakness overtook her and she stumbled back onto the log.

She wasn't prepared. She didn't even say goodbye. "What about the plans we all made?" she whispered to herself as her breathing became difficult. Her heart began to beat louder and louder. Then, a ringing in her ears took over. Can Kingsley hear this? she pondered as she covered her ears with her small hands. Looking around to flee, she heard—

"Princess Lola, I will not leave you. I will help you sort all of this out. Please allow me to take you to our family cottage."

"No. I must get to Mōsa at once!"

Kingsley knelt beside her. "Let me take you to our cottage further down the path." With amber eyes flashing and a crooked smile, he said, "My mother makes the best rabbit stew you'll ever have, and you look like you need a good meal and some rest. "

"I must get home."

"The moonrise is just an hour or so away and unfortunately, traveling after moonrise has become too dangerous. Please let me help you, Lola."

Startled at the use of her informal name, Lola said, "Just one night. Then, I will be off to Mōsa in the morn."

"Agreed," he said, his sparkling eyes connecting with hers. The fireflies in Lola's belly fluttered when his golden gaze landed on her.

Standing, he held out his hands to help the tiny but mighty princess to safety. "Come." She began to walk when she abruptly stopped. "Wait! Wait! You said Luna was gone. Where is Sole?"

Kingsley, smiling brightly, said, "I will tell you everything over Ma's rabbit stew, Tesoro."

"No! You will tell me now!" Her eyes flashed, but King didn't budge. Lola's shoulders sagged.

"Fine, I will go with you, but first you must tell me why you keep calling me Tesoro. What does it mean?"

"Tesoro means 'my treasure' in my mother's native tongue. I found you fair and square, and that makes you Tesoro. Now let's go. Ma's rabbit stew is waiting."

***

"This isn't a cottage. It's a fucking castle," Lola proclaimed. Seven skinny, square towers surround the castle in a near-perfect circle connected by enormous, vast walls of blue stone, which was only found in the Ventane Woods and the Grimerg Rise Keep. Simple windows scattered thinly across the borders in an asymmetric design and enormous crenelations perched atop the towers for archers and artillery. Lola had never seen the Ventane Woods look so royal.

"Did you say your last name was Do'Ramos? You're from the House of Do'Ramos?" Lola inquired.

"Well, I thought you'd never ask," King said with a hint of arrogance and a devilishly crooked smile. My apologies, Princess Lola, I may not have been forthcoming with—"

"Your Highness," A handsome guard dressed in royal blue interrupted. "Your father has been looking for you."

"Your Highness?" Lola repeated.

"Thank you, Thad. I am sure he has been."

Turning to face her, he bowed. Then, graciously kissing her right hand, the prince smiled. "I am Kingsley Do'Ramos. The second-born son of the Aurora court, Earl of Swords, last of his name, and Governor of War of the Ventane Woods. But like I said, my friends call me King," he finished with a charming wink that pissed Lola off.

Standing before a vast gate built at the shore of the rose-colored Sirena Sea, the giant metal doors the handsome guard stood in front of appeared to be the only entrance to the castle. Four enormous towers sat on the edge of the seashore. Then, Lola heard the sudden creak of the gate. They slowly swung open to reveal a tall beauty with a fresh, cheerful face and chestnut hair tight in a high ponytail. First, the girl's narrow hazel eyes watched rapidly over Lola's face. Then, they softened over her cheekbones.

Arms crossed, she said, "Well, brother, you are sure of a long discord with father. But, unfortunately, it appears that you chose hunting again over the council meeting."

"Fuck!"

"Language!" shouted Lola and the girl in unison.

"I think I might like this one," Kingsley's sister whispered to him as she pushed past to greet the newcomer.

She rushed a curtsey. "I am Princess Sirena, his favorite sister."

"You're my only sister."

"Oh, shut up!" she said, hitting her brother in the arm. "Now, will you not introduce us, brother?"

Sighing in defeat, King began, "Princess Sirena, please meet Princess Lola Sirena Porte of Mōsa, the Last daughter of King Axel and Queen Lygia." Slowly, Sirena's eyebrows raised and her mouth hung open. "Shut your mouth, sister, for fear a firefly may get caught in it," Kingsley said as he smiled at his sister.

Closing the distance between them, Sirena approached Lola softly. "Welcome back to the land of the living, Princess. I am truly sorry for losing your people and those you loved. Where have…" She stopped suddenly as an equally beautiful woman approached them. If Lola didn't know better, she would think Sirena and this woman were sisters. Upon the woman's regal entrance, she kissed Kingsley on the cheek and he replied, "Hello, Mother."

Mother? Lola thought.

"Your father has been looking for you…" The Queen suddenly stopped and stared at Lola as if seeing a ghost. Then, she grabbed her hands and said, "Lola, daughter of my dearest friend Lygia, you are welcome here." Tearfully, the Queen embraced Lola as she whispered in her ear, "We thought you were all lost forever." She gently touched Lola's chin. "My name is Alina Do'Ramos, and your mother was my best friend. I swore to her that should evil fall on Mōsa, we would care for you as our own."

Lola at first refused to cry, but the tears came anyway, and she allowed the Queen to embrace her as a mother would. Her tears rushed over her in waves of despair. Wrapping her arm around Lola, Queen Alina demanded that her son Avenn's old room be set up for her next to Kingsley and Selina's quarters. "Make sure a warm bath is ready for her. And Sirena, please grab her one of your gowns."

"I will get one right away," Sirena said excitedly as she ran off.

"I will heat our rabbit stew and get you nice and fed. Then you can tell us all about your ordeal." Lola turned to face Kingsley. Although she had just met him, she feared not being by his side. Breaking the distance between them, he took her hands in his and said, " I will see you this evening. Ma and Sirena will take good care of you." Lola didn't know what she felt. All she knew is she needed food and rest before tomorrow, when she would head home. Thad, the handsome guard, led Lola away to escort her to her quarters.

Turning to face her son, Alina noticed he didn't take his gaze off Lola. Alina whispered, "She is as lovely as her mother. As brave, too. Don't worry about her, son. She is just going to freshen up. I'm sure she will grace you with her presence at supper. "

"Mother, I…I mean, I don't…she…."

"Please stop before you hurt yourself," the Queen said with a smirk. "Your father awaits you in the study. He is in a foul mood, and I am sure you can guess why. Maybe your discovery of the Princess of Mōsa will lighten his mood. Now go!"

Kingsley didn't want to enter the study. Since his brother's death, he and his father had been at odds. Never before had a first son died before a second son. But here they were. Kingsley was never meant to be King. He'd had a plan. He would complete his time in the Sanctum, marry the girl of his dreams, Mya, and be the war governor for his brother Jaden. The Darkness changed all of that.

He'd never forget the day his parents summoned him from the Sanctum to break the news. He knew it was serious the moment he realized his father King Heath had come to accompany him back home.

CHAPTER 3

Solitude and magick

Lola relishes the sight of the inviting, copper tub brimming with steaming hot water.

It is a true blessing, a sanctuary for her weary body. With a sense of gratitude, she gracefully slides into the comforting embrace of the tub, escaping the confines of those clothes that clung to her skin like a layer of filth. The water envelopes her, seeping into every pore, helping her cleanse herself of the grime and weariness that plagues her.

Cleansing herself of this day.

She lets out a long sigh and closes her eyes. The water is enveloping her body, soothing her tense muscles and nearly calming her racing thoughts. She was grateful for the bath's privacy; it is the first chance she's had to be truly alone.

Nearly, though, is her mind distracted from the weight of her worries. The longer she sits in silence, the longer she continues to breathe, the more her thoughts keep drifting to her missing sister. Her family.

Lola isn't just mourning and feeling doleful.

The fear that grips her heart is almost unbearable. She feels tears welling up in her eyes, but she quickly submerges her face in the water to hide them.

Emerging from the water's warm embrace, Lola takes a deep breath as it cascades down her body. The scents of the milk and bath oils, with juniper berries, lilac, and mugwort, are helping her relax, physically unwind. It feels like the warmth is seeping into her bones, and yet she can't let go.

She can't afford to let her guard down; she's allowed herself this moment of respite. Now she has to think. Plan. She tries to gather herself, to steel her resolve for the challenges that lay ahead.

You're a warrior. So, what are you going to do?

Leaving first thing in the morning would be best as she hates goodbyes. If she is quick and clever about it, she can be gone before the royal family awakens at sunrise.

She needs to get to Mōsa; how exactly will she do that?

She'll need a horse and then a ship to cross the Sirena Sea. And if she leaves inconspicuously, that's a journey she'll be making alone, no help whatsoever. If her math is right, it will take at least five moonrises to make it to Mōsa during the solstice.

Kingsley had offered to join her, before he told her he

was a Prince. He probably didn't mean it...

Even if he does mean it, is he really going to be able to just up and leave his kingdom? Helping another royal is certainly noble, but he has responsibilities of his own. Foreign affairs come second to internal ones, even in a time of crisis. But...

Does Kingsley really want to accompany her?

Something is enthralling about him. Perhaps it's his appearance. Or, simply his ability to be a confident lion at one moment, then a shy, lovable dog at the next. She'd been agitated with some of his behavior due to exhaustion and stress. Give him a fair assessment, Lola.

Kingsley felt safe. Why is she trying so hard to deny this?

He had found her and brought her all this way. She won't forget his heart, even if childish behavior from men generally got under her skin.

That is something to take into account, though. Kingsley is a man. They are both royals, but there are certain rules. Expectations. Lola prefers to do things on her own. If the Prince of Kingsguard Reef is guiding her, it will be a challenge to ignore him, especially when she needs his help.

Her needing him will surely make Kingsley happy.

And, he may be that confident man he was back in the Ventane Woods, talking and walking beside her all the way to Mōsa. How annoying...

Lola lets out a long breath again, still attempting to rest.

The water is still hot. Should she need to add more, the maid had kindly readied a pot of water hanging in the small fireplace in the corner of the room. It'll probably start boiling soon. That is something to focus on, as well as adding a few more drops of oil to soothe her senses.

But her mind wanders again, pondering new scenarios and asking other questions. Questions like, what had happened to her over the last three years?

Where was she and why can't she remember it?

A gentle knock on the door startles her, pulling her out of the pit of thought.

Queen Alina enters after Lola calls her in. In her hands is a silk azure gown. She gives Lola privacy as she steps out of the bath, letting her drape a towel over her body and hair before handing her the dress.

As the queen reaches for the clothes, Sirena kindly offers, "I wanted you to have something fresh to wear for the dinner this moonrise. I hope you don't mind if we wash your clothes for you?" Her smile is warm and gentle.

But suddenly, Lola gasps, surprising both of them. "No!" she exclaims, pulling the clothes away from the queen's grasp.

"Forgive my haste," Alina says quietly. The queen steps back as Lola holds her soiled clothes close to her chest. "I know it's strange," Lola begins, taking a deep breath. "But they hold the secrets as to what happened to me. I can't

31

say why exactly, but my body has felt unsafe to inhabit ever since I woke up in the Ventane woods."

Lola picks the dirty raggy tunic and pants off the settee, cradling them in her hands.

"I experienced discomfort, loss and the Holy Mother knows what else in these threads. It will take time to remember what happened. This is the only evidence I have of all this time I've lost."

Alina gently holds Lola's hands and assures her she understands.

"Then it's settled. We will not wash them until you ask us to."

"Thank you."

Once the silk dress is slipped on, Lola looks at herself in the mirror. She can't believe her eyes. The azure gown's satin-like silhouette flaunts a plunging v-neckline, with clear crystals outlining the heart-shaped bust. She feels her breasts bulging out of the frock, but this is not a new problem for Lola. Although the youngest of three sisters, Lola is the most shapely, resembling her mother's figure. The sheath skirt opens with a slit that flows into a train. As horrid as she'd felt inside, she has a moment now to feel beautiful in this lavish gown.

To feel like a princess again.

Feeling beautiful has always come easy to Lola. Since she could remember, everyone told her how much she resembled her mother. She had puffy, pouting lips that were blossom soft. The resemblance was uncanny, her deep mahogany skin, short, muscular limbs, round face, and raven-coiled long locks cascading to her waist.

Staring at herself now in this foreign place, her eyes, once chestnut brown, no longer reflect her mother.

The tinge of green is new. They're her eyes, but they've transformed.

Dressed in Sirena's gown, Lola sits on the settee. The tall, blonde chambermaid who drew her bath returns, softly combing and drying her hair, then lightly powdering it with rose-petal powder and fashioning it into a dream.

Her long tresses are now in one large braid around her head and forming the shape of a crown. Another gentle reminder that she is still the Princess of Mōsa and would be recognized by the House of Do'Ramos of Kingsguard. The longer she spends gazing at her reflection in the mirror, the more the expression slips on her chestnut face.

The beautiful dress and hair can't mask the despair.

Realizing Lola's fragile state, Alina refuses to leave her side. She instructs the chambermaid on what will work best for moisturizing her skin, guaranteeing that Lola has the best of care.

The moment the maid exits through the ornate doors, Lola takes advantage of her alone time with the Queen.

"Can you tell me what happened?"

The corners of Alina's kind, emerald eyes crinkle. She sits beside Lola on the settee, wrapping an arm around her.

"It was spring in Mōsa and a perfect evening for your sister Sole's mating ceremony."

"Were you there?"

"Yes, child."

"Then why don't I remember you?"

"Like many painful memories, you have begun to unpack those, and that will come soon. I hope we can carefully help you along the way."

She sighs, thinking back.

"Your sister was a sight to behold. As Sole entered the Expanse the bioluminescent waters glowed a beautiful teal adding to the beauty and romance of that night. She looked absolutely majestic. She looked like a fairy. Every-one had remarked they'd only seen her in glamorous gowns or golden body paint on special occasions."

The Queen swallows and brushes a spiral lock of hair from Lola's face. She follows this with a small, somber smile.

"Typically, Sole wore her hair in a tight bun, never revealing its true length. Paired with her spectacles, many villagers didn't understand what Nasir saw in her. At this moment, the idea of a girl who would rather read a book beach side while the other children swam was gone."

Alina's laugh warms Lola down to her bones.

"That's probably why she never learned to swim. On this moonrise, before them stood the woman Nasir always saw; for him, she was forever beautiful. And we all witnessed it that night."

"I remember pieces of that evening," Lola says, starting to envision it all. "Lola's face falls, the sparkle from her eyes fades and is replaced with a mist of tears. She isn't sure if she wants to know the truth.

"When did it all go wrong?"

"King Heath, our son Avenn, and Sirena made the decision to sail back to Kingsguard. We had an important Kingsguard Reef high council meeting scheduled in six moonrises, so we couldn't stay for all the festivities. Additionally, we were eagerly anticipating Kingsley's return from the Sanctum and didn't want to miss his arrival, as he had been away for a considerable amount of time."

"The Sanctum?" Lola asks hesitantly. She knows it is something she should remember. But it's foggy.

"Yes. The Sanctum is where all second-born children are sent on their seventh birthday to be trained in battle, master a skill, and bend the knee to their first born sibling. All second-borns remain there for seven cycles returning home on their 14th year."

"It sounds like a harsh place."

Whispering, Alina shares, "I never wanted to send my boy there. But that is a story for another time."

She draws in a soothing breath.

"Now, where were we…ah yes. When morning broke, that is when we first heard the screams. Making our way through Kingsguard and the Ventane Woods, that's when we saw them. Many fell ill. Many more perished."

Her bottom lip quivers.

"We returned home to learn that our Avenn had been consumed by the Darkness while he slept." Her tears fell fast as Lola reached for Alina's hands, saying, "You don't have to tell me more."

"Yes, I do," she whispers firmly. "At that moment, I knew two things. One, our son Avenn was gone. And, his light now shines in our garden at every moonrise."

Lola remembers that Western tradition tells the story of how fireflies may be sacred at times, as they carry the spirits of loved ones who have passed on to be with the Holy Mother.

"King Heath and I made haste to the Sanctum and brought Kingsley home. I fear he may never forgive us for the burden of the crown he must now carry."

Lola thinks of her sister Sole. Did she feel the same about being the heir to her parent's throne, even though she was a second-born daughter who was not groomed for a crown?

She was groomed for war. Lola promises herself at this very moment that she'll make her way back to her eldest sister. Sole will need help reclaiming Mōsa, returning it to the land it once was.

"Do you know what happened in Mōsa? What happened to my parents?"

With solemn eyes Alina slowly begins.

"After word got out about the many dead in Mōsa, we learned that your sister had found her mate, Nasir, dead on their mating night. Princess Sole fell ill shortly after discovering his remains. Many said her grief allowed the Darkness to consume her."

Lola and Alina are both in tears now. Alina says she is so sorry, but it is necessary to get everything out.

"Your father's next in command, Masile, made the decision to isolate Mōsa from the rest of Transea. Maisle had learned that Sundom was on a search for a cure, and he asked for their aid. Sundom refused due to the hatred King Aiden still held towards your father."

Lola struggles to contain the rage surging within her magick. The green glimmers start to intensify, and the revelation about Sundom's lack of compassion and preference for vengeance in such a critical time is incredibly painful to bear.

"Things got worse when both you and your sister Luna fell ill and were consumed by the Darkness. Then the Misa..." She can't bring herself to finish her sentence.

With the kindest expression she can muster, Queen Alina

continues, "But your sister Sole slept for many moons until one day her eyes flickered open. Your father had decreed that the eldest living daughter at the time of his death would become Queen. So, the moment your sister Luna passed away, Sole became his successor."

The memories of her father's warm smile brought tears to her eyes. Her Papi, as she affectionately called him, was a brave man with the heart of a lion behind his gentle eyes. How could someone so strong be taken away so suddenly?

"After that, we learned that Nisa refused to leave Sole's side. Many nights, she was dragged out of your parents' room, where Sole lay. Despite trying to shield her from the plague, it was unsuccessful. Poor girl. She insisted on caring for your sister."

Caressing Lola's cheek, Queen Alina whispers, "When you and Luna succumbed to the Darkness, news spread throughout the land that Sole was the only living daughter of Mōsa."

Lola's tears began to cascade down her cheeks like waves, threatening to wash away the delicate pink powder that the chambermaid had carefully applied to her face. The gravity of it all makes her feel like her heart is collapsing. Finding it hard to breathe, she reaches for Alina, who holds her as tight as she needs to ground herself.

"But Sole survived, and she awoke…with magick," Alina says, embracing Lola again.

"A healing magick, they say. That very magick saved your people, and many of us."

"Sole has what?" Lola asks, wiping the tears from her face.

"Sole has magick."

CHAPTER 4

Now our enemies
find rest

Entering the great hall with Queen Alina, Lola was taken aback by the sheer size of what Kingsley had referred to as a cottage. Huge braziers hung from each of the sixteen obsidian columns in the immense hall, their light wrapping the aisle in a warm radiance and illuminating illustrations of battles on the oblique ceiling. Stone effigies that looked down upon the slate floor reminded Lola of tales her father told her of the knights of Kingsguard Reef.

Generations ago, the knights of Kingsguard stood 170,000 strong Her father told her that when they marched in unison, their ferocity drowned out all other sounds. Each knight possessed shifter magick. The exodus west is when magick began to dissipate, and with every generation, grew rarer and rarer until finally, there were no more shifters left.

Stepping onto the azure rug with her black velvet heels, Lola made her way down the center aisle leading to the ostentatious dining table. Between each banner hung lit torches that illuminated the statues of mighty Kingsguard Knights below them.

Grand, washed glass windows framed by azure velvet drapes allowed just enough golden sunlight to make the room appear warm and inviting. Lola had never seen anything so grand and gaudy in Mōsa.

Overwhelmed by the pennant banners with ornate tapestries hanging from the walls, Lola was saddened to see how privilege, possession, and power had consumed the once brave people of Kingsguard Reef.

A radiant table of jade lay before a giant painting of the previous ruler. Kingsley's grandfather, perhaps?

Sirena noticed them enter the great hall first and shouted, "Lola, come sit by me!" Looking towards the doors, the two men rose to their feet.

Kingsley looked exquisite in his navy dinner coat and white tunic, revealing the muscles hiding underneath. Clean shaven and eyes bright, his crooked smile made Lola's body tighten.

Kingsley's attention shifted from his conversation with his father and cousins Bishop and Thad. His cock hardened upon seeing Lola.

He had never seen that dress look the same on his sister. The slit of it went up to Lola's thigh, exposing flashes of the smooth skin of her short, toned legs every time her black heels hit the marble floor. A low 'fuuuck' fell from his lips as he watched her make her way towards him.

"Well, are you going to just stand there, son?" the king whispered as a smile reached his lips. Kingsley hadn't noticed her perfect skin before, but something made it glow like the sunset in the Ventane Woods. There was no mistaking it; the women of Mōsa were a beautiful sight to behold. Her lips were blush red and her braids fell low down her toned back. Along with the rest of the room, Kingsley lost his fucking breath. His cousins Thad and Bishop were silent and started moving in her direction, but King got there first, escorting Lola to the enormous jade table.

Closing the distance between them, Kingsley offered her his arm; he escorted Lola to her seat, but not before whispering warm words, his eyes smiling. "Hey Lola."

"Hello, Prince. When will you address me by my formal name?" she said.

He started to say something semi charming when Bishop cleared his throat, sporting a look on his face that was halfway between a sneer and a grimace. He raised a hand to Lola saying, "Holy mother, do all the women on your island dress so inappropriately?" Jabbing his brother on his elbow, Thad said, "Remind me to visit Mōsa more often."

"Inappropriate? Because I walk confidently or because I'm unashamed of what the Holy Mother has given me?" Lola retorted. She wasn't about to let this dolt lecture her on what constituted modesty. "If that's the case, then yes, the women in Mōsa dress inappropriately. If we have something worth showing, we don't hide behind our clothes."

Lola gave Bishop a once-over, her eyes landing just below his waist. Then she shrugged.

"Others do."

Sirena, who was taking a sip of wine, practically lost it all through her nose. After composing herself, she gave Lola a supportive nod.

"I like her, Bishop," she blurted out.

Jabbing his brother Bishop with his elbow, Thad remarked, "Brother, remind me to visit Mōsa more often." That comment had Lola wanting to smile. But the feeling faded. Knowing what she knew now, what Mōsa would there be for him to visit?

The gentle touch of King's hand on her lower back caught Lola unaware. She needed to steady herself before her knees buckled under his gaze.

Upon reaching her seat, Lola was greeted by a smiling King Heath, Sirena, and Thad. Bishop's grimace never left her. She wouldn't disrespect the Do'Ramos family by body-slamming one of their kinsmen onto the table, but she would certainly take the time later to find out what the fuck his problem was.

Kingsley kindly pulled her chair back and Lola's eyes glossed over the wolf chiseled on the backside of the wood which matched one carved into the center of the table: a symbol of their family crest.

King Heath's silvery, shoulder-length hair was pulled back to reveal a radiant face with shining golden eyes that watched wearily over Lola, acknowledging her pain. A blade had left a mark that stretched from just under his left eyebrow, ran across his nose, and ended on his right cheekbone, leaving a compelling memory of a battle—against the Sunguards of Sundom, perhaps. Lola made a note to ask Kingsley about the scar once they were alone.

Queen Lygia had often spoken of King Heath as a true adventurer and mighty warrior whose enormous stature intimidated others, despite his kind eyes. Under different circumstances, Lola would love to ask the king about his many battles. Although she was of the Misa warriors—the most feared female regiment in the Western Isles—she had not seen war like King Heath had.

"Welcome, Princess Lola. We are honored to have you as our guest for as long as you like."

"Thank you for your kindness, Your Highness," Lola said as she curtsied before sitting.

"Please, in this room, call me as your mother did: Heath."

"Th…thank you, Heath."

Sitting beside Sirena felt inviting, but Lola was also directly across from Kingsley, and his amber eyes told her everything she needed to know—that she could not be alone with the polished prince of Kingsguard Reef. He was handsome enough, but equally as arrogant. She had many suitors in Mōsa, and although she found several of them quite handsome, none of them were a match for her in combat. Being the only princess in four generations allowed to train with the Misa was not something Lola took for granted.

Men like Kingsley were good for a romp, but she couldn't have that distraction right now. For the first time in her life, she needed to devise a plan on her own, and that plan did not include him. Men like Kingsley didn't really have substance; they couldn't be trusted.

Lola had only met one man she could truly trust, and that was her father. Sitting with Kingsley and King Heath, she wondered if maybe they did have what it took for her to trust them like she had her father. A sense of deep sadness took hold, transporting her to the days before the Darkness with her family. Who had attended the vigil for her parents when the Darkness took them? Had the Do'Ramoses? Had they seen the Darkness firsthand?

Lola wondered how she could sit there, laughing and drinking mango wine, knowing that her parent's deaths had been nothing short of brutal? And how could these people sit here beside her telling jokes, drinking, and dining, right after breaking the news that her family lay cold in the ground? It's almost as if the Darkness had never touched

Kingsguard Reef. But Lola would not allow tonight to be just another dinner. Tomorrow, she would be gone, so that only left her tonight to get the answers she needed about what had happened over the past three years.

Taking one last big gulp of mango wine, she asked the one question no one wanted to answer.

"Tell me about Mōsa."

The silence in the room was deafening as the entire table stopped drinking and eating. It was Kingsley who answered her first. "Much has happened in Mōsa since you...since you've been gone. You see—"

"Lola, what would you like to know?" interrupted King Heath.

"I already know many of those I loved are gone." Lola's voice was cracked and raw. Queen Alina gently reached to still Lola's shaking hands and took over for her. "I have explained to Lola that Luna is gone, that she was the last one to be infected, and that from what we heard, her death was swift. That King Axel and Queen Lygia were consumed early, and that Princess Sole..." She paused as if unsure how to continue.

"How can Sole have magick?" Lola broke the silence. "How is it possible?" Magick did not exist prior to the Darkness. It had been generations since anyone had possessed such a gift. So why Sole? Why now?

"We still aren't sure how she has magick," the king

answered. "But we know that her power healed many that were close to perishing from the Darkness. Your people fought valiantly and"—he locked eyes with Lola—"many of our scouts say that the hardest struggle was seeing the Misa warriors fall. We aided as many as possible, as did the Sanctum, and at times even Sundom aided as well, but to no avail—the Darkness ravaged everything in its wake until Sole woke up. None saved as many as she did, but even her magick wasn't enough to rid Mōsa of the Darkness."

Lola swallowed a lump in her throat at the tender memory of the Misa warriors and of her home. She forced the heartache aside and scanned over what King Heath had said.

"Sundom provided aid?"

"Yes," Heath confirmed. "And when Sole awoke, High King A'Dien of Sundom called her to court."

Lola reminisced about her mother, Queen Lygia, and her elite female warriors, the Misa, trained to perfection in the Kingdom of Mōsa. Desperate to join them, Lola convinced her mother to train her at age twelve. Despite brutal training, Lola excelled, seeing it as her path to escape domestic life. Meanwhile, her sister Sole found love with Nasir, but tragedy struck when he succumbed to the Darkness, a plague that ravaged their family. Lola later discovered that Sole had awakened to magick, offering hope amidst the despair.

"Sole's in Sundom?!"

Fear gripped Lola, tying her stomach into a million knots as the thought of Sundom's oppression washed over any aid they had attempted to provide to Mōsa. Standing to her feet, she sputtered, "How could she be in Sundom? I must go to her at once. She is in grave danger."

King Axel and Queen Lygia always warned their daughters never to enter Sundom unprotected. "Sundonians are not to be trusted," her father would say. "The promises made by a Sundonian only ever lead to death."

"Princess, please sit down," Kingsley whispered softly as he touched her shoulder and startled Lola, who hadn't noticed him get up. As she returned to her seat, King whispered, taking a deep breath, "Your eyes were about to flash. You must be calm, or they will know about your magick."

She sat still, but she wasn't listening to him. All she knew was that she had to do everything possible to find her sister and protect her.

***

Kingsley

Seeing her emerald eyes flicker with magick, Kingsley knew he would have to do something to calm her before his father realized she was a mage. Easing her tensions, Kingsley assured her that Sole was not alone.

"She has five Misa Warriors accompanying her."

Thanks to the Holy Mother, his family had not yet noticed the shimmer of magick in Lola's eyes, but he feared her secret would be revealed this very night. The Sanctum had sent an edict declaring themselves the Holy Mother's army against magick. If they got word that she was a mage, no one—not even Kingsley himself—could keep them from coming for Lola. If they did, he feared they would never see her again. He would do everything he could to protect her.

He couldn't tell her the rumors that the Sanctum had been making its way to Sole when they learned of her magick, but that the King of Sundom had sent for her just in time. Kingsley didn't know why he worried so much about Lola's safety, but he did.

Eyes darting back between his mother and father, he wondered when they would tell her the rest. How would they tell her? Taking a sip of his honey wine with his hands steady, he continued,

"Princess, there is—"

"That is enough for tonight, son; I am sure Lola needs rest," his father said with a forced smile. "We can resume this in the morning."

"Father, I think—"

"Enough, son," the king said, more gently this time.

"Do you ride?" Sirena turned to Lola as she abruptly changed the subject.

Lola scrunched her brows in confusion. "Do I ride?"

"Yes. Do you ride horses?"

"I do," she replied sheepishly. Readjusting to conversations about everyday happenings would take time. She wanted to actually scream. She wanted to know more about her people and her sister.

"Yes. I do ride."

"I hope you are better than Kingsley; he always boasts about what a great horseman he is and—"

"I do not!" he interrupted.

"You do!" replied Sirena and Queen Alina in unison.

The room erupted in laughter at Kingsley's expense. Then he did that thing Lola loved to hate; he looked at her with that crooked smile.

"Then that settles it! King and I will take you riding first thing tomorrow. Won't we, King?"

"Of course, if the princess likes to ride, we can take her. What do you say, Princess? I promise I won't ride too far ahead."

Although the Misa preferred to walk barefoot to battle, every war maiden learned to ride horses in varying positions. Apparently, King didn't know that. Lola was both an agile fighter and rider. She couldn't wait for Kingsley to see her in action.

"I'd love to go riding before I make my way back to Mōsa," Lola said a little louder than she intended.

The laughter ceased around the ornate table. Then,

breaking the deafening silence, Sirena nervously said, "We'd hope you would rest some more with us before returning to Mōsa."

Heath continued, "Princess, I understand your eagerness to return, but Transea has changed since you have been away."

Lola steadied her gaze, intent on getting her answers. "How has it changed?"

Heath sighed, and then continued flat and steady, "We hear things in the East have been tumultuous at best. Since the death of King A'Dien, his son King Rill Alacor has inherited the throne."

"King A'Dien is dead? How? When? That is good news, right?" How could she not be thrilled to learn that her father's ruthless enemy had been struck down? Over the last four generations, Transea was divided into the Eastern and Western hemispheres. The eastern hemisphere was home to Sundom: a dry desert scorched by two suns during the day and cursed with bitter cold at moonrise. The people were elves with pointy ears, beautiful bright blue-gray eyes, and sunkissed copper skin. Just north of the Dark Wilds, Sundom was covered by crystallized sand as far as the eye could see, save for a scattering of rocky beaches and jagged mountains. It was the most barren land in Transea. The people of Sundom lived off weaponsmithing, trade, and the spoils of war. Sundom's blades of Alacor could cut a rock in half in one slice. They were vengeful, cold-hearted people whose only reputation came from weaponsmithing, rape, colonization, and war.

Breaking Lola's thoughts, King Heath continued. "Lola, there is something we must tell you." The tone of his voice told her it wasn't good news. "King A'dien's death was no accident." He paused to look at his son. "Our informants tell us that Nasir killed him."

Lola felt no sadness for the tyrant's king's untimely demise, but she was confused. Nasir was peaceful, generous and kind.

"Nasir? What do you mean? You told me he was taken by the Darkness." Lola went numb with shock, the weight of the past three years and all that had occurred finally setting in. Heath and Alina's voices echoed in the grand hall as they explained how Nasir had woken up from the Darkness—how he'd changed. He, too, possessed magick. But rather than use his magick to heal, like Sole, he'd chosen to kill.

"Princess, when the Darkness swept across our land, it changed those it infected."

Lola nods, haunting fragments of memories now returning.

He was responsible for the deaths of many, including King A'dien of Sundom and ultimately, the death of his twin sister, Nisa Asha.

Hot tears streamed down Lola's face as Heath spoke. "He has stolen part of the Sungard regimen of Sundom and he's journeying to Mōsa to claim the throne."

This was too much for Lola to take. Her head was spinning, and her palms were sweaty. She had woken up to a nightmare. How could Nasir, of all people, harbor such violence? Nasir was her sister's mate and best friend. The Nasir Lola knew would never do anything to harm Sole or Nisa. How could he have killed his sister? They were more than just close. "This can't be true!" she shouted to the King, refusing to believe such ludicrous claims. But deep down, she knew they had no reason to lie to her.

The King explained what Queen Alina had shared with her in her rooms and then told her how, during Sole's journey on the Radiant, she and Rivian, the Second-Born Prince of Sundom, fell in love. She learned of her sister's capture and how Nasir had been in Sundom when they arrived, seemingly himself. "And then one night, Nasir revealed his true intentions. He wanted Sole…"

"Of course he did, he's her fated mate," Lola said, voice clipped and raw. "Sole could never give up Nasir for a Sundonian."

Sirena took over for her father as she said, "I wish I could tell you that he was the same, but he changed."

"Aren't we all changed after the Darkness?" Lola asked no one in particular. "I refuse to believe he turned into a monster. How could the very same gray eyes that always looked upon her with love be the same eyes that killed Nisa?"

Silence enveloped the table as her question was met without an answer. What explanation was there?

"Our informants say he journeys west to claim the Western Isles as his own," Kingsley told her. "He is expected to arrive here in the next twenty days." His tone affirmed that order could prevail over this chaos. King Heath leaned forward. "We also received word that Sole is making her way here to stop him. She is now allied with Sundom, uniting with one focus: to kill Nasir Asha and secure the Western Isles," the king noted, conviction and anger creeping into his voice.

It was not a secret that Sudom and Mōsa were enemies. Mōsians originated from Sundom, but when the then King of Sundom, King A'Dun, attempted to assassinate Lola's grandfather, a civil war broke out, forcing her people to find refuge in Mōsa. Since the division, Mōsa grew to be a mighty force in commerce. Selling their fine silks, water, and beautiful bioluminescent gems made them an economic force to be reckoned with. As the Mōsian people prospered, other Sundonians made their way to Mōsa, seeking asylum from a tyrannical regime. That was before the Darkness.

"It is important you understand why we must protect you. King Rill crowned your sister the Queen of the Western

Isles. Many here see Queen Sole as a traitor for joining forces with Sundom and will stop at nothing to overthrow or even kill her."

Lola didn't know if she would ever get used to hearing her sister referred to as Queen Sole. Being a second daughter, she was never expected to take the throne. "If anyone knew that you were alive...well, we fear for your safety," Heath said.

Lola would make her way back home; her people needed her now more than ever. Voice soft and measured, Queen Alina continued, "You must be aware of the many dangers that may lie ahead. The Sanctum Priest, Ezra Sarlee, has appointed himself the destroyer of magick. He believes the Holy Mother vanquished magick four generations ago because it was evil. He now seeks to ensure it does not rise."

"Especially since he doesn't possess it," Sirena whispered, taking another sip of honey wine. And there lay the truth of Ezra Sarlee's vengeance.

Prince Kingsley Do'Ramos

CHAPTER 5

*The language
of fireflies*

"Please, Princess, don't leave. I have been thoughtless. We can sit by the fire and drink some honey wine while my king and queen play the same hand of cards they have been playing for the last nine moonrises." That made her smile a little.

"I guess I'll stay," Lola told Kingsley as she settled to lounge beside the hearth in the great hall. "I'm sure I can endure your company a little bit longer."

He even held the goblets sexy. Holy Mother, help me. Lola had to focus. Sitting here by the fire with this perfect specimen of a prince would be no easy feat. His body looked relaxed and comfortable, but his molten eyes were on fire as they locked on her.

He took pity on her and asked, "How are you taking the news about your sister?"

"Alright, I suppose. It doesn't surprise me that she has

a plan. Sole always had a plan…" Her eyes were far away again, back to that night when her sister's dreams had come true—when she married the love of her life only to wake to his cold dead body hours later. As her thoughts spiraled, the memory of finding Sole comatose began to creep back into Lola's mind.

"A penny for your thoughts?" King whispered.

Taking one gulp of honey wine and then another, she replied, "I'm thinking about fireflies."

"Fireflies?"

"Yes. In Mōsa, we believe that our dead are carried away by the fireflies. I believe you have the same tradition here?" King nodded and gestured for Lola to continue. "As the Darkness grew, I remember the amount of fireflies did, too. When I was confined to my quarters, I would sit beside my window and watch them outside. Night after night, there were more and more. Tragic…but beautiful as well."

He leaned back in his chair, taking in the sight of her with a newfound appreciation. There was a look in his eyes, one that Lola hadn't seen before – a mix of admiration, wonder, and something deeper, something unspoken. It was as if he was seeing her for the first time, truly seeing her.

For a moment, time seemed to stand still as Kingsley allowed himself to drown in the beauty of her presence. And then, without a word, he simply nodded, a small smile playing at the corners of his lips. There was a mystery in that smile, a silent acknowledgment of something unsaid.

Taking another sip of his wine, King stood to his feet and started pacing. "There have been rumors that Sole plans to face Nasir and imprison him."

Lola's eyes darted back to Kingsley. She understood more of why he did not tell his parents of her newfound power.

"If the world has gone mad as you claim, then that is exactly why I must return to Mōsa. My people have been left unprotected, and I will not hide while they are used as pawns," she said too fast and too loud.

"There is no denying you are your mother's daughter," King Heath remarked from the other side of the room. Lola couldn't tell if that was a compliment or not.

"I will accompany the Princess to Mōsa," Kingsley declared. The room fell silent as Lola realized Kingsley was not at all what she expected.

"I assure you all," Lola began calmly, "that I need no escort." With her magick, she could find a way to defend herself.

"Father, you cannot expect me to leave the Princess of Mōsa unattended," Kingsley insisted, voice thick of conviction. "It was I who found her, and I feel responsible for her."

Tight as a plucked wire, King Heath replied, "You are the heir to this throne. Should something happen to you—"

"It won't!" Kingsley snapped.

"Son, you must understand that we fear for your safety," Queen Alina reasoned in an effort to keep the men civil. Kingsley took a deliberate step toward his parents.

"And what of Lola's safety? Her parents were taken by the Darkness, her sister is our queen, and you'll let her leave unprotected?"

"Enough!" The King shouted, raising a hand to command silence.

The room obeyed, and Lola watched the King force out a stressed sigh. The one person who'd shown her nothing but kindness.

They waited for him to speak when Lola swallowed a string of replies. I am the sister of the High Queen or I am of age and can travel as I wish. But she knew now wasn't the time to discuss this. "Your majesty," she said, "perhaps we can revisit this conversation tomorrow when we have rested and after we have gone riding."

The King nodded and pinched the bridge of his nose. "Forgive our outburst, Princess. We can wait to discuss this until tomorrow. For now, get some rest and know that our home is your home. Sirena will accompany you to your rooms. Kingsley, the Queen, and I have much to discuss."

"Please don't feel bad," Sirena assured Lola as they walked to Lola's quarters. "You don't understand much about my father and Kingsley's relationship. Just know Father means well."

Lola nodded and the two carried on in silence, their footsteps echoing down the empty corridor.

"So tell me," Sirena said. "How do you feel about my brother? He seems to be quite fond of you." Sirena asked what she wanted when she wanted, regardless of whether or not it was the right time.

"Fond? Oh, no! I assure you we are just friends. You probably see a man overprotective of a woman he believes he saved. I assure you that I needed no saving," Lola clarified.

"That may very well be true, but I know my brother, and I have never seen him like this for anyone except..."

Lola stopped in her tracks. "Except who?"

"Oh, forgive me, I have said too much, and Kingsley would kill me if he knew we were talking about her."

Lola didn't know why her stomach tightened at the thought of there being someone else. Not that she was interested in Kingsley, but if he was promised to another, their flirting definitely needed to stop. She refused to be the reason for two mates to fall apart. She saw how beautiful true mates could be. Her parents, as well as Nasir and Sole, had been great examples of true love. She would never jeopardize something like that.

Her voice hardened as she spoke, "If Kingsley is promised to another, I shouldn't be left alone with him." Transean custom forbids mated individuals to spend time alone with another who is not their mate.

"No, you have it all wrong. He was, but Kingsley's entire life changed when my brother Avenn was taken by the Darkness. He was brought back to Kingsguard Reef to prepare for a throne that was never promised to him. To make matters worse, Kingsley and Mya could no longer wed because it's forbidden."

Frustrated, Lola asked, "Forbidden?" How long would it be like this? Relying on others to tell her history she should already know. When would she begin to remember what she had forgotten about her world?

"Heirs to the throne are not allowed to marry second-born children. What that law never prepared for was the death of the firstborn. Before the Darkness, firstborn children didn't typically die prematurely. King was devastated, and now he and my father are at odds because of it."

"I'm so sorry. King must be—"

"I must be what?" Kingsley's voice cut through the hallway.

"Sirena, go to your rooms," he demanded abruptly.

"King, I didn't mean to…"

"Go! Sirena, we can talk about this tomorrow."

Entering her room, she wished Lola a good night as hot tears began to fall down her face.

"Goodnight, Sirena," Lola said, grumbling as she faced King.

As soon as Sirena shut her door, Lola burst out, "How could you do that?"

"Me?"

"Yes, you!"

"Your sister loves you! Shit, your entire family loves you, yet somehow, your disdain is obvious. I know you have lost much in your life, and for that, I am sorry." Tears pricked at the corners of her eyes. "When you have lost your parents, sister, and all those who were dear to you, then tell me how you are entitled to make everyone around you miserable. I have lost everything—my future and my past! So forgive me if I don't feel sorry for you!" Storming towards her door, she suddenly turned back to him. "I would give anything to be with my family again! While you just throw it away! Goodnight, prince Do'Ramos," was the last thing she said, standing at the threshold, before slamming the door in Kingsley's bewildered face.

CHAPTER 6

The price of pleasure

As the moon's vibrant light filtered across her bedroom floor, Lola lay still on her enormous bed of cedar, her body tense with grief and doubt. Swaddling herself in the sheets and comforter didn't ease her restlessness or lull her mind. She needed to get out. She needed to walk. It would help her clear the cloud hanging over her head. So, slipping on the riding outfit Sirena gave her, Lola surrendered to the nagging feeling and headed out to the courtyard. The dark cape, far too large for her frame, dragged on the floor behind her as if she were a girl wearing her father's clothes. She knew it had to be Kingsley's; she could smell chocolate, mingling with the fragrance of fresh rain and a sprig of cinnamon.

That was his scent.

The last thing she wanted was his presence. He was an ungrateful, arrogant prick and she would have nothing to do with him.

Sneaking past the guards and the prince, she managed

to make it to the road leading to the Ventane Woods. The suns had not yet painted the sky with the pink and orange of dawn, so she knew she had enough time to take a stroll and return before she was missed.

It had been ten years since Lola had ventured down this road.

As Lola cautiously stepped into the enchanted winter forest, her eyes widened with wonder and her breath caught in anticipation. She heard tales of the mystical forest and even visited it as a child, but nothing could prepare her for the breathtaking sight that unfolded before her.

The forest floor was a carpet of pristine white, adorned with delicate snowdrops peeking through the glistening snow. Each tiny bloom beckoned Lola closer, their fragile beauty a testament to nature's resilience in the harshest of seasons. Their delicate grace captivated her.

Her gaze shifted upward, and there, towering above her, stood green trees, their branches reaching towards the heavens and casting enchanting shadows upon the snowy ground. But what truly stole Lola's breath away was the radiant glow the double suns cast upon the forest. Their golden light filtered through the branches, creating a dazzling interplay of light and shadow.

As Lola took hesitant steps forward, the snow beneath her feet seemed to respond to her presence, shimmering and glowing with an otherworldly luminescence, as if each snowflake held a secret enchantment. Their gentle radiance lit her path, guiding her deeper into the magickal realm.

Every rustle and whisper of the forest drew Lola's attention, as if the woodland creatures were whispering their welcomes. She caught glimpses of elusive creatures, their fur or feathers kissed by the soft glow of the snow. They moved with a grace that mirrored the enchantment of their surroundings.

Overwhelmed with awe, Lola found herself completely immersed in the forest's ethereal atmosphere. The crisp winter air with its hint of magick, ignited her senses with the scent of pine and the gentle touch of a chilly breeze. This was a place that defied reality, where dreams and imagination melded seamlessly with the tangible world.

In this moment, Lola knew this realm of wonder spoke to her magick. With each step, she embraced the enchantment that surrounded her.

The morning dew reminded her of the times she and her father, King Axel, would rise early to catch the day's first light. Now, Lola journeyed this road alone. And this wouldn't be the only path she'd have to face on her own. She would be alone from here on out if the people of Mōsa truly were gone. She wanted to trust Kingsley, his sister, his parents, and the people of Kingsguard Reef—that they'd told her the truth—but at the same time, she couldn't bear that truth and hoped they were lying, even if they themselves didn't know it.

Fighting tears, she reminisced on times with her friends. Her Misa sisters, her Porte sisters, all those the Darkness has stolen from her. Aurora—Rory—her oldest and dearest friend.

She loved walking the woods with Lola late at night, swooning over the stillness of the hour and enjoying the sky before dawn broke.

Had the Darkness taken her, too?

"Somehow I have left them all behind. Where have I been all this time?" she asked the early morning breeze that ran through her curls.

The forest began to wake up, leaves rustling and birds chirping as the first of the twin suns stretched and peered out from behind the mountains on the horizon. The sky was a deep shade of purple, the suns unapologetically contrasting with their bold orange and red hues. The air was nice and cool, a light mist rising from the forest floor. In this dense wood, she wasn't as alone as she first felt.

As both suns slowly continued to ascend, they illu-minated the tree trunks with a warm, golden glow. The light danced as it filtered through the leaves, littering the forest floor with dainty shadows of each branch. Soon, the floor was awash with a kaleidoscope of colors—greens, oranges, reds—and splatters of dew and frost. The bird-song grew louder, their morning greetings filling the air as they welcomed the new day.

The ascent of the Transean suns eased her restlessness.

"I thought I might find you out here, Princess," a voice behind her said.

Kingsley. Lola whirled around.

"It seems as though I am not the only one who can't sleep this moonrise." His warm golden glare took in every inch of her. Great. Her knees locked up again.

Kingsley Do'Ramos, second prince of Kingsguard Reef, certainly did cut an imposing figure as he walked up to Lola. At six-foot-three, a lean but muscular build stretched him out even more. Lola couldn't help but be taken aback by him.

Though it was barely sunrise, his eyes still gleamed with an inner fire. His short brown curls were a little wild. Bedhead. But he was messy and he didn't care. Even his hair had an air of conceit. Lola still couldn't decide if she liked it. If she liked him.

Despite everything he had been through, his ingratitude remained unchanged, and Lola, who had lost everything herself, couldn't bear to be near him.

"Come walk with me," he murmured.

She stayed still.

Turning back to see her unmoving, he sarcastically asked, "Are your feet feeling unwell, Tesoro?"

His voice ignited a flash of green in her eyes. What was

it about him that made him so unbearable?

"Do you speak to all women in this manner?" she retorted.

"No, just you," he replied matter-of-factly.

"Well, Your Highness, I'll have you know that—"

"After humiliating me in front of my sister, my guards, and the entire castle with your rebuke, the least you can do is accompany me for a stroll in the woods," he interrupted.

Had she been so loud that the entire castle overheard their conversation last night? Her cheeks flushed with embarrassment. Once again, she had spoken her mind without considering the consequences. The Holy Mother might have known she was right, but that didn't excuse her lack of tact.

"While I don't regret what I said, I do regret saying it so loudly," she admitted, crossing her arms as a chill gripped her.

"You are forgiven!" he declared.

"I never sought forgiveness, Prince."

"It's close enough. Besides, your outspokenness didn't make it any less true. I can be difficult," Kingsley asserted. "Now, would you please walk with me, Princess? Help me salvage my troubled reputation," he requested, his eyes twinkling with mischief.

Maintaining her crossed arms in protest, Lola walked ahead of the prince, an act uncommon for women in

Transea. But if Kingsley knew anything, it was that Lola Porte was no ordinary woman.

"So, Princess, tell me more about Mōsa. I haven't been there since my time before joining the Sanctum."

Out of the corner of her eye, his sharp features and the edges of his mouth were waking her up.

"Mōsa, is a beautiful place. A place that I plan to protect with my life. My people are strong and proud, and they will stop at nothing to protect their land and their people."

Kingsley nods thoughtfully. "I can see why you miss it. So, how do you plan on getting back?"

As usual, Lola didn't have a plan. She was great with a bow and sword, yet strategy was not her strong suit. Even during training, it had been pointed out to her that Lola thought more with her heart. Out of her sisters, she tended to be the most impulsive. Emotional. It was something about herself she was highly critical of. She is Queen Lygia's daughter, after all.

Her mother was tactful, organized, and diplomatic; and, she led by example in innumerable ways.

Now, more than ever, Lola needed to learn how to follow in her mother's footsteps. Figure it out. Somehow, she'd find a way. Perhaps she should have given herself more time…she needed resources. She needed maps. She didn't know the terrain around her, or what sorts of dangers to be prepared for. Kingsley was a nuisance, but he wasn't dumb. He could give her the information she needed if only she just took a deep breath.

He probably assumes I don't know what I'm doing. Not that she'd given him much else to go off of...

"Princess? Are you feeling alright?" Kingsley took a sheepish step toward her. "Maybe your journey to Mōsa can wait for a couple of days. So you can think this all through. You may need to rest, and I am sure, mother—"

"Stop!" she exclaimed. What she didn't need was him reading her mind!

Even the trees stood still at her command, their leaves coming to a halt despite the light breeze.

"I will stop questioning your desires, Princess. I don't think it's unreasonable for you to want to return home. But I have to insist on joining you on the journey to Mōsa."

He smiled rather mischievously.

"I even have some ideas of my own."

"You don't need to pity me."

"Pity? How is this pity?"

Lola sighed, shrugging as she looked over his shoulder.

"I don't know. I guess I'm still not sure what to expect from you."

He nods slowly.

"I am sorry for my actions last night, and I'm sorry I've been...scattered. But I promise you, you won't find any pity here." His cunning smile returned.

"Really? What will I find then?" she asked in jest. He softly placed his hand on her shoulder, close enough that she felt a surge of energy race through her body.

"Hopefully," he said, "an admirer and friend. If you'll allow me, Tesoro."

"An admirer?" she repeated.

"Your grit, Lola. It's very…entrancing." His voice quivered just a hair as he complimented her, and he lowered his hands to his sides but stood tall. After last night, he certainly chose his words with care…

His attempt at being kind misted her with warmth, wicking away the cold morning air and kindling her heart in her chest. She didn't want him to be a nuisance. She wanted this warmth between them to last.

"I fear the Mōsa I remember is gone, King," she said honestly.

"We're never prepared to lose the things we love most." He smiled deeply. "I know it's not fair. But that's why I try to savor what I have. And not take those around me…for granted."

She nodded.

"I'm sorry I said otherwise," she said with her head down.

He shook his head with a dismissive hand gesture. "Now it's forgotten." Then, he grinned. "I also always prioritize pleasure."

He flicked a curl behind her shoulder, slipped his hands

into his pockets, and started walking ahead.

"So what's the plan?" he asked, beginning to whistle.

"You really want to know what I'm thinking?" She asked, quickly following him.

"Oh most definitely. Because, let's think this through, Tesoro. You haven't slept since you arrived. If you're exhausted before we even begin, you won't make for a great traveling partner. So, what is your plan? To rest before we leave? Or to get you to your sister and off this ratchet island on yearning alone?"

"Ratchet? You refer to your homeland with such disdain."

Apart from Sundom, the Western Isles hadn't been too bad. And she hadn't even seen Sundom with her own eyes...

Kingsley let out a heavy sigh.

"I, too, don't feel I have the luxury of resting, Lola." There was a hint of bitterness in his tone. "I've been on the move ever since Avenn died. Just trying to make sense of everything, to figure out how to lead a kingdom I never wanted to rule. And I haven't had the aid I've wanted."

She knew he was referring to his father. He bit his lower lip as they walked.

"As for my comment about my island, let's just say the pleasant things wear off the longer you're here. But I'm not leaving your side until we get you to your sister and make sure you are safe."

He offered a small smile.

"Has my rambling given you enough time to come up with a plan?"

She couldn't help but chuckle, but her smile quickly faded. "No."

"May I offer a suggestion?"

Sighing, she gave him a semi-reluctant nod.

They stopped near the edge of a glade. Not unlike the part of the forest she had awoken in, this glade was full of grass and frost-coated flowers. The wind swirled icy water in pools with. Twigs snapped as more critters scurried about. The Ventane Woods sure were lively.

Kingsley breathed out through his nose and reached over, tucking another long coiled strand of hair behind her ear.

This cocky little prince sure insists on being close, she thought. Still, she'd be lying to herself if she said the sensation of his fingers brushing her ear wasn't soothing.

"Princess," he said. "You could use a couple more nights of rest, some nourishing meals, a plan, and the company of a king. And it makes no sense for the two of us to travel all the way to Mōsa unattended."

Begrudgingly, she agreed.

"Well then. Have you got a plan, Prince Do'Ramos?"

"Let's keep walking," he told her, ignoring her question. "We're almost there. Once we reach the river, we can follow it downstream to the coast."

"I'll take that as a no," she teased. Then she sighed, continuing to follow him. Suddenly, a rustling in the bushes made her jump.

Kingsley was instantly alert, reaching for his sword. But then, a small cory darted out of the bushes and scurried away. Lola let out a nervous laugh, relieved that it wasn't something more dangerous.

As they resumed their walk, Kingsley's hand brushed against hers. Another jolt of energy. He had to be doing all of this on purpose. She turned to him and, in a moment of intimacy, their eyes met.

"Kingsley," Lola said softly. "Tell me your plan." He stayed silent until they finally reached the clearing. "There's a way we can go to Mōsa." His voice was low and serious. "We could take the Sirena Sea. It would be dangerous, but it's the fastest route."

"I like danger," Lola proclaimed.

He grinned at her, mischievous again. It dawned on her that she was alone, again, with the handsome Prince of Kingsguard Reef. In the forest. Standing in the clearing overlooking the cliffs on the coast, Lola took in the sight of the sea and wondered if he was serious. The reckless plan had her heart skipping a beat more than their seclusion together.

"Do you really think it's a good plan?" she asked,

uncertain.

Kingsley nodded. "I do." He confidently stared down the waters that rhythmically lapped at the sand, pulling out and rushing in again. It was winter, but not even the cold or snow could stall the waves.

"But we're not leaving today. We need to make sure we have everything we need and that we're prepared for the journey."

"You are right; I could use some of your mother's stew. Oh, and Prince?"

"Yes?"

"Never touch my hair again. It is customary that the only man to ever touch a Mōsian woman's locs would be her mate."

"Is that so?" he asked. "I apologize."

He closed the distance between them, heart racing in anticipation. He had felt the chemistry when he touched her fingertips, her shoulder, her hair. When their eyes met, he gave her a moment to adjust, and took the chance to read her expression. She didn't pull away. And he'd been wanting to do this since he first met her.

He'd been craving her lips.

"So, what can I touch?" he whispered. He leaned in. "I promise you, Princess. You will get home, and you will be safe."

Now she leaned in. He could feel the heat of her sweet

breath on his face.

For a moment, everything else faded away. All that mattered was the intense desire he felt for Lola. He had never felt like this for any other woman, not even his former fiancée.

His hands moved up to cup her face, pulling her in closer.

He couldn't think straight. He didn't even know what the fuck he was doing. This gorgeous, tiny woman was grieving and all he could think of is how he wanted to cloak her. Protect her, watch her…sort her out.

Their lips were inches apart. The trees and leaves swayed. The suns had risen, the sky almost as beautiful and vibrant as Lola's aura. He could feel the electricity in the air.

And then, the faint sound of metal clanging and horse hooves traveled from the direction of the castle. "Prince! Princess!" a voice hollered.

Kingsley's eyes flew open. He immediately pulled back from Lola, stunned, and cleared his throat. Disappointment etched across both their faces. They both turned toward the source of the sound and saw a group of soldiers approaching. Kingsley quickly composed himself, taking a step back from Lola and resting his hands at his sides, hoping their privacy hadn't been completely invaded. He wasn't sure how much the soldiers managed to see.

A strong fire still burned inside him. He wanted her badly.

Now that disappointment was starting to feel agonizing. Being denied. If this was to continue happening, it was only going to further stoke that fire.

Lola turned and saw the soldier at the front of the small pack, the one who likely called out to them. He had a big grin stretched across his chiseled jaw.

His eyes were the same honey color as...

"Cousin!" Thad announced as he strode in front of them. "My apologies. Have I interrupted you?" His brows perked up slightly on the word interrupted. "Aunt Alina is demanding your attention for the sobremesa."

Kingsley sighed. "Princess Lola, you may remember my annoying cousin Thad."

"It's good to see you again, beautiful," Thad greeted with a wink.

Lola narrowed her eyes.

"What did you just say?"

Thad chuckled, taking a step closer. "I'm sorry we've ruined your little playdate, but you had a lot of the people at the castle quite worried."

When he saw Lola's expression, he raised his hands defensively.

"I'm sorry, Princess. I'm something of a joker." Lola stepped away from Thad and stared him down.

"I'll have you know that Mōsian women are not mere toys to be played with," she warned through gritted teeth, her voice a potent mix of fury and disgust.

"And it would do you well to remember that."

Kingsley stepped forward, placing a hand on Lola's shoulder.

"Thad, that's enough. Lola is not someone to be trifled with," he stated. Her stance alone left no room for doubt. She slid Kingsley's hand off her shoulder and faced Thad on her own.

Thad held up his hands again in surrender.

"Alright, alright, I get it. I was just teasing." His tone was laced with amusement.

Lola glares at him for a moment longer before turning on her heel and walking away.

"I will accompany you," Kingsley said, briskly walking after her. His next comment was almost a plea.

"We are set to go riding today."

"I don't need anyone, and we will not be riding today," she scoffed.

Kingsley followed her at a distance, his eyes lingering on her retreating figure. He could feel the heat rising in his cheeks as he thought about what had almost happened between them. He knew that Lola was right. Mōsian women were not toys. Women were not his toys. He knew that he needed to be careful around her, to show her the respect she deserved, but it was hard when all he wanted to do was pull her into his arms and kiss her senseless.

Thad caught up and walked beside him, laughing to himself. The soldiers followed behind, awkwardly escorting them back to the castle, though Lola—whom they were supposed to be protecting—was in the lead.

"Well cousin, I fucking like this one," Thad smirked. "She's different from your other friends."

As much as Kingsley hated to admit it, Thad's suggestion that he was a womanizer hit uncomfortably close to home. Despite his breakup with Mya, Kingsley couldn't deny his habit of always having a first daughter by his side, or sneaking off for a quick tryst in the stables. It was a realization that made him cringe with shame. He'd been out of control since his world had fallen apart. That was still no excuse. The thought of Lola discovering his indiscretions filled him with anxiety. What made his mind buzz more is he couldn't quite pinpoint why he cared so much.

"Shut your fucking face," King ordered his cousin. "That's the long lost Princess of Mōsa. Besides, she wasn't part of my plan. Or did you forget, Thad?"

The plans for his future weren't even his, but that didn't seem to matter to anyone else. If they were his plans and he had the choice, he'd love to make her his. Or at least, have a chance with someone he felt so different around. He still didn't know what he wanted. This princess had thrown him for a loop.

For now, all he could do was steal glances and imagine

what might have happened in the woods if they hadn't been interrupted.

CHAPTER 7

Riding into danger

Kingsley's hope for an hour's rest before heading to the stables was shattered by the bright sunlight, hunger, and his growing frustration about his moment with Lola in the forest. He wasn't sure what upset him more: the fact that they'd been interrupted, or her final words to him: I don't need anyone.

As he made his way through the labyrinthine halls, his thoughts continued to swirl in a tempest of uncertainty and longing. And then, as if guided by an unseen force, his feet carried him towards Lola's chambers. He knocked and heard her muffled, "Come in!" from the other side of the door.

"Good morning, Princess. I hope you managed to sleep some," Kingsley said as he entered her rooms.

She wouldn't tell him that sleep had evaded her. That the thoughts of her family and friends had kept her awake, and that their moment of closeness in the forest hadn't helped either. Instead, she said, "I slept as well as can be expected," as she stood to take one last glance in the mirror. Securing her long, chestnut braid, she caught him in the reflection and sucked in a breath; those brown-green eyes pierced her. Refusing to let him know what she was experiencing, she broke eye contact. "Where is Sirena? Will she be joining us today?"

Kingsley turned away from Lola and ran a hand through his brown wavy hair. "No," he said. "It seems that my sister has fallen ill."

Ill? Had the Darkness reached Sirena as well? A deep panic flashed across Lola's eyes. Understanding her distress, Kingsley urgently replied, "She isn't really ill; she's mad at her idiotic brother for yelling at her. I heard he's an ass."

Catching her breath, tilting her head, and smiling, Lola said, "I'm pretty sure he is." They both stood there for what seemed like an eternity. Then, finally, Lola broke the stare as she made her way to the desk.

"Are we going riding, or are you too worried to ride with a Misa warrior?" Lola shot King a challenging look as she reached for her riding gloves.

"Ho, Princess, I am many things around you, but worried isn't one of them."

Lola had never been more thankful for her mahogany skin, or else the prince would know she was blushing, and she would have none of that.

Reaching for her hand, King gently placed it in the crux of his elbow as the two made their way to the stables.

***

The horse groom met the prince at the entrance of the enormous white stable. The stable had always been a place of peace for Kingsley. Maybe he found solace here because horses didn't care if you were a prince or a pauper. They only cared if you were kind. Only his immediate family had ever come to this place. Bringing Lola made him uneasy. As much as her company intrigued him, he didn't want outside opinions to dampen his safe haven.

"Henry, I'd like you to meet our guest, Miss Lori. She is an old friend of the family visiting from Sundom." Lola and Kingsley remembered what King Heath had instructed. No one, not even the servants, could know who Lola truly was. Therefore the alias, Lori Reefwood.

"It's wonderful to meet you, Miss Lori. I'm Henry, the groom for these thirty-nine horses," he said, his breath steaming in the crisp morning air.

Henry was a short man with olive skin, deep-set brown eyes, a receding hairline, and a bright smile. Kingsley had spent much time with Henry as a boy, learning how to ride like a prince. Avenn had been a skilled rider, but Kingsley had always struggled...until Henry took him under his wing and made him the best horseman in all of Kingsguard Reef. Kingsley looked forward to showing Lola what he could do on a horse. Surely she couldn't be as good as he was.

"It is a pleasure to meet you, Henry," Lola said. "I adore horses and know what it takes to care for them. Our own groom in Mo…back home taught me how to ride and care for a steed. You, sir, must be quite kind hearted for all these horses to love you."

Henry smiled as he stared at Lola awkwardly, and Kingsley became annoyed. "Henry, did you get what I asked for?" Kingsley asked.

Startled as if coming out of a dream, Henry shook free of his trance and replied, "Yes, Sir," as he made his way to stalls eight and nine.

Following Henry, Kingsley itched to start riding and to get the princess alone again. They had much to discuss. Lost in thought, Kingsley hadn't noticed when Lola separated herself from him, drawn to the most beautiful horse in the stables. She stood on her toes and reached up high to pet the gorgeous gray merle stallion.

His stallion.

The stallion was named Cross because he was ordinarily cross with all others aside from Henry and Kingsley. But this princess had enamored him like she had done with everyone else in Kingsguard Reef.

Kingsley couldn't blame them. Although in a tight long

braid now, her full long locs of cinnamon brown often cascaded over her shoulders ethereally, and her glowing smile and piercing green eyes captivated anyone she came across. The glow of her deep mahogany skin made every man in Kingsguard Reef stop and stare. She was fucking beautiful, and his cock knew it, too.

Her pink, pouty lips were blossom soft, and he knew if he got too close, she would ruin him with them. Every time she bit her lower lip while she was remembering something, or licked them before she insulted him, his cock wanted to say hello to her in the worst way. But he knew he would never do so. She simply wasn't part of the plan.

"I think I'll ride this one," Lola voiced cheerfully.

"Oh, Miss, that is a fine horse, indeed. But you see, that is Prin—"

Interrupting Henry before he exposed what a child he could be about 'his horse,' Kingsley spoke, "Saddle up Nova—his sister's horse—for the lady, won't you, Henry?"

Henry's nervous stare was sure to give Kingsley away.

"Is this your horse?" Lola asked.

Fuck, will this woman ever let him get away with anything?

"Yes. He is mine."

"Well, he is quite a beauty. Will it be hard for you to see me best you on your very own horse?"

Her lips smiled that beautiful smile, and he took a step closer to her. "We shall see about that," Kingsley replied defiantly. That's when he heard voices approaching. Her voice.

Mya entered the stables beside his mother. How he wished he could hide. He had loved Mya since they were children. They endured the Sanctum together and were promised to be wed until Avenn was taken by the Darkness. Then he lost his best friend, his love, and his plan.

Feeling uncomfortably close to Lola as Mya approached, Kingsley took a few steps back.

"Oh, there you two are," the queen exclaimed. Turning to face them, gut churning, Kingsley said, "Hello, mother. Mya."

"Hello, King," Mya said, and he was undone.

***

Lola couldn't remember what they were talking about. All she knew was that Kingsley went from charming to cold in an instant.

Dark green, long hair neatly coiffed to reveal a full, striking face—milky soft skin and strong cheekbones. High-set hazel eyes watched delightfully over Kingsley until landing on Lola and dissolving into a cold, dark gaze.

"It's a pleasure to see you both," Kingsley said cordially. "Mya, what brings you to Kingsguard Reef?"

"Have you forgotten?" she replied.

His quizzical look indicated that he had no clue what they were talking about. If King didn't know, Lola definitely didn't know.

"It's the Solstice, dear," Alina reminded him.

"The Solstice?" Lola whispered to herself as memories of winter solstices with her family flashed into her mind. Beautiful moments along the Sirena Sea with her people as they released the lanterns of renewal. The Solstice was when the two suns appeared to reach their lowest point in the sky, giving the appearance of one sun standing still. Lola closed the distance between herself and the group standing beside Kingsley, holding back her tears as she forced herself to greet Mya.

"Hello, I am Lo...Lori, I am visiting from Sundom."

"How rude of us, Kingsley," the queen remarked. "Mya, Lori is the daughter of an old family friend who has come to spend the winter Solstice at Kingsguard Reef."

"My pleasure, Miss Lori," Mya said coolly with a formal curtsy. "Surprisingly, in all the years I have known King, he has never mentioned you."

With that comment Lola's intuition was confirmed. Ugh! She couldn't stand petty people, but she knew exactly how to handle them.

"I am surprised he didn't mention me." Lola took swift control of the conversation. "We have been close for quite some time. Haven't we, King? We recently ran into each other by chance, and he hasn't been able to get rid of me since."

She turned to face Kingsley, brow arched. She enjoyed watching him squirm again.

"Ah...yes. We are old friends, My."

Lola didn't know why she was so agitated at his use of her pet name. But she was.

"Lori," Kingsley told her, his eyes a little agitated. "This is the friend Sirena mentioned last night. Mya and I were at the Sanctum together before...well, before."

So this is Mya Sarlee, Kingsley's former betrothed. There was no doubting her beauty.

She was certainly fit for the Do'Ramos family. The way Mya and Kingsley still looked at each other made it clear they'd deeply cared for each other at one point. Maybe they still do, Lola wondered as her belly turned.

The awkward silence that followed revealed that Mya was even more tense as she looked both Kingsley and Lola in the eye. Her initial judgment of 'Lori Reefwood' was palpable.

As usual, Queen Alina chimed in to save the day, and Kingsley couldn't be more grateful.

"Kingsley, weren't you going to take Lori riding? We won't keep you."

"Yes," he said louder than he intended to. As if on cue, Henry returned with Cross in tow.

"Awe, there's that blasted horse. Does he still hate every-one?" Mya asked Kingsley.

Sliding her riding gloves back on, Lola left Kingsley alone with Mya to ask Henry how she should handle Cross.

"He's a stubborn one," Henry confessed. "But if he gets away from you, just whistle for him like this and he will come running."

Lola practiced her whistling and nailed it on her third try.

"Do you need assistance with the saddle, madame?"

"No, thank you, Henry."

Lola reached up and gently gripped the saddle. Although she had never used a harness when riding in Mōsa, she appreciated not having to worry about chafing.

"Cross is quite huge!" Lola uttered to Henry as she stabbed her foot into the black stirrup and hauled herself up. Sitting atop Cross, she didn't move for a moment. Her beauty and regality has the others staring.

Taking a satisfying breath, she glanced at Kingsley with a smile, then quickly darted her eyes to Mya before making direct eye contact with him again.

"Are you coming, King?"

And, just as quickly as she asked the question, she was off.

Cross glided effortlessly across the ground. Lola admired his dapples of black and his dark gray merle coat, recognizing that he was a younger stallion. He flew out of the stable like he was running towards something. No hesitation. Her heart and Cross's beat as one as they raced through the forest.

"Prin…Lori! Slow down!" a voice yelled behind her. Finally,

She figured he wouldn't be able to resist breaking away from Mya to catch up to her. Slowing down, Lola observed Kingsley as he chased her, riding as if he was one with the horse, his lean body swaying with the stride of the graceful animal.

This man has to know how incredibly handsome he is, right?

"Why did you take off like that? You nearly frightened my mother half to death."

Shit…

She hadn't thought how the queen might have felt seeing her act like that. That was the impulsivity she needed to work on. But for fuck's sake, she couldn't stand one more moment listening to Mya speak.

"I will apologize to your mother when I see her next." They slowed to a gentle trot, side by side.

Cross snorted.

"I thought Cross was about to toss you off his back, but he seems very comfortable with you." Arching his eyebrow slightly, his lips smiling wickedly, he couldn't help but comment, "You are one fine rider."

"I beg your pardon?"

"I meant you ride well."

"Really? That's what you want to say?"

She didn't know why she loved to see him sweat. Changing the subject, she asked, "So, handsome prince, where are we off to today?"

Eyes smiling, it dawned on Kingsley what she had just said. "Wait, you think I'm handsome?"

Realizing she wasn't going to answer him, he continued. "I thought we would go to the creek. The one you mentioned you and your family went fishing along when you were a child. Unfortunately, it isn't near, but seeing as you are a fierce rider, you should be able to make the journey."

He grinned again as he commanded his white stallion to ride hard and fast, leaving Lola in his dust.

But not for long.

They rode slowly and talked, even laughed, and for the first time since waking up in the forest, Lola felt a semblance of peace. They rode through the Ventane Woods and then headed down a hill to a wide creek.

The forest was enormous, opaque, and primal. Lola loved it. Winter strangled the land as the suns filled the bright sky. Rays of light burst through the forest canopy of rowan, oak, and cypress, allowing a gallimaufry of snowdrops, winterberries, and black tulips to twinkle among the thick layer of snow-covered fallen leaves below.

A discord of wild noises, most belonging to small creatures, brightened up the frosty forest and drowned out the
occasional roar of a large animal trying to assert itself. The
creek was just as she remembered it. The early stage of
winter had brought a slow tranquility to the area.

Lola came to a stop, catching her breath as she watched
Kingsley close the distance between them. Kingsley was
magnificent as he moved through the enchanted forest.
She was captivated by his every move. Tall and lean, his
dark curls falling gracefully on his forehead, and his lips
flushing red from the cold, he exuded a magnetic allure
that drew her in. As he gracefully dismounted, a surge of
passion coursed through Lola's veins, setting her heart
ablaze. In that moment, it was as if the world around them
had faded into a blur, leaving only him—the embodiment
of perfection—in focus. His every movement was a tanta-
lizing dance that left her breathless and yearning for more.
The air crackled with an electric intensity as their gazes
locked and time stood still. She could feel the magnetic pull
between them, drawing her irresistibly closer to this alluring
man. He was a hypnotic charm that left her spellbound.

With each step he took, her pulse quickened, and a rush
of emotions overwhelmed her. Her senses came alive,
heightened by the sheer desire that coursed through her
veins—the fire burning within her soul. She fell deeper
into his grasp, willingly surrendering to the intoxicating

enchantment that bound them together. And yet she knew he was not part of her plan. Someone needed to tell her pussy that.

She knew, in that moment, that something extraordinary was happening to her—was it her magick, or was she simply under the spell of this perfect man? "Come here," Kingsley said as he lifted her by the waist off the horse.

Lola knew how to dismount a horse with no assistance. But she wanted him to assist her. It made her feel silly; the touch of his warm hands on her waist had her almost shaking. They stood there for a moment locking eyes before Kingsley broke the silence.

"Come here," he said with a smirk. "What for?"

"Come smell this winter blossom." "Why?" she asked playfully.

Taking her hand in his, King continued.

"Because, Princess Lola, this is the smell of my childhood."

Bending over, Lola gently caressed the beautiful white blossom and inhaled its sweet scent. Looking up, she saw his honey eyes drinking her in.

"Let's make a fire," Kingsley suggested, already walking away from her to collect wood.

Lola was thankful he had brought her here. She needed a morning away from lying about who she truly was. She needed a moment to let go before continuing to process her losses—and her newfound magick.

With ease, Kingsley set a fire.

"Henry gave me this satchel with some sustenance and herbs should we need medical attention. I told him not to worry, but he's been fussing over me since I was a lad."

The satchel contained various kinds of cheese, jam, honey, a small kettle for making tea, and three warm loaves of bread.

"It was truly kind of him to prepare this for us," Lola said. "I will have to make sure to thank him when we return."

"Be careful, Princess. I fear if you give Henry any more attention, he will ask to court you," he joked.

After building a small fire to keep them warm, Kingsley rested on a fallen tree a calculated distance away from Lola—for fear of how he'd behave if he were closer. Kingsley prodded Lola's memory with a casual inquiry, "So tell me, Princess, when did you learn to ride so fiercely?"

Lola took a seat on the opposite side of the fire, the young flames flitting through the air between them. She stared into them, eyes smiling.

"I first learned to ride as a girl," she told him. "That was when my queen mother allowed me to train with the Misa warriors. From age five to ten I learned combat drills on our horses. Although none were as big as Cross. As I got older, I rode horseback nearly every evening, and once I rode ten miles at a fast gallop. How about you, King?"

Kingsley loved the sound of his nickname on her lips.

Kingsley's eyes drifted back to a time long passed. "I first rode as a boy. Henry taught me. Then, while in the Sanctum, we had riding lessons that later turned into violent combat lessons."

"My sister Sole told me that the Sanctum is horrid." Lola waited for his response, but King's demeanor told her he wasn't ready to discuss that with her. Besides, he hardly knew her. Lola knew what would make him talk. "So, tell me about her?"

His eyes locked on hers as he asked, "Who?"

"Mya. She is quite a beauty. Has she always been that lovely?"

"I'm sure you don't want to hear about my tired old love story."

"Of course I do!" she insisted. "I mean, we literally have all day. Or did you want to go back and face your ex, her family, and all the gossip that comes to walk at you as you awkwardly try to survive the Solstice?"

Leaning back on the log, he said, "Well, come here, get closer; this is a long story, and it's going to get colder soon." Lola rolled her eyes but obliged, moving over to him to share the warm, hunter-green travel blanket Henry had placed in their satchel.

Kingsley shared how he met Mya, how he'd always thought of her as his best friend until her twelfth shadowborn day, when she blossomed into a beautiful young lady. While at the Sanctum, they became like family, then fell in love. His eyes glistened when he spoke about his brother's death and how that forced him to make many hard decisions.

One of those decisions came by way of his father. Kingsley and Mya would not wed. A bitter law in Transea forbade second-born children to marry an heir to the throne. According to Transean law, Kingsley's mate would need to be born a first daughter. His lips tightened as, for a moment, he remembered how he had lost everything he loved.

"Enough about me...tell me about you, Princess. I am sure many lads wanted to spend time with the beautiful Princess of Mōsa."

"Did you just call me beautiful?'

"Stop avoiding the question, Lola."

The way he said her name in that low, deep, gravelly voice sent goosebumps prickling over her skin.

"No suitors. Just training, family, and my people. Boys were an unnecessary distraction. Besides, if I was going to fall in love, it would have to be like the love Sole and Nasir share. Used to share..."

With a sigh, Kingsley couldn't help but chuckle. "Ah, the luxury of choice," he mused, his gaze lingering on her. "You truly are fortunate, Lola."

Her laughter danced in the breeze as she countered,

"Fortunate, perhaps, but not without debts owed. You forget, Prince, that my journey here was paved by your hand."

A playful grin tugged at his lips. "And yet, you're determined to leave just when things are getting interesting."

Lola's expression softened, a flicker of vulnerability crossing her features. "I must go," she insisted, though her distant gaze betrayed her as it revealed a reluctance to leave.

Kingsley's smile faltered slightly. "I fear you may forget us if you go," he admitted.

Her eyes met his, and a silent understanding passed between them. "Tell me, Prince Kingsley, do you think the people of Mōsa will ever accept me as their war maiden?"

"They will," he replied without hesitation. "Because, little firefly, I believe in you.

Lola's eyes glazed over and her jaw went soft as she stared at him. Tension hung in the air and their unspoken feelings lingered, waiting to be acknowledged. They were impossibly close to each other, and if not for the rustling in the woods behind them, she might have done something stupid just then.

Twigs snapped. Footsteps pattered. Something was coming.

CHAPTER 8

Dire encounters

A clouded dire wolf approached the fire, hair raised and teeth bared. Lola and Kingsley had to work together, and they had to act fast. Kingsley's blood ran cold.

"Aren't dire wolves extinct?" he muttered, keeping his voice low so as to not enrage the creature. It had been four generations since anyone had seen one. Lola took a measured breath.

"Apparently not."

What was one doing here now? King Heath had told Sirena and Kingsley stories of the dire wolves when they were children. They were the symbol of their family emblem, after all. Kingsley knew these monsters were filled with powerful magick and, if this one took a chance on them, he and Lola would surely die. But he couldn't allow anything to harm her. Not ever.

Rising to his feet, Kingsley drew his sword just as the wolf charged him, knocking him off his feet. Terrified, Lola tried to summon her magick, but it wouldn't come. The horses neighed and fought against their bindings. Lola rushed to Cross, freeing him into the wilderness. That's when she heard the bloodcurdling screaming of the other horse. Crimson sticky blood covered the white stallion. The dire locked his enormous jaw around the defenseless horse's midsection. Collapsing to the ground, the stallion stared at Lola as it took its last breath, eyes glossing over but never closing.

Taking in the horrifying sight, Kingsley reached across with his right hand, gripping the handle of his brother's sword just below the guard. He drew it out, and snapped it forward.

The gray beast unleashed a soul-piercing growl that reverberated through the air, its gaze fixed directly on Kingsley. With agile movements, the wolf's paws swiftly shuffled, granting its immense body the balance required to evade the sharp blade. Then, at the last moment, Kingsley drew the sword up over the head of the beast. The gray wolf sloped down to the right, but the blade never pierced his flesh.

With one leap, its enormous white fangs bit into Kingsley's shoulder. "Lola, run!" Kingsley grunted as he collapsed to the forest floor. And she did run—to catch him as he fell. She looked deep into his eyes with her own, and flashing emerald was the last thing Kingsley saw before everything went black.

***

The giant wolf only wanted one thing: to devour her. Its massive skull was nearly two feet in length, and it's bloody teeth bared.

But Lola refused to run. Distancing herself from the beast, Lola cautiously stepped back, crunching on the leaves underfoot. The wolf charged her, using its head to throw Lola against an oak tree. It crushed her ribs on the right side. As she fell in a heap on the ground, she heard something crack. Not sure if it was her leg, Lola forced herself to stand.

As her rage rose, so did her magick, the will of it consuming every part of her. Suddenly, everything was clear. From the individual leaves on the trees to the worms crawling on the ground. It was as if her magick allowed the strength of her ancestors to course through her veins.

As her heart beat, it pulsed magical energies into the forest around her. A small but clear blue-green blast of waves shot from her tiny hands. Lola paired her newfound magick with the only defense she knew: her Misa warrior tactics. Her training had taken her from daughter to soldier, from woman to weapon. Finally, she was Misa, and she was ready for war.

Lola took Kingsley's gilded sword from where it had fallen amongst the leaves. Waves of her magick pulsed through the blade as she raised it steadily. The dire's menacing growl would have shocked her to her frigid bones, but rather than run from it, she faced it, her eyes flashing. It was up to her to save them. As the wolf slowly approached, Lola shifted the sword from one hand to the other. The steel was heavier than she was used to, but it would do. As she and the wolf paced, Lola whispered the Mōsa motto, "Here, before, now and after."

Then, with two swings of the blade, her magick slashed and removed the head of the horrid beast. Blood sprayed and stained the snowdrop blossoms. Heart racing, Lola took rapid breaths. She turned to Kinglsey and wiped the blood from the blade on her gray riding coat. Kingsley whispered, "First, you take my horse, and now my sword." His breathing was strained but he still managed to chuckle. "Lola, you are a wonderfully wicked woman, and I think I like it?"

Lola heaved Kingsley to his feet.

"King, we must make haste. I fear your shoulder is in worse condition than I thought." There was blood everywhere. Lola had never been squeamish around blood before the Darkness, but now, the smell of blood made her stomach turn.

"You look a little pale, Lola. Did the dire hurt you?"

"No. I am sure it's just my magick rising. The blood is making me a bit nauseous now. At any rate, we must get you back to Kingsguard Reef; you need to have the physician tend to your wounds."

"I'd rather have you tend to my wounds," he said as he licked his delicious lips. He leaned his arm over her shoulder for balance. Lola's stomach flipped to have him this close.

"Do you know what I think?" His words slurred.

I'd listen to anything rather than my own inappropriate thoughts, Lola thought.

"What do you think, King?"

His mouth turned up a fraction of an inch, Kingsley uttered, "I think the men of Mōsa were complete fools."

"Fools? Why would you say that?" She arched one eyebrow.

"Because I would have given anything to grow up alongside you."

His words proved more arousing than Lola cared to admit. Trying to make light of his flirtation, she said, "You, sir are clearly delirious from the dire's bite. We must get you home."

"This is not about the bite," he said with quiet intensity, making eye contact with her. "Lola, you are magnificent, and anyone who can't see that is a fucking fool." His good hand briefly touched the back of her neck as he lifted the collar of her riding coat. She ignored the way his touch titillated her and focused on getting him home.

Lola whistled sharply, and Cross swiftly galloped back to the battle scene. She helped Kingsley onto the horse first and then swung herself up in front of him. He slumped against her back—from blood loss or just the need to be close to her, Lola didn't know. The suns were setting in the east, meaning moonrise would be upon them soon enough. They galloped into the dark woods in the hopes they could make it to Kingsguard Reef before the starlit skies consumed the Ventane Woods.

Lola guided the steed across the freezing river, through the mist, and past the small wooden bridge they'd crossed on their way. She hadn't realized how far from Kingsguard Reef they had ventured. How had she not noticed? Talking with Kingsley had distracted her. He had distracted her.

"King, I will get you home but you must stay with me. Stay awake." Kingsley's slumped body found refuge on her shoulders. "Lola," he mumbled. "I fear that sleep will take…me soon." The end of his sentence dissolved. He was getting so cold. The forest was far-reaching, dark, and ancient, but Lola knew she would have to find somewhere for Kingsley to rest until morning.

A mixture of sounds—the distant howling of ravenous beasts—echoed through the brisk night air. Closing her fingers and squeezing backward on the reins, Lola halted the stallion near a flat, serene parish surrounded by the mountains of the Sanctum. Its natural barrier would allow for Lola to keep a warm fire burning without threat of the harsh winds blowing it out entirely. She hopped down from Cross and gently helped Kingsley dismount, then raced to lay him by the wall and cover him with the hunter-green blanket they had shared moments before the dire wolf attacked.

Kingsley slept soundly while Lola tried to stay awake to safeguard the prince. But sleep clawed at her weary muscles. She loved her newfound power, but it drained her strength like nothing she'd ever known.

Lola shuffled closer to the sleeping prince and tucked him in once more. As she gently caressed his forehead, swiping his chestnut hair from his sweaty face, Kingsley jolted awake. Fisting her hair possessively, he drew her within inches of his perfect lips. Before she knew what was happening, his arms were around her, and their lips crashed together. She again felt the rush of helplessness, the sinking surrender, the surging tide of her magick that left her twisted. Lola was drowned in desire and despair. She had been kissed before, but never like this. His insistent mouth separated her sweet, shivering lips, sending wild tremors down her spine as his tongue aroused desire she had never known existed. And before her mind told her this was wrong, she kissed him back. Still fisting her hair, King gently bent her back to give him access to her neck, and he kissed her there, softly at first, then with a swift scale of intensity. Lola clung to him as if he were the only solid thing in the world she has woken up to. Sliding his hand down her neck, Lola could feel her magick rise to the surface. She pushed it down deep until she was out of his embrace. And then Kingsley was gone, and she was alone in the dark. "Kingsley?" she whispered, touching her lips, but all she could hear was his feet slowly shuffling away from the crackling fire. Her heart pounded.

****Sanctum, three years ago -

Her words trailed off abruptly. The warm, golden hues of the mountaintop sunset in her mind's eye suddenly darkened.

Her eyes, moments ago alight with joy, now stared vacantly ahead. Her pupils dilated, transforming her gaze into dark, haunted pools. A slight tremor began in her hands.

The air around Lola seemed to grow thick and oppressive. Goosebumps raised on her arms, and the color drained from her face, leaving it ashen and drawn.

In her mind, she was no longer safe. She was back there, in that moment of terror and despair that had changed everything.

Lola's breathing became rapid and shallow, her chest rising and falling in quick, jerky movements. A bead of sweat formed on her temple, slowly tracing a path down her cheek like a solitary tear.

Her body tensed, shoulders hunching as if to make herself smaller, to hide from the horrors playing out in her mind. The relaxed posture of moments ago vanished, replaced by rigid, barely-contained panic.

She had grown accustomed to the smell of piss and shit around her...This wet, dark cell was the place of her nightmares. The lone window—high up the wall—never let in the cold air, but she could feel the sun's warmth as a stripe of light crossed her filthy feet.

His silver gaze consumed her as the guards grabbed Lola, tossing her to the filthy ground and strapping her to ropes on the floor. Lola refused to show them any fear, even if her spine felt like it had collapsed. Laying amongst the decay, excrement, blood, and vomit, Lola closed her eyes. She needed her mother's strength and encouragement now. But her mother, her sisters, and her Misa war maidens were gone. She would have to face these monsters alone. Alone is something she had never been. Lola had never felt this empty.

The voice that she heard night after fucking night was back. Curt and filled with a dark rage, he asked, "Are you ready to show me your magick, Lola?" His familiarity with her name made her want to spit in his face.

Fists balled tightly, eyes staring blankly, Lola replied, "I have no magick, asshole. You'd think you would know that after all this time." He gently caressed her wet face with his rough hand and whispered, "I can get you out of here, my dove. I can make all of this go away. You have to make it rise, and I will do the rest."

"If I had magick, I would use it to destroy you. Did you forget who I am? I am the Mōsian princess. I am Lola of Porte House, battle maiden, the snake of the great expanse and last of my name."

His laughter echoed in the dungeon.

"You keep telling us you have no magick, but wake up every morning fully healed. There is magick in you, girl, and we will see it extinguished," the hooded monster whispered coolly. He pulled at her ankles and wrists and wound the rope around the crossbars at her head and feet. Lola was once again in agony. Night after night, she endured this. There were nights she would have gladly revealed her magick to welcome death, but it would not show itself. The loud pop of snapping cartilage had her gasping for breath. She had grown too accustomed to these sounds.

A sudden jerk of the wooden handle yanked the ropes around her arms and ankles even tauter, but she would not scream; she would not give him the satisfaction.

"The prophecy alerted us to the rise of magick, but I never would have foreseen such a perfect specimen as one of its wielders. Did you know of the prophecy, princess?"

"Keep talking; your breath will kill me before your soldiers do." That earned her a slap from the beast. A warm, metallic taste filled her mouth. "The book contained precisely what we must prepare for."

With his voice low and gravely, he recited the prophecy, "When the three are reborn, the bond shall bring forth an age of magick and an era of sorrow. When you woke from the dead with those glowing green eyes, we knew you had magick. We knew then that you were one of the three. The master wanted me to behead you right then and there. But, unfortunately, I couldn't do that to such a beautiful face. And so, I made a vow to the master that I would extinguish your magick so long as I could take you as my bride." Lola swallowed a string of profanities as vomit rose in her throat. Her captor and torturer was to be her mate? She would kill him before ever letting him touch her. Lola never wanted to marry; she wanted to dedicate her life to becoming a Misa battle maiden. How had things changed so much? The beautiful life she lived amongst her people was becoming a distant memory with each passing day. Closing her eyes to push her magick deep down, Lola could hear the rushing waterfall just outside the massive granite door that marked the entrance to the dungeon. Focusing on the waterfall, the serene plants, and the vines that grew in this dark place, Lola found peace beyond all the pain.

She was weak, but her will was strong. Since waking this magick, Lola knew she would be a target. She also knew this magick could be her saving grace. If only she knew how to use it. Silence deafened her while the ropes pulled on her limbs. Pain shot through her naked body, and she was sure that soon, all the blood in her body would burst out her fingertips. Then the ropes relaxed, and her blood rushed back. A distant voice urged her to answer it. Then, finally, she could hear again. "Speak up!" the monster yelled. Voice cracked and raw, she recited…"Here, before now, and after," as her magick rose to the surface. Her blue-green eyes pulsed, her connection to Life Magick surging. Long, sly vines slowly made their way to the three soldiers' ankles undetected, wrapping around like the very ropes restraining Lola herself. The men were lifted high off the ground, and before they could shout or even move a muscle, Lola commanded the vines to cover their mouths. Her magick pulsed as it called to the roots deep beneath the surface of Transea. She willed the roots to halt just inches before piercing their hearts. Reciting the Mōsian people's chant once more, she ensured it was the last thing the men heard. "Here, before, now and after," she said. She closed her eyes and unleashed the roots into the hearts of the men, setting herself free at last. The vines crawled back to her, prying the ropes from her arms and legs. The roots came to her aid as she attempted to stand, lifting her upright and supporting her until she could stand alone. Grabbing a black tunic off one of the corpses, she slipped it over her naked body, climbed the root, and allowed it to carry her through the window and out of the dungeon. She hadn't planned for the magick to take so much energy from her, but it had. Leaving her exhausted, her vision faded to black. The roots that carried her receded from where they came, dropping Lola midair—far too high above the ground. Branch after branch sliced her arms and her face as she plummeted from the tower, falling for a slow eternity before hitting the ground hard. She was beaten and bloody, but she was free.

CHAPTER 9

Vows in the moonlight

Lola's screams pierced the night sky and broke Kingsley's heart. He would do anything to stop it. The pain from his bloody shoulder prevented him from holding Lola any tighter than he already was. He held her while her piercing screams slowly died into soft cries and whispers of nonsense, rocking her back and forth and cradling her head with his bad arm, but he didn't care. He didn't know how long he was asleep before he heard her gravely voice say, "What happened?"

He brushed her hair out of her face and whispered, "I'm not sure. You must've been having a nightmare. Can you remember anything?"

She tried to sit up, but the forest spun before her eyes and gravity dragged her back down onto King's lap. He held her close. "Just stay here a bit longer until the world rights itself. Now tell me, what is the last thing you remember?"

"I…I don't remember." She drew out the word don't, and he knew she wasn't being honest. He was tired of being patient and giving her space. He wanted to protect her, but he couldn't do that if she didn't tell him her truth.

"Lola, I need to know. First, you have to tell someone what happened. Then, how else will we help you so you can help your sister?"

Finding the strength to slowly sit up on her own, Lola refused to look at him. Instead, she wrapped her arms around her legs and slowly rocked herself. "King, I don't know. I can talk about it." Her voice was cracked and raw. "They took me, touched me, left me naked, bloodied, and beaten. Every night my magick healed me, and then they beat me again."

Kingsley's blood ran cold. He gritted his teeth with a dark rage and asked, "Who did this to you?"

"I don't know, I don't know!" she cried out. Her searing tears streaked down her distraught face, emerald eyes pulsing as her magick demanding release. But Lola would not allow her magick to cause harm to King. So she pushed it down and took several deep breaths to compose herself.

"Can you remember anything about the place or the people?"

"It was a dungeon, I think. The people that held me kept referring to it as the tower."

"Were there any sounds you can recall?" he asked impatiently.

"Yes. There was rushing water near the tower…I could

hear it at night, and when the guards came to…see me. Their boots…"

Snapping her from going back to that horrible place in her mind, Kingsley urged her to continue. "Lola, what about their boots?"

"Their boots were wet," she said, detached. Scooting closer to her, he put his arm around her shoulder. She flinched, and it broke his heart. Kingsley had witnessed similar responses to abuse in the Sanctum. Some of the boys in his unit were sent away to be "fixed" only to return… different. He could see that same far-away look they all had reflected in Lola's eyes.

Her memories were coming back in a flood, and he didn't know how to help her. "It's not your fault," he assured her.

Lola turned to face him with red-rimmed eyes. "What happened to you was disgusting and, in every sense of the word, wrong." His voice walked the line between bitterness and incredulity. "What they did to you…it's inconceivable. I promise I will find who did this, and they will pay." Then, just as Lola opened her mouth to say thank you but that she could take care of herself, he locked eyes with her and whispered, "Don't ask me to leave you alone with this because I will not."

Lola swallowed a lump in her throat and pressed her eyes shut, tears streaming down her cheeks. She nodded numbly, knowing there was nothing she could do to stop

King from guarding her.

The muffled clopping of horse hooves against the snow-covered ground had Kingsley leaping to his feet. He held his bloodied arm close as he squinted into the forest. Galloping their way towards the dying embers of their bonfire was Bishop. They were safe. More importantly, he knew Lola was safe.

"King, King?" he shouted from the distance. Taking one last look at the beautiful princess with copper skin, King shouted back, "Bishop!" He knew his family would come. He just wished they hadn't come in this moment; one look at Lola, and they, too, would see it. That she was ruined. King Heath would know something horrible had happened, and he wasn't sure he could keep this secret from his father.

"They will be here soon," he whispered as he gently helped Lola up from the ground. "I promise you I will make this right. I only ask that you trust me."

"What do you mean, trust you?"

"I don't believe I found you in the woods by happen-stance. It was destiny."

"Wiping the tears from her face, she asked, "What are you asking of me, Kingsley?"

"I need to tell my mother and father what has transpired. What you have learned about your captors."

"Absolutely not," she said, eyes pulsing.

"Do you trust me?"

"I will not have all of Transea knowing that the Misa warrior princess was taken captive"—her voice cracked—"and that she was afraid."

"Lola, anyone would be afraid if they were held under such conditions. I'm asking you to trust that my mother and father will do anything to protect you. We must tell them what you have remembered. You must let us help you make this right."

Nodding, she agreed to do as she was asked. "You are wrong, you know," she said. "There is no fixing what has happened to me."

Before Kingsley could tell her otherwise, Bishop, Thad, several guards, and the king and queen circled their horses around the campsite. Jumping off his horse, King Heath ran to his son. "Son, are you well?" He didn't wait for a response before checking every part of Kingsley's body as if he were a boy who had just scraped his knee. It was a tender moment Lola would never again have with her father. King Heath's gaze fell on his son's mangled arm.

"What happened to you?"

Kingsley gently drew away from his father.

"Father, there is much to tell you," he said as he looked at his mother, who was with Lola, wiping the tears that kept coming. "Something terrible has happened to the princess. I will wait to share it until we return, but no one will stop me from making this right for her. I need your word that you will help me solve this injustice."

His father recognized the look in his son's amber eyes. It was the same look the king got when he would do anything to protect his queen and his children. He knew he would help his son; he just didn't know how and at what cost.

After making it back to House Do'Ramos, Lola, Kingsley, the queen and king, and his trusted cousins, Thad and Bishop, were informed of the dire wolf attack. Both Lola and Kingsley omitted the crucial element of the story: how Lola had saved them with her magick. The royals sat in quiet despair at Lola's tragic recall of her time in the tower. She explained how the guards were hooded. How she never saw their faces, just their eyes. They never used names, and all wore black. The only guard she could remember was the one who beat her and took liberties with her every night. The silvery eyes that pierced through darkness under his hood was something she would never forget.

"But how did they take you from Mōsa?" Queen Alina asked, wiping her tears. Lola shook her head and shut her eyes. She truly had no idea.

"Those were dark days filled with much grief and turmoil. I don't know how you made it there, Princess Lola," the King began, "but I do know that at some point, there was no more room for the bodies that succumbed to the Darkness. So Mōsa had to make hard choices, and some bodies were transported to the Western Isles to be disposed of."

The room fell silent again, remembering how the Darkness had nearly destroyed Mōsa.

"That may answer how she was transported out of Mōsa, but it doesn't explain why she wasn't returned when they realized she was alive," the king said to no one in particular.

"The night is late, and Kingsley needs to have that wound tended to," Alina insisted. "And I am sure the princess could use a warm bath and a cup of Eliram lavender tea to help her rest. We can discuss all of this again in the morning."

Nodding, the king agreed.

"One more thing, son." King Heath cleared his throat. "It is decided you will accompany the Princess to be reunited with her sister."

Eyes wide in relief and surprise, Kingsley blurted out, "Thank you, Father." His cousins chuckled at his eagerness as Kingsley's lips formed a tight line.

"And the pair of you will accompany him!" The King exclaimed to the brothers. "Thad, please escort the princess to her quarters."

"No!" Kingsley shouted. "I mean, my king, I would like to escort the princess to her quarters."

"Oh no, you don't," his mother chimed in. "You are off to the infirmary, young prince. Your arm needs tending to. We have a ball in two nights' time, and we need you mended or at least mending."

Taking one last look at Lola, King closed the distance

between them. Then, facing her tear-streaked face, puffy eyes, and full lips, he brushed her loose hair behind the ear and said, "I'll see you tomorrow. Thad will make sure you get to your room safe." They stared at each other for a few seconds longer than they probably should have.

"Umm, humm," the King gestured. "Let us all find rest this evening. Tomorrow we will sort all of this out." With that, Lola walked out of the room on Thaduis's arm. Kingsley hated to see her on anyone's arm other than his, especially Thad—a charming prick who would do anything to get a pretty lady.

***

Lola sat in the warm copper tub the chambermaids had prepared for her and sobbed. Her wet hair coiled around her face as flashbacks of the dungeon continued to plague her mind. Her magick had saved her night after night in that horrible place. Healing every scar, every physical wound. But it couldn't make her the woman she was before.

Lola knew Kingsley would protect her from the first time she met him in the woods. She didn't quite understand why this made her feel safe. The gravity of her situation weighed heavy on her. She had been changed forever, and she would get revenge. The Holy Mother would swing her sword and make her strong to destroy the people who did this to her.

He had kissed her. He had kissed her hard. What if she could have a different life? How did she get so attached to a boy she'd met just a few weeks ago? She shook her head and let her thoughts go elsewhere. There were more critical questions Lola had to ask herself. The Darkness had stolen everything from her. She wasn't the same person anymore, and for the first time since learning of her sister's survival, she wondered...what if Sole wasn't either?

A gentle knock on the door made her flinch. The ache in her chest filled her with anxiety as she climbed out of the copper tub and wrapped a silk robe around her wet body. Taking deep breaths, she tried to settle her rapid beating heart.

Walking to the door, she told herself, "You are no longer in the dungeon; you are safe; you have magick."

Creaking open the walnut door, she found Kingsley on the other side—freshly washed, his hair still dripping wet. He smelled of lavender, honey, and spice. Then, smiling that crooked smile, he said, "How fair is the tea?"

"Prince, I do not think it wise for you to be found in my room at such an hour. You must go."

"I will go. But first, I wanted to give you this."

He drew his hand out from behind his back, holding a short dagger, made of Ventane steel. The blade was bio-luminescent and a strikingly familiar hue of aquamarine.

"This is Mōsian steel?"

"Yes it is," he said, eyes smiling.

Lola shifted the weight of the blade between her hands, examining its curved guard and pommel. This was a well-balanced masterpiece. The second best steel in all of Transea, second only to Sundonian steel. The weapon was the perfect representation of two worlds—hers and his—colliding, but she would rather die than tell him that's what she was thinking. Lola stared at the blade and lowered herself to sit on the settee. "My grandfather gave this to me when I was a boy. As I got older, my hands outgrew its grip. He called it the Champion's Choice."

Smiling as he sat right beside her, Kingsley continued, "When I was a boy, he told me tales of how one could use this magical blade to crush their enemies! He told me that the aquamarine steel possessed old magick. Staring at her as she examined the weapon, he whispered, "I want you to have it."

Bright-eyed, she looked up at him. "What? No, I could never take something your grandfather gave you. Never." She handed the blade back to him.

"Well, that is good to know that you won't take it. That's why I am giving it to you," he said slyly. "Besides, you are the only true champion I have ever met. You survived death, captivity, you faced off with a dire..."

Kingsley placed the blade back in her hands. "You,

beautiful Princess, are a champion to me."

Lola was enamored with this stunning weaponry—and possibly with the prince, too. The blade was wide with a curved crossguard, creating the ideal weight balance. The cross-guard had an ornamented lion paw on each side, the Do'Ramos family's symbol. "It has sat in my night drawer for many years. I think I've found a good home with you. It would also make me feel better if you carried protection. The day he gifted it to me, my grandfather told me, 'The greatest fighters of all are the most deserving of this weapon.' Lola, tonight, you have proven more than once that you are a fierce fighter. I couldn't think of anyone more deserving than you to call this blade your own."

"Thank you, King," Lola said with a small but honest smile. "You really didn't have to. I promise you it will never leave my side."

"You are a unique woman, Princess."

"What makes you say that?"

"I have encountered many women in my lifetime."

Lola's jaw tightened at his mention of other women.

"None of those women were brave enough to face what you did and come out the victor. I give you this blade because there is no greater woman I know that will put it to good use. You amaze me, Lola Porte."

Clasping her hands in his, he continued, "I vow to you on this night. I will find who did this to you and slice their balls off. What they did is unforgivable. I will send scouts out in the morning to start exploring these woods in search of the waterfall. There are three in the area that we know of. Once we locate the one you spoke of, my father will send my guards and me to retrieve the monsters who did this to you. Their crimes will not go unpunished."

Twirling a loose strand of her long, chocolate hair between his fingers, Lola thought he might kiss her again. She was sure of it.

But...rising from the settee, he put his hands on her shoulders and asked, "May I hug you?"

Nodding, she whispered, "Yes." She stood, and for a long moment, they held each other. The butterflies in her stomach flipped and her entire body tightened in his embrace. Before they parted for the night, he walked her to her bed, kissed her on the cheek, and tucked her in.

Lola's eyes shone bright like emeralds. "Your eyes, they are glowing," he whispered. "One day, I'll figure out why they do that."

Stepping through the doorway, Kingsley turned at the sound of his name.

"King," Lola called softly from the bed. "I think it happens when there is danger...and when I am happy."

"Princess, did you just admit that I make you happy?" he asked with that crooked smile.

"Good night, Prin...goodnight, King."

CHAPTER 10

A Mōsian court

Princess Lola stood before the gilded mirror. Light from the flickering candles casting a warm glow on her face as she fastened the clasp of her golden necklace. Her heart beat like a raucous drum in anticipation of the Solstice Ball.

As she looked out of the window, a small potted plant sitting on the windowsill drew her attention. It was wilted and dry; her chambermaid hadn't watered it in a while.

Without thinking twice, she reached out to touch it. Closing her eyes and focusing her magick, she visualized it coming back to life—the brown fading, replaced with emerald green, little buds forming and ready to flower. A gentle, green light emanated from her hand, enveloping the plant in a soft glow.

The leaves rose up, then the stem stood taller.

Healthier.

Lola smiled in satisfaction of her accomplishment. She knew she had to be careful using her magick with others so nearby, but she couldn't resist the urge to help this plant in need.

If it had been as neglected as it looked, no one would notice what she'd done anyhow.

She returned to the mirror, taking in her reflection.

Her gown was a sight to behold, crafted from some of the finest velvet she'd ever seen. It shimmered like moonlight on the Great Expanse in Mōsa. Its rich dark green hue exuded mystery, as though she could hide in the forest with it. It flowed in a graceful cascade down to the floor and showcased Lola's curves with a heart-shaped neckline. Her raven braids descended down her back, each strand adorned with a golden clasp, while a black stole draped elegantly around her shoulders, providing warmth in the chilly night air. Her dark skin glowed in the soft light. However, her luscious ruby lips, tightly pressed together, unveiled her unease.

Sirena had helped plan her attire, along with the aid of Consuelo the chamberlain. The Princess of Kingsguard Reef gushed over the wardrobe Lola had at her disposal, ecstatic when they had finally settled on this green number. She saw her snagging everyone's attention, yet again.

"I fear my brother and cousins will find it impossible to resist being captivated by your radiant presence," Sirena shared, brimming with excitement.

Lola didn't want anyone's attention tonight.

"I would far prefer the exhilaration of riding Kingsley's

horse, rather than subject myself to the advances of men who seek nothing more than momentary dalliances," she declared.

"One thing is certain, my brother can't keep his eyes off you. I don't think I have ever seen him this enamored, not even with Mya."

"Darling, you underestimate your charm," Lola whispered to Sirena. "Let's not forget that you look absolutely spectacular tonight. I can't help but wonder who will be utterly smitten by you this evening," Lola exclaimed with a sassy wink.

Sirena wore a stunning ruby velvet gown with a plunging neckline, complemented by her dark, pinned-back curls and a golden wolf pin that she wore on her gown. Sirena waved her compliment off humbly.

"You may very well be my biggest masterpiece!" Sirena exclaimed as she gazed upon Lola's completed ensemble.

"Kissing her on the cheek she whispered, "I will see you at the ball. Don't be late."

"You never know, I might get lost on my way there," Lola uttered in frustration.

Ignoring Lola's sneering, Sirena exuded an air of undeniable elegance and magnetic charm as she exited the room. Before she crossed the threshold, she called back, "Don't fret, your escort will be here shortly to ensure you arrive on time."

"I need an es…" Lola began to say, but Sirena ignored her and shut the door to her room.

Lola shook her feeling of unease. No amount of dressing up and feeling beautiful, no amount of compliments would make the reality of the ball any easier. She was going to have to be on the whole evening, even if she lacked the energy to do so.

She looked at the plant in the window. Right.

Despite her reservations, this gown was necessary for her diplomatic role.

She has a mission to accomplish; acquire support for Mōsa, and for Sole. She had to be charismatic, and magnetic, never revealing who she is. She had to be confident.

Taking in her reflection again, she smiled deeply. She did look beautiful. This dress was yet another weapon in her arsenal. She was a warrior, first and foremost. Misa warriors knew how to make the most out of any resources they had at their disposal. If she was to garner the attention and respect she deserved, she couldn't be any more prepared.

She was in command.

With a flick of her locs, she prepared to leave the comfort of her chambers, her confidence rising as rapidly as her revived plant. The gown flowed behind her like a river of darkness.

Only one last thing to do.

She had to ensure that the Champion's Choice, the Mōsian blade Kingsley gave her—was on her at all times. Sheathing it beneath her royal gown, secured close to her left thigh, Lola adjusted the fabric around it and stepped out into the bedroom, the bathroom doors sweeping away behind her as she walked through the entryway.

"Is there anything else you need, miss?" her tall, fair-haired chambermaid asked as Lola entered the room.

"No. Thank you for assisting me Eva," Lola replied.

She meant it.

Lola was starting to understand why Sirena liked getting all dressed up. She was right. It made her feel powerful, knowing she looked her best. But, doing so required help, and getting her hair done was somewhat of a guilty pleasure. In Mōsa, women gracefully embraced the tradition of allowing their locs to cascade freely, embellished with glistening golden clasps interwoven in their braids. However, in the midst of this sea of flowing hair, Sole, her sister, had always stood out. With meticulous care, she had often gathered her ebony strands in an intricate updo, skillfully crafted, to keep her hair from falling into her face while engrossed in the sacred tomes and ancient scrolls of their forebears.

"Oh, no need to thank me, miss," Eva chirped. "It is my job to make sure you look perfect for the ball." She couldn't be a year or so younger than Lola, but she'd been more diligent than the forgotten princess could have asked for. She had run out of time. The grand hour arrived, heralding the magnificent Ball of the Solstice. The drums sped up, matching Lola's anticipation.

This world was so different from Mōsa. Back home, no one bowed to one another. Even the royals were taught to dress and bathe themselves. Still, with all that personal training, Lola could barely style her own locs, which is why she often opted to wear them down.

Eva positioned Lola in front of another mirror so she could adjust her stole one final time. The fabric hugged Lola's shoulders in all the right ways. Eva was about to say something else when a figure in the doorway interrupted her.

"Are you ready?"

Lola looked behind her reflection in the mirror to see a young woman with honey-molten eyes, chestnut skin, and a surplus of attitude staring at her intently from the door frame.

Her hair was a beautiful light hue of pink.

Those eyes, oh yes! Another Do'Ramos, perhaps? "Lady Martin," Eva said as she curtsied.

The purple-haired beauty eyed Lola up and down, her arms crossed.

"You're attending the Ball of the Solstice in that outfit?"

As Lola's brows raised, Lady Martin quickly wagged a

hand.

"What I mean is, isn't this a bit…grandiose for a Mōsian woman? Aren't you accustomed to the wild? The sand and dirt? Things that have you more dressed down?"

Who the fuck was this Lady Martin, leaning in on Lola's private moments, judging her attire? Lola hadn't seen her around the castle, and looking at her negative stance, she was glad for it. Lola applied one final layer of red tint to her lips before replying, "I assure you Lady Martin, I am just as ready for the wilds in this ensemble as I would be in any other. Though, I tend not to meddle in the trivial matters some nobles seem to concern themselves with. I'm sure you don't, either."

Her final words dripped in clear, pointed sarcasm. It was Lady Martin's turn to raise her eyebrows. "My name is Melia, Kingsley's cousin," she said. Sirena had mentioned her cousin Melia, but she hadn't mentioned that she was so stunning. Her gaze was full and assertive and her angular features were as sharp as her tongue.

Her honey eyes would be graceful if they weren't so cunning, watching Lola suspiciously. Several moles spread seductively on her left cheek. Her sleek copper legs peeked out from beneath her black gown. No doubt she'd enchant any ballroom attendee. But it was her ashen pink curls that made her a true beauty.

"You may have met my brothers, Thad and Bishop," she

said. Lola nodded without diverting from her own reflection in the mirror. Sirena had mentioned her escort would arrive shortly, but the last thing she'd expected was this crude woman.

Her presence towered over the whole doorway.

Lola wasn't about to feel boxed in.

If Melia intended to be assertive, then Lola would dominate.

She turned to face her.

"I am Princess Lola Sirena of Porte House. I am sure your brothers told you of my identity."

What sense was there in withholding the truth even if Melia didn't know who she was? Besides, Lola wasn't afraid of some woman who preferred to glower and cross her arms than have a civil interaction.

"I appreciate your honesty," Melia uttered as she sauntered into the room. An awkward silence held the chambermaids captive. Finally, Melia took the reins and spoke.

"It wasn't right what happened to you."

"What do you mean?" Lola asked.

"Princess, we are a tight-knit family. Not one of us is unaware of the torment and captivity you endured. When you and King arrived, it seems Sirena practically screamed it from the turrets."

Stepping closer to Lola, she continued.

"So, I'll repeat it. It wasn't right what happened to you." Lola was stunned. This woman ignited her magick rage. She couldn't help but feel enraged by the Do'Ramos family. How dare they broadcast her pain?

The desire to leave as soon as possible clawed at Lola.

She's not the enemy, she told herself. At least not for the time being. Get it under control.

Lola returned to the mirror, not giving Melia the satisfaction of eye contact.

"My past is of no one's concern. I really don't know what business it is of yours."

"You should know the Do'Ramos family comes from a long line of warriors. But, unfortunately, we have a terrible knack for wanting to protect the weak, and shit like that."

Eva, who'd been busying herself tidying up, frantically bowed out and attended to something else.

"Weak? Did you just imply that I, a Misa Warrior, am weak?! I will assure you that the one thing I am not...is fucking weak," Lola proclaimed as soon as they were alone.

A vexatious smile spread across Melia's face. "Good! You should know, Princess, that neither are we. Once Kingsley finds out who did this to you, he will destroy them. Even if it means destroying himself in the process."

"No," Lola demanded. "I don't want anyone involved in this. Once I get to my sister, we will sort this out."

"Well until then, you are under our protection. Something

you ought to be grateful for."

"Oh, Melia," Lola said, refusing to use her proper title. "I am quite grateful."

Melia tilted her head to look down at Lola with an infuriating smile.

"I can see why 'ol King is enamored with you."

"Enamored?" Lola turned away from the mirror and walked right up to her. "I don't care for your implications!"

"Oh, you will soon learn, Princess, that I say as I please. And, I acknowledge what I see." She shrugged.

"Kingsley is a good person. Damaged, cynical about his future, and maybe a bit skeptical that a woman like you would even attempt to get close to him, yes. But he is still a good man and one day he will be a good king."

Lola was about to kick this woman's ass. The only thing holding her back was her commitment to the evening. No good would come of a fight before the ball. So, in an effort not to choke on her tongue, she said nothing.

Melia strode over to the fireplace and eyed an hourglass on the mantle. Her long nails tapped the wooden base. She threw a rueful look over her shoulder.

"Kingsley's love life has been open for the world to see, for quite some time now—the good and the bad parts. Now, most onlookers pity him."

Melia crossed her arms. Her expression slipped ever so slightly. Sadness, maybe?

Lola was annoyed at the thought of his people pitying him. "He doesn't need anyone's pity. And he especially doesn't want yours," she spat.

If Melia was a caring person, she was hiding it deep down.

Lola realized she'd been holding her breath. She swallowed a string of profanities and decided it was best to make her way to the great hall. Let this woman have her weird tantrum from her high horse.

What a waste of my time.

But Melia was determined. Following Lola and ultimately passing her with her long legs, the tall beauty came to a halt in front of Lola, forcing her to stop in her tracks.

"We are a small kingdom," she said, keeping her voice down. "And we care about Kingsley. We want to see him happy, and not just because he's our future king. In case you haven't noticed, he's not just charming, he's fucking hot. Many women would kill to be his choice. The one he does choose ought to realize what that means."

She carried on until the end of the corridor and paused, looking around to ensure no one was near.

"He deserves happiness. If he won't find it with you, you leave him be."

Lola scoffed again, stifling a laugh.

"Well, then Lady Martin, let me conclude this ridiculous discussion. I am unsure why you have convinced yourself that I am seeking to become either the source of Kingsley's joy or his worst nightmare. But let me be very clear that I have much more significant endeavors that demand my attention. I'm not sure if you have heard, but the Darkness is killing our loved ones. Rather than focusing on your cousin's romantic endeavors, I am far more concerned with greater pursuits, like regaining my father's throne."

She pursed her red lips.

"Soon, I will be off to be with my sister. And you, your family, and your kingdom will become a faded memory until I decide to dredge it up again. Do you understand?" Lola spat, her eyes raging green.

She didn't wait for Melia's answer before turning and strutting toward the great hall.

Even if Kingsley was ready to explore something more, Lola wasn't. Besides, King wanted Mya. She was the one who could make this right.

All the emotions had churned up that fizzy, energetic heat in the pit of Lola's stomach—an energy that was entirely comforting and untamed all at once. Lola didn't need a mirror to know her eyes were burning. She felt them shifting. As she walked down the hall she looked out the windows and saw the thicket of trees densely surrounding the castle. She started to imagine the roots from the trees, those mighty branches bursting through the windows, eking out and spreading through the castle, snatching up Melia, guards, Kingsley, and everyone who had managed to annoy her since she'd arrived in Kingsguard Reef.

Lola examined the trees further. The leaves and branches had started to sway. Was that the wind? Or was it her?

Breathe, she told herself. Don't bring what you just imagined to life!

As her time alone before the ball continued to slip away, Lola kept focusing, trying to ward off these feelings of unease. She had been careful to keep her magick under wraps so far. She couldn't draw too much attention to herself. Even with her regal attire, she was hoping over the course of the night, she'd be able to blend in with the crowd, enjoying the festivities without risking any incidents.

"Princess!"

She turned to see Thad, beaming and marching down the hallway from the Ball, which was just around the corner. Soft music stretched out from behind him.

"Are you coming? We are waiting for you!"

This was precisely what she didn't need—another Martin sibling to add to her malaise about partaking in this Ball.

She bit her tongue anyway, stifling her attitude. Over the last several days, Thad and Lola had spent time connecting and laughing. When Thad was initially assigned to be Lola's guard, he approached the task with duty and professionalism.

However, fate had a different plan in store for them. Their

shared experiences and moments of vulnerability built a bridge of understanding, quickly revealing the genuine person behind Thad's stoic facade. And amidst the laughter and heartfelt conversations, Lola had found solace in the presence of her new...friend. There was no need to be hostile to him. Underneath his charming, noble exterior, he was quite sweet.

He had asked so many questions about her disappearance, her time in the Ventane Woods, and Kingsley's rescue. He wanted to know how much she remembered, and what she needed in order to move on. To forget and push forward, to become the strong princess that she had once been.

He was one of the only people in the castle who seemed to be wary of the lingering Darkness in the world. That Lola was destined to be involved in it, whether she wanted to or not.

It was hard not to appreciate his friendship.

Once he reached her in the hall, Thad blinked, taken aback by her beauty and her green gown. A taste of shy awe played across his face.

"My..." was all he said.

"My apologies, my Lord," Lola sighed. "It's been a long day."

"Has it?"

"Yes. Perhaps it will be better now that you're here." Now,

Thad looked horrified. Dramatically so.

"Now I know something is really wrong. You are being too nice to me. I knew this would happen, I just knew it!"

"You knew what would happen?"

"I knew you would fall in love with me. You might not care, but I don't want to double-cross my cousin. Let's put a stop to this at once."

"You are ridiculous." She rolled her eyes. Thad grinned, continuing to tease her.

"You need to go back to breaking my heart with every bit of venom you can throw at me, and I will go back to admiring you from afar."

"I thought you were all concerned about your cousin," she replied. "Isn't admiration even from afar a risk?"

He snorted.

"When I acted concerned I was lying."

It was hard not to admire his mannerisms. His silky brown locs, even before the Ball, looked slightly unkempt. That was how he was—natural—and it suited him just fine.

He also had those damn Do'Ramos eyes—honey brown, nearly ablaze when you caught their attention. Yet, they didn't burn like Kingsley's eyes. His eyes captivated her. She had no clue how they've been seared into her mind, even when she didn't want to see them. But, they were imprinted there nonetheless, refusing to let go of her.

Maybe Thad was what she needed right now.

The perfect distraction.

Charming enough, easygoing, and clearly confident, he wasn't looking for love, just a good time. And it was clear he liked to work his way under his cousin's skin. If she was going to focus her energy on anyone to get through the Ball of the Solstice, Thad would be the perfect choice. He'd wash Kingsley right out of her mind.

Thad shot her a crooked smile as she took a step closer, albeit dimmer than what she was used to from King. "Save me a dance," she told him. Then, she passed him, ready to enter the great hall. He hurried after her, extending his arm.

"Now, now, Princess, you should know better. I must escort you in."

"How strange that the women here need escorting," she noted, brushing the skirt of her gown as though brushing Thad himself off. "In Mōsa, women enter a room on their own. My father would say, I believe my daughters to be beautiful and brutal. Either version can stand alone in a room."

Thad hastily replied, "I am sure you can do this on your own. But, what if I'm the one who needs the escort?"

She couldn't keep her red lips from curling up into a smile.

"You're very quick on your feet."

Standing beside her, he placed her small hand in the bend of his elbow. Then, they glided toward the music, crowds, and the extensive Solstice feast. "Let's go drive my cousin mad," he whispered. She could feel him winking in his head. "You are trouble, Thad Martin."

"And you love it, Princess Lola. Besides, when Kingsley sees you in that dress, he will surely be undone. I for one can't wait to see him unravel."

"Watch your tongue," she teased. He patted her gloved hand.

"You can deny it, but neither of you can hide it."

"Hide, what?"

"What you feel when you're around each other. Everyone can see it." His jaw tightened with that remark.

"Something you all insist on addressing, but do nothing whatsoever to assist in."

"Well, I'll be helping Kingsley now," Thad stated. "A little competition will shine a light so brightly on things he'll have nowhere to hide."

Fine, Thad wasn't going to help her forget about Kingsley. But meddling with him, just a bit, was the next best thing.

***

"Why must mother insist on pairing our Solstice feast with torment?" Kingsley whispered to Sirena as they stood alongside their parents, smiling cordially while receiving guests for the first ball of the week.

The energy in the room was stiff. Dignitaries arrived with their families in a show of solidarity to House of Do'Ramos. The receiving line took place in the great hall. It was an elaborate display of holiday frenzy.

"Take heed, brother, before Mother hears you and injures your other arm."

"She would, indeed!"

He stood tall, dressed in his finest attire. His luxurious velvet emerald jacket was tailored to perfection and adorned with intricate golden embroidery. Beneath it was a black regal tunic. The entire outfit was pulled together by a heavy umbra steel gilded crown atop his head, studded with black glittering jewels that sparkled under the ballroom's chandeliers. Umbrasteel could only be found in the mines of the Ventane Woods. Although he didn't usually wear his crown, it was expected of him during the Solstice parties.

He loved the jacket.

He hated the crown.

However, the black sling that held his injured arm in place was a stark contrast to the elegance of his attire. He had to be mindful not to move it too much, something that wouldn't be easy with all the dancing and formalities he had committed to tonight. He resisted the urge to groan. The weight of the crown put pressure on his neck, causing his posture to wane. Despite this, he kept his composure dignified, greeting the guests with warm smiles and gracious words.

"So, tell me brother, what are you going to do about your little problem?"

"My problem?"

"Yes, your problem."

Bemused, Kingsley had no idea what his inquisitive sister was talking about.

Rolling her eyes, Sirena whispered, "What are you going to do about Princess Lola?"

"There is nothing to do. Father has agreed to allow me to leave to accompany her to her sister. I will bring Thad and Bishop with me."

"Ugh! you are insufferable," Sirena proclaimed. "I meant, what are you going to do about your feelings for Lola?"

"Feelings? I assure you there are no—"

"Will you stop! Anyone who is in the room with the pair of you can see something is there. I think she may be your perfect match.

Jaw tightening, King locked eyes with his sister. Who was he fooling? His sister knew him best of all. She wasn't wrong.

"I get thirsty just looking at her, though it makes no sense," Kingsley confessed to his sister.

"I couldn't be any happier for you, King!" Sirena squealed so only her brother could hear, reeling her excitement back the moment she remembered the formality of the atmosphere.

"You deserve something of your own," she said, calmer. "Not something that was forced upon you."

She bowed to another family from the South. Once they continued down the line, she jabbed Kingsely with a final, whispered comment.

"Admit it! You are lovelorn!"

"What? I'm not fucking lovelorn," Kingsley protested. His statement didn't keep the blush from creeping up his neck. When Sirena noticed, she tweaked her nose and smiled, comfortable in her smugness.

"You may hate me for saying this, but she is better suited for you than Mya ever was. I never liked her. She was too nice. A fake."

"Don't congratulate me just yet. The princess has no idea how I feel for her. She thinks I am spoiled, arrogant, and insufferable."

"And she's right," Sirena choked out with a mischievous smile.

Kingsley asked quietly, "Who's side are you on?"

"I am on your side." They turned back to the line of guests, Sirena's giddiness beaming under her guise of prestige.

Each of the sixteen obsidian columns was beautifully wrapped in holly, flickering flames of lighting fixtures illuminating the immense hall. The gorgeous crimson rung ran from the aisle down through the center, and atop it sat a lustrous table where the guest would dine. Ornate place settings framed the long centerpiece of snowdrops, black tulips, and holly on a black velvet runner that sparkled in the glow of the candelabras.

As they made their way through the line of guests, Kingsley and Sirena were surprised to see Mya's family in attendance. Kingsley had not seen Mya's father since King Heath had called off the betrothal over a year ago.

"Well, this is awkward," whispered Sirena before smiling and saying, "Lord Ezra, it's been too long." Ezra and King Heath had been good friends as young men. Both rose to power before they were ten and eight; they'd been forced to grow up fast. The years and politics had strained their houses significantly. As the high priest of the Sanctum, the boarding school for all second-born children, and the High priest head of the Holy Mother Church, Ezra had close ties to Sundom. In the past weeks, there had been whispers of Ezra's involvement in the disappearance of alleged mages. King Heath shared a recent edict that the Sanctum was 'collecting' those who were suspected of having magick, referring to them as abominations. Kingsley had to keep Lola safe no matter the cost. Hopefully, she wouldn't draw too much attention to herself tonight.

As soon as the thought crossed his mind, he spotted her. There she was, entering the hall on Thad 's arm in the most stunning green gown he had ever seen. The entire room stopped to stare at her.

"Kingsley, did you hear me, boy?" Ezra asked.

"I beg your pardon, Lord Sarelee. I was momentarily distracted. What were you saying?"

"I wanted to introduce you to Lord Sebastian Krauss."

With an outstretched hand, the man insisted, "You can call me Sebes."

"Welcome to Kingsguard Reef, Lord Krauss. This is my sister, Princess Sirena, second lady of House of Do'Ramos."

Bowing gallantly, Sebes gently kissed Sirena's gloved hand.

"It is a pleasure to meet you, Lord Krauss," Sirena replied nervously.

He was a regal man with a beautiful head of ashen hair that flowed to his shoulders. Kingsley frowned at his remarkably handsome face. His glinting silver eyes clearly watched over Lola as she approached. At the main hall's entrance, Lola finally caught a solid look at the opulence of the room's decor and the extravagance of the guests' attire. Heads turned in their direction, the gazes of nearly everyone in the room upon her and Thad. She may have underestimated the response the crowd would have towards a stranger.

She knew she looked good, but it still caught her off guard.

Focus. Don't get embarrassed. Leverage your attention.

Tonight, she had to befriend a room full of strangers should her sister need their alliance in the future. Having escaped from Melia, and with a handsome man on her arm, she had the space to feel radiant. The admiring stares of those around her certainly didn't hurt.

Thad guided her towards Kingsley and Sirena. Stood beside them was Mya, her entire upper body as stiff as an oak board.

Lola couldn't help but admit how stunning Mya looked in her red gown. The silk fabric shimmered in the candlelight, intricate beading and embroidery adorning her bodice. Her billowy skirt was suited for a dance. Kingsley and Mya standing beside each other did look like the perfect royal couple. Her poise was sharp enough to draw attention on its own. But not Kingsley's attention; he hadn't taken his eyes off Lola since she rounded the corner.

Lola suppressed a giggle. Watching him squirm, surrounded by gorgeous women, was amusing, no matter the context.

As Thad led her further, Lola was transfixed by the grandeur of the stunning Solstice display before her. Merely staring through the entryway—not even having set foot inside the room yet—was a treat for the eyes.

When they finally stepped inside the hall, she didn't turn to the line of Do'Ramos family members—no, not just yet. What caught her attention was the garden through the sprawling windows and open, glass doors. In the distance, beyond the dancing crowd, was a frosted field of grass enclosed by fragrant bushes and shrubs, still healthy, with a single, majestic tree rising. Snowflakes danced in the cool night air. The smaller flower bushes were just as proud, highlighted with soft candles lit in jars playfully scattered throughout the greenery.

The central tree—a poplar—stood tall and regal. She'd been told it was the pride and joy of the House of Do'Ramos, that it had stood there for over four generations.

Lola took a deep breath, yearning to take in the scent of the garden and the magick that seemed to permeate the air. The lush colors of the plants, even under the snow, filled her with vibrant energy. She couldn't help but feel a deep connection to it all.

Don't get too carried away, she told herself. Keep it hidden.

The night was chilly, but the doors to the garden stayed propped open as guests walked through in their mink stoles and wool overcoats. Two roaring fireplaces burned on each side of the great hall.

Mōsa only had two seasons: the rainy season and the summer. A brief memory surfaced in Lola's mind of visiting Kingsguard Reef so her mother could spend the Solstice with Queen Alina. Lola must have been very young back then.

In those days, she had not met Kingsley. He'd already been sent off to the Sanctum. Lola shuddered at the thought of the place. Sole had spent a few months in the Sanctum before their father was informed that she was being abused by the Sundonian children.

Surrounded by beautiful holiday decor and the warmth of the fire, Lola's heart ached for her family. If only they could be sharing this time together.

"Holy Mother! You are stunning in that dress!" Sirena called from the receiving line of guests. Lola hoped her cheeks weren't as red as they were hot. Sirena tended to be loud when she was excited, a somewhat embarrassing habit. And she was excited most often when Lola was around. The worst part of it, however, was that Sirena's ill-timed proclamation had burst out just as the quartet finished their last melody. Those who hadn't caught Lola's entrance before were definitely staring now.

Never mind, she was a princess. How was one meant to ever grow accustomed to so many people flat-out staring at them? At least in Mōsa, no one bowed to her. They called her by her first name. It made her feel real, and made any reverential gazes more tolerable.

"Doesn't she look amazing, Kingsley?" Sirena asked as she elbowed her brother. He looked like another dire wolf had descended upon him, only this time he didn't know what to do.

Now that she had a chance to really look him in the eye, Lola wasn't sure what made her belly tighten more: his stare or the fact that Mya had briskly taken his arm the moment Lola had turned to them.

"I told you that dress would unravel him!" Thad whispered triumphantly, a cherubic smile spreading on his face.

"Hush Thad," Lola retorted through gritted teeth.

She could feel him snickering as he politely released her from his arm. Kingsley broke from his position in the receiving line, forcing Mya to let go of him. Lola wondered if he remembered the kiss they shared in the woods. He had been so unwell, delirious from the dire's bite. But, reading his eyes now…

"You must forgive my sister for being incredibly loud," Kingsley said, barely masking a deep swallow before he spoke.

"She's been that way since she was born. Ill-mannered and annoyingly thunderous."

He stood right in front of her.

"But Lola, she is never wrong. You are a vision." Mya scoffs, but doesn't look too offended.

Lola's mouth had gone dry. There were dozens of responses cycling through her head, but the words refused to come out.

Saving her from utter humiliation, Thad interrupted. "Cousin, I couldn't agree more. Imagine my happiness when she decided to accompany me to the Ball this evening."

Lola almost choked on her own spit at Thad's bold lie. He had walked her through a door. Despite her comment about a dance, she had no intention of attending the entire event with any one person.

Kingsley's jaw tightened beneath his polite smile. She wasn't surprised about his annoyance with Thad.

Or, maybe she was the one who had annoyed him.

All she wanted was to mosey over to the tables in search of good food. And, for this night to be over.

"It appears that you are healing nicely from the wolf bite," Lola told King. "I am glad."

She meant it, even if her stomach did twist at the mention of that night.

"They have bandaged me up every hour on the hour. But all is well. How are you faring, Princess?"

Lola wanted to tell him the truth—that she hadn't slept, that her isolation from him was difficult, but necessary. It would be a relief to tell him of the memories that haunted her when she tried to close her eyes at night. She wanted to tell someone.

But this was not the time or place for such conversations. Instead, she lied. "I am well."

"That is a lovely color on you," Mya interrupted. "Even if it is last season's green."

If looks could kill, Mya would be a quiver of poisonous

darts. Lola set her in her sights, praying the woman wrapping her arm around Kingsley's—yet again—hadn't ignited her eyes.

So, this is how she wants to play this. All is fair.

"I wouldn't know one season to the next, but I'm learning quickly," Lola stated. "But you and Kingsley were in last season, too, correct? Thank you for giving me such a clear touchpoint."

Lola guides Thad to the dance floor, but not before eyeing Mya's arm and remarking over her shoulder, "A bit of advice; old habits die hard."

Thad quickly cleared his throat next to her, a rush of air coming out his nose as he desperately suppressed a laugh.

Lola didn't know this dance, but it was either make a fool of herself to music, or kill Mya where she stands. And one of those would arguably draw more attention.

She'd had enough of prissy women ripping her down. Why couldn't everyone be like Sirena?

"You like to sting like a wasp, don't you? I think I am falling madly in love with you," Thad proclaimed.

"Is this all you people do? Dress up, talk, and needle each other for fun?"

"Oh, Princess, we are much more superficial than that."

"How can I take this house seriously?" Thad was teasing, but Lola was truly frustrated. "Look at them all. Smiling, laughing, as if the Darkness is not consuming the world."

Thad's face stiffened then.

"Did you forget my cousin Avenn and our stepmother were both taken by the Darkness?"

His nostrils flared slightly. As if he were disgusted.

"It may not look like it, but no one in this room has forgotten."

"Forgive me, Thad. My mother always told me I don't think through what I am going to say before I say it."

"You mean like back there with Mya?" he asked with a wink, softening his expression again. "That was quite magickal if you ask me. You, too, are quick on your feet."

"I am sorry. I was asleep while everything I loved in the world was being stripped away. I forgot that those who were awake have also suffered."

"How could I stay mad at you?"

Thad pulled her in closer as they danced, guiding her through the steps. His hand was warm on her back. Comforting.

"Is he staring at us?" he asked.

Peering over Thad's tall shoulder, Lola immediately made eye contact with Kingsley who did, in fact, look upset. "Ugh! Why did you make me look over there? Did I do something wrong?"

"Not at all. My cousin is a great man who doesn't necessarily see what is right in front of him. Sometimes he needs a nudge."

"This is a nudge?"

Thad spins with her. "Maybe it's a shove." He grinned.

Thad and Lola fell silent, letting the music guide them from turn to glide. Before she knew it, she had the hang of the traditional Kingsguard Reef dance.

She felt lighter. Free. Then, just like that, it all slipped away.

"Don't look now, but a very perplexed prince is coming this way," Thad whispered. "Are you ready?"

She had no clue what she was supposed to get ready for, but the closer Kingsley got to her, the more and more untamed she felt.

CHAPTER 11

Royal temptations

"Princess, may I have this dance?" A very handsome Kingsley asked. Even if Lola wanted, she simply couldn't draw her eyes from his princely charm and the grace he sported in his tailored jacket.

"I fear your cousin has spun me one time too many times," she confessed. "I may be a bit tired of dancing to another song."

Grabbing her arm, Kingsley whispered, "Would you leave me here on the dance floor alone?" His crooked smile roused something within her, but she flashed back to the beginning of the evening.

"I think you should ask your fiance if she wants to dance with you."

"Oh, I see. You're jealous."

"Jealous?" She spat out a bit louder than she would have liked.

"You heard me!"

Grabbing her waist and blocking her from the view of

the audience—that was now staring at the handsome couple—he said in a low voice, "Be careful, my princess; your eyes are glowing."

Closing her eyes and taking three deep breaths, Lola settled her magick. She fixed her gaze on Kingsley and whispered with gritted teeth, "Let's get this over with."

The floor was cleared for the prince to take his first dance.

"Why aren't the others dancing?"

"Well, you see, whenever the royal family steps on the dance floor for their first dance, the floor is cleared."

"Wonderful," she said sarcastically.

"You and I have much to discuss."

"About what?" she said as she eyed the ever-growing crowd around them.

Gently turning her chin to face him, he whispered, "Lola, we must talk about your memories, the dire wolf, and our kiss."

"Wh…what kiss?"

"Is that all you heard, Princess? Interesting," he asked, his mouth turning up a fraction of an inch.

"I've never killed a prince before, but it's not above me," she quipped.

Laughing out loud, Kingsley brought her in closer. "We will have this conversation tomorrow. We also need to discuss our journey to your sister. My father believes that going to Mōsa may be too dangerous at the moment. And it may not be our destination anymore. Queen Sole sent word that she has settled in Grimerg Rise. She has asked that you be escorted there. Father sent word to her that we are to make arrangements for your departure."

"What?" Lola's eyes went wide and she pulled away from him. "I must prepare. I must leave at once." She attempted to leave the dance floor, but Kingsley gripped her waist tighter.

"We will leave in three nights," he told her. "Your sister commanded that we await your escorts."

"Escorts?" She asked, perplexed.

"Yes, she is sending a handful of escorts to take you to Grimerg Rise. They'll be here at sunrise. Father has advised that the queen wait to extract you after all of our guests have left from the Solstice celebrations, in order to not raise suspicion.

"Sole," Lola whispered to no one in particular. She was excited, but apprehensive as well. She and Sole were once very close, but now they would be what? They'd both been touched by the Darkness and had magick bestowed upon them. They'd both changed. Tears collected in her eyes.

"Lola." Kingsley's gentle whisper brought her back to the dance floor.

The concern in his eyes told her she was not alone in this.

"Are you well, Princess?"

"Not really," she muttered through gritted teeth. "You just told me my sister, who I—not long ago—thought dead or lost to me, and who is now the queen of the Western Isles, is sending a small Sundonian army to bring me home. No I am not well."

"My father has also granted me leave to escort you to the Rise," Kingsley said, only prodding Lola further.

"Didn't you just tell me that my sister would be sending an entourage for me?"

"Yes. I did," he said matter-of-factly.

He spun her once more as the music sped up and the crowd stared intently, and Lola was reminded of the many pairs of eyes still on them.

"Then there will be no need for you to escort me any-where. I will be safe with my sister's trusted guards."

"I can't do that."

"You can't do what?"

"You are mine…I mean…my responsibility, and I will see you safe."

Two more spins and the music slowed. Now, their dance felt more intimate. Lola couldn't understand why her heart felt as though it was going to beat right out of her chest. Kingsley's firm hands held her closer and closer.

"I will see you safe," he whispered again as the song came to a gentle end. They stood there for a moment, eyes locked in a firm embrace. The crowd roared, bringing them out of their trance. Then, walking off the dance floor, they rejoined the young royals.

"You looked like angels!" Sirena told Lola as she grabbed her by the elbow. Let's go get some ale. I am sure you are parched."

The two princesses left the group and made their way to the lanky server, who held a golden platter of tall flutes of honey wine. Lola downed one glass and then another. She had no idea why Kingsley mystified her so, but he did. No one had ever made her feel that undone. No one.

"It's a shame you are leaving soon," Sirena said. "You and King need more time to get to know each other."

"Why on earth would we need to do that?" Lola replied.

"Because if you saw what I just witnessed on that ballroom floor, what everyone in this room just witnessed, you would know that you both make a beautiful match."

"Don't be silly, Sirena. I am no princess hoping to rule. I am ready for war. I have no time for…liking someone."

"What about loving someone? Because I just witnessed it wasn't just like. It was something more."

Before Lola could reply, the ladies were interrupted by someone who Lola could only describe as simply alluring. Silver, well-groomed hair gently hung over his fresh, cheerful face, and his intense stare made Lola a bit uneasy as he approached, quickly towering over both women.

"Ladies, happy Solstice."

"Hello, Lord Krauss," Sirena said politely.

"Please, call me Sebes," he said, voice low and border-line sexy.

Lola grabbed one more flute of honey wine and took a sip to help her relax.

"I don't think we have had the pleasure of being introduced?" Sebes said, turning to face Lola.

"Oh, how rude of me. This is Lori Reefwood. She is visiting from Sundom for the Solstice."

Lifting her gloved hand, Sebes kissed it ever so gently. Lola could feel the heat of his breath settle into her hands, and her heart pounded.

"It is a pleasure," Lola said.

"Will you be here long?" Sebes inquired.

"No, Lord Krauss. I will be leaving in three moonrises. I am waiting for my escorts, and then I will be off."

"Sebes, please. Lord Krauss is my father," he said, eyes smiling.

"Then, before you leave, may I ask for this dance?"

Lola wasn't quite sure what to do. When she had been dancing with Thad, she hadn't thought much of what King-sley thought. She didn't know why she worried how this dance would make Kingsley feel.

He is nothing to you, Lola, she told herself. Wanting to prove herself right, Lola allowed the handsome Sebes to escort her to the ballroom floor once more.

The slow romantic song allowed Sebes to hold Lola quite close. Then, setting some space between them by "accidentally" stepping on his feet, Lola continued, "What is your station, Lord Krauss? Sorry—Sebes."

Actually, I am the senior guard at the Sanctum. I am primarily responsible for protecting Lord Ezra Sarlee and his family. "Well then, my apologies are in order," Lola whispered coolly.

Eyebrows arched, Sebes asked, "What do you mean?"

"You have to protect Mya Sarlee. My condolences!"

With a loud yet charming laugh, Sebes said, "Thank you for that!" as his eyes tear up from his uncontrollable laughter. Then, after composing himself, Sebes continued. "I haven't laughed that hard in a long while. The last few weeks have been quite difficult, and today has been especially challenging. Until you, that is."

Lola knew it was time to get some air. The dance with the Sebes left her out of sorts. When her dance was over, Kingsley was nowhere to be found, but Thad came to her rescue and offered to take her out of the hall. She thanked him with wide eyes and a sigh of relief.

Lola didn't bother with her fur overcoat; she was still so warm from the dancing and the crowd. The cool night air kissed her bare skin.

Within the garden, a magickal Solstice Bal was unfolding.

Revelers wrapped themselves in dark furs, merging regal elegance with the primal embrace of the frost-kissed woods.

Overhead, strands of glittering lights hung from the branches, casting a soft, enchanting glow upon the festivities below. They shimmered like stars, illuminating the garden with their mesmerizing radiance.

A gentle breeze rustled the leaves and carried the music through the air. The haunting melodies echoed through the Las Damas Garden, captivating all who listened.

Lost in thought, Lola recalled the last time she saw snow, when Kingsley had been bitten by the dire and she had painfully reunited with the memories of her captivity. Would the snow always remind her of that horrid night?

"It's beautiful, isn't it?" Thad asked.

"It is haunting," she said, wrapping her arms around her waist. She probably should have put on her overcoat. Seeing her need, Thad took off his velvet dinner jacket and draped it over her shoulders

"Thanks, Thad,"

"So now I have a nickname? I warned you not to fall in love with me," he said, eyes smiling.

"You are an ass. But I like you, Thad!"

"Was that a compliment?" Thad asked.

"No! It was just a fact."

"Ah, so first you danced with Lord Krauss, and now you're

falling for me? Looks like you're on a mission to shatter my cousin's heart tonight!" Thad said with a sheepish grin, his eyes twinkling mischievously.

"What are you talking about?"

"You dancing with Lord Krauss," Thad explained. "No one saw that coming. You made a smashing pair, even if he does work for the enemy."

"The enemy?"

"You may have heard I am not a fan of the Sanctum."

"I hadn't heard that. But I am not either. I saw what the Sanctum did to my sister. It changed her. She once told me that the Sanctum is where you go to learn about the evils in the world. I was so happy when my parents brought her back home and proclaimed that none of their daughters would ever step foot in the Sanctum again."

The pair began to walk towards the great hall. "The Sanctum was hard on Bishop," Thad told her. "He wasn't as lucky as your sister. My parents are traditionalists to a fault. Although Bishop is charming and funny, he has a hard side that few can penetrate."

Suddenly, a loud laugh pierced the night sky, snapping their attention to the castle steps leading into the Solstice Ball. There, Kingsley and Mya stood in an embrace. And that's when Lola saw it. Kingsley and Mya were kissing. It wasn't a gentle kiss—no—but a lingering, passionate kiss full of desire.

Lola's blood went cold, but she suppressed the sick feeling in the pit of her stomach and marched up the stairs towards the great hall as if Kingsley and Mya weren't there. Thad followed close behind and whispered, "Holy shite!"

As Lola stopped directly in front of the two, Mya broke away from the kiss to catch her breath. Kingsley looked drunk enough that he could barely stand on his feet, but Lola didn't give a shit.

"I think I've seen all I plan to see this evening," she said, swallowing a lump in her throat. "Thad, will you escort me to my quarters?"

"Of course."

As if taken out of a trance, Kingsley's half-opened eyes dragged over to Lola as she stormed up the stairs. "Lola, wait...what are you doing here? Thad, I told you to stay away from her!" he exclaimed.

Before Thad could respond, Lola whirled around. "How dare you?" she shouted. "You may have saved me, but that does not mean you own me! I am a free woman."

"You didn't say that when I kissed you in the woods!"

Lola froze.

She slapped him—hard. Lola actually slapped the future king of Kingsguard Reef, and in seconds, soldiers had flanked Kingsley to protect him from...Lola.

"How could you?" Lola said, voice cracking.

The prince, stunned and slow to react, touched his

163

reddening cheek and said, "You're right. Keep whatever company you wish. You seem to have managed just fine this evening. Suitor after suitor at your beck and call." His words punched her in the gut, and he immediately regretted them when he saw the look on her face. Lola's heart broke. Feeling the weight of his words, King recoiled inwardly, realizing the depth of his accusation. Aware of Lola's traumatic past in captivity, he cursed himself for being an asshole. In that regrettable moment, consumed by his own insecurities, he had succumbed to the urge to hurt her as he had been hurt by seeing her in the arms of Lord Sebes.

"You have no say on who I frolic with or whom I fuck!" Lola's voice shook.

"Wait, Lola…" he slurred. "I didn't mean that."

"Everything I have said, I meant," she spat.

As if on cue, Sebes stepped out into the cold.

"Oh dear, have I interrupted something?" Sebes said.

"Nothing of importance," Lola replied, eyes still on Kingsley.

"May I escort you somewhere?"

"Yes! Please."

"Lord Sebes, my guards will escort the lady to her quarters," Kingsley said with a royal tone Lola had never heard him use.

Stopping abruptly, Sebes turned to face King with a tight jaw.

"Prince, I fear you may have had too much ale this night. Maybe it is you who your guards need to escort."

They stood there in silence for a beat until King commanded, "Max, Philip, escort the lady to her rooms." When the soldiers didn't move, Kingsley shouted, "Now!"

Before the guards could take Lola away, Sebes asked her, "May I call on you tomorrow?" loud enough for Kingsley to hear. Glaring at Kingsley, Lola said, "Yes, Sebes you may." With that, she exited the cold terrace, pushing her way through the dancing crowd and out of the great hall. Her magick began to rise. She could burn this entire castle to the ground. In the empty corridor, she flashed her emerald eyes while the guards hurried after her. Hot tears streamed down her cheeks as she whipped open the door to her room and slammed it behind her. Flopping onto her bed, she concentrated on breathing deeply and controlling her magick. Sleep came to her as her wet tears dried.

CHAPTER 12

Rude awakenings

Sitting at the royal family's jade table, Kingsley silently begged the Holy Mother for relief from the headache crushing his brain. It only worsened when Melia, Bishop, and Thad jovially joined him for breakfast.

"Cousin!" Bishop yelled louder than necessary as he slapped King on the back.

"We missed you last night after, well after..." Melia said as her mischievous smile filled her face.

"Leave him be," Thad corrected his siblings. "He was dumped not by one, but two beautiful maidens last night. He deserves to nurse his hangover in peace and quiet," he said as he slammed the large walnut doors to the dining hall.

Sitting beside him, Bishop whispered, "Cousin, I must say you turned a dreadful night into a dream of drama and debauchery."

Eyes rolling and lips pressed into a tight line, Kingsley grumbled, "Fuck off, will you?"

"Now, is that any way to talk to your favorite cousin?"

Bishop jokingly questioned.

"You may be my dead cousin if you make me draw my sword!"

"Good morning, son," Queen Alina said as she and King Heath entered the dining hall. "I see you drunk yourself into a stupor. I suggest you have some tea with the ale. It will do you some good. Then we can talk about how you will make this right with Lola."

"Her sister is the Queen of the Western isle," his father said. "We cannot risk conflict so early in her reign. I expect you to handle this today."

Kingsley's hands grasped at his hair and slid down his face, covering his eyes with his hands, desperate for relief from the sharp, head-splitting pain. Ordinarily, the pain wouldn't be more than a minor nuisance, but right now, it was far more than that. Was it shame? He didn't know, but he needed to sip his fucking tea and bathe before confronting Lola.

Kingsley gritted his teeth and let out a short grunt. Forcing down two sips of tea, he grumbled, "Mother, have you seen Sirena this morn?"

"She went to check in on Lola," his mother said, intentionally refusing eye contact.

"Great," he grumbled. "Those two together will be the death of me."

The dining hall erupted in chuckles at his words. Even

Heath broke a smile. King couldn't help but smile at the pair of those women conniving together.

The laughter subsided as a rapping on the door echoed throughout the hall. Darius, the king's most trusted guard, entered. Walking straight to King Heath, he whispered something in his ear.

"Let them in," Heath told him.

Darius left the way he'd come. Heath looked around the table and said, "I expect you all to be on your best behavior. High Queen Sole's escorts have arrived for Princess Lola. And for the Holy Mother's sake, Kingsley, sit up straight."

Of course Lola's escorts would arrive precisely when Kingsley was not at his best. Nothing could save him from this nightmare.

Three people entered the room. The most notable was a dark-skinned woman with hazel eyes so closely resembling Lola's that Kingsley couldn't stop staring at. Could this be her sister?

The King addressed the woman first. "Welcome to Kingsguard Reef. I hope your trip down the mountain was pleasant."

"I wouldn't call it pleasant," the young woman replied.

Black, curly hair pulled back to reveal a thin, radiant face. A scar stretched across her right cheek—a seemingly painful reminder of a battle she might have won.

"Your Highness, I am Aurora Gamble, head of the Misa

Army for the High Queen Sole Porte of Mōsa, healer of Transea, yielder of magick. I have come to retrieve Princess Lola."

"Darius, please go tell Princess Lola that her escorts have arrived," Heath said before turning back to the newcomers.

"Please sit. Won't you join us for breakfast? I am sure you have had a long journey. We have made up your rooms so that you may find rest when the time is right."

The man with brown hair and a strange mustache said, "We will rest, but not until we have seen the Princess. We will wait here with you." He gripped the pommel of his sword.

Turning to face the Sundonian that was speaking, Aurora said, "This fine guard is Luce Dragonmore, right hand to the second son of Sundom." He could have quickly passed for one of the Lords of Sundom if not for his pointy ears—a dead giveaway of his Sundonian genes. Elves who could not be trusted, that's who they were. Kingsley narrowed his eyes at the man.

Shoving Luce in the shoulder, a pink-haired, pointy-eared woman beside him said through gritted teeth, "We would love to join you for breakfast."

The way she gripped her sword told Kingsley that she was a warrior, too. She was a beautiful woman, but her cunning gaze let the whole room know she could fuck up your life with one swing of her sword. Glancing over at Bishop, Kingsley thought his cousin might have seen an angel by the look on his face. Whispering to Kingsley without taking his eyes off of the pink-haired beauty, he whispered, "It's official; I am in love."

"Careful, cousin, that one might slice your balls right off," Kingsley muttered back.

The silence was deafening. Thank the Holy Mother for the Queen. "This is my son Kingsley," she said. "The Prince of Kingsguard Reef. These fine gentlemen are my nephews, Bishop and Thad. And this beauty is our niece, Melia."

"It's a pleasure to meet you all," said Luce, visibly lingering his gaze on Melia.

"My father tells me you will stay until the Solstice festivities are over?" Kingsley asked, wanting to know if what his father had promised was true.

It was Luce who replied first. "We have been ordered to stay until the Princess tells us she is ready to leave," Luce said. Kingsley nodded.

"When you decide to make your way back up the mountain, my father has agreed that I should accompany you—I mean…the princess to make sure she arrives safely."

"There is no need for that," Aurora said. "We will see to her safety now."

"I don't think you understand; I am going."

The pink-haired woman spoke. "I failed to introduce myself earlier; my name is Kia. Luce and I are part of the

Sunguards of the house of Sundom. We can assure you that her safety is our top priority."

"I think my cousin is explaining that he and my brothers will assist you in keeping her safe," Melia chimed in.

"Lady Melia, is it? "

"Yes," Melia added with a solid eye roll to match.

"Thank you for your concern, but we will not be taking any additional people with us on this journey. It is a risky endeavor, and besides, we have rationed provisions for our journey home."

Interrupting loudly, Kingsley said, "Provisions will not be an issue. We will accompany her because I will not leave her alone until she is safely with her sister."

"I beg your pardon?" Luce admonished.

Standing abruptly, Kingsley said, "You are from Sundom, is that correct?"

"Yes."

"So then you know that Lola believes Sundonians to be her enemy. You haven't met her yet, but I assure you she will do what she wants, when she wants."

"Trust me, we are aware of the power the Mōsian woman holds, and we are up for the challenge."

"She will decide who will accompany her; anyone that forces Lola will answer to me," Kingsley added.

Luce opened his mouth to reply when a knock on the door made everyone fall silent. Lola entered the room.

Kingsley's smile instantly faded as Lola refused to meet his honey glaze.

Turning to King Heath, Lola said, "Your Highness, you asked for me."

"Yes, Princess Lola, Your sister Queen Sole has sent a small party—"

"You mean a small army," Bishop interrupted.

One intense glare from the king shut Bishop up. "They have come to take you home," he finished.

Locking eyes on the three strangers, Lola gripped the blade that Kingsley gave her. Kingsley couldn't help but smile once more. Fuck, she was incredible. Everything about her warrior demeanor turned him on. Luce noticed it, too, putting his hands up. Lola refused to let go of her blade in a room full of her enemies. "Princess, if I may…" began Luce.

"You may fucking not. How do I know that this is not a trap? That you aren't holding my sister captive?"

With a calm tone, the pink-haired woman stepped closer to Lola and replied, "Because your sister would sooner cut his balls off than let any harm come to you. So she gave us this note to give to you…"

She cautiously held out a piece of paper for the princess to take. Lola snatched it quickly and scanned the note, immediately recognizing the penmanship. It was neat, precise, and perfect, just like her sister's.

"How do I know—"

"Lala," the dark-skinned woman's voice interrupted.

"Who said that?"

In a room full of Kingsguard Royals and Sundom guards, hearing her childhood nickname took Lola right back to Mōsa. She knew that voice. It had come from the third stranger sitting at the table, back turned to Lola.

"Who are you?" she asked. Her voice cracked, revealing how desperate she was to be with her people once more.

Standing from the table, the stranger turned to Lola. Hot tears streamed down Lola's face as her emerald eyes landed on the scarred face of Aurora Gamble, her dearest friend. Seeing Rory restored the hope she dreamt of finding since waking up in the Ventane woods.

The women ran to each other and embraced for what seemed like hours. The smiles that permeated through the tears they both shed told the story of tragic loss, deep love, and unbelievable resolve.

"Rory?" Lola uttered with a plea. "Is it Sole well?"

Rory knew her friend better than most. She knew what Lola was asking. Was Sole harmed by the magick?

"She is well. Wait until you see what she has become." Staring at Lola's green eyes, Rory continued, "I see she is not the only one who has changed."

"Lola, my dear," Queen Alina said as she made her way to the two women. "Why don't we bring some tea and fresh bread to the king's study where you and your guest can have more privacy."

Wiping her tears, Lola nodded.

"Before you leave," King Heath said. "I would ask that Prince Kingsley accompany you to the study and that he be brought up to speed on all the matters of the Western Isles."

"Princess Lola," Aurora said, "Is that alright with you?"

Lola's knees almost buckled when she turned to face Kingsley for the first time since entering room. She swore this man got more handsome with every passing day. His molten eyes pierced her deep. She was infuriated with him and somehow she knew that he saw her pain, and all she wanted to do was run into his arms for comfort. But that opportunity had since passed. He didn't belong to her. And she did not belong to him. Sole needed her to be prudent and ensure Mōsa's alliances were in place. If her sister was to take over Mōsa again, she would undoubtedly need Kingsguard Reef as an ally. So, against her better judgment, she replied, "Yes. The prince can join us," never taking her eyes off him.

The five of them exited the great hall: Mōsa, Sundom, and Kingsguard Reef, together. Sole had found a way to tie Mōsa with Sundom and now Kingsguard Reef when for generations before, their parents had failed. She didn't know how Sole had done it , but she would soon find out.

CHAPTER 13

Dangerous alliance

"Who the fuck do you think you are?" Kingsley asked, his jaw tight.

"My name is Luce Dragonmore," he said, crossing his arms. "Let that be the end of that, Second Prince."

"Let's get one thing straight, sun boy, from what I know, Lola doesn't know you, so we don't have to trust anything you fucking say," Kingsly stated.

"We? Last I checked, the princess was not betrothed. What is your motivation here, Prince?" Luce spat.

"Enough!" Rory shouted.

"How will we ever get through tonight if you are both swinging your dicks around?" Kia grumbled as she pulled Luce back towards the bookshelves in Kings Heath's study.

Seeing Lola's eyes begin to flash, Kingsley swiftly made his way to her. His instinct was to wrap his arms around her, but he knew there was much to discuss about the previous night before she would trust him again.

"Lola," he whispered, "Your eyes are flashing." Crossing

her arms, Lola said simply, "Yes. I know."

Turning to face Lola, the three guests looked as if they had seen a ghost. "What?' Lola asked in frustration.

"Lo, It's just that Sole's eyes light up when she gets pissed off. Except her eyes are violet."

Lola sunk into the chair beside her. With everything that had transpired, she needed a moment to sit and digest that information.

Kingsley pulled out the matching chair that faced her took his seat beside her. She rolled her eyes at him, deciding it was too much effort to ask him to move. Instead she looked at Rory and said, "Tell me everything."

Lola listened as Rory told her how, after Sole had awoken from the Darkness, she was summoned by King Adun Alacor of Sundom to heal him. But when they arrived, the king was dead, and the new king had held them hostage. "The King and Queen informed me of how Sole and Nasir have both changed. But hearing you say it, as someone who witnessed it with your own eyes…well, I still can't believe it."

"Believe it, Princess. Much has happened in your absence," Luce interrupted.

"What's his problem?" Lola asked Rory.

"Like us, he has lost much. He just happens to be an asshole, too. The Darkness changed things for him."

"The Darkness changed things for everyone," Lola said

to no one in particular.

"I see stubbornness runs in the fucking family," Luce clipped.

Lola couldn't deny the irritating soldier's perfection, his physique like chiseled stone. In a previous existence, she would have been entangled with someone like him. Despite his captivating appearance, in the present, he remained irritating.

"Luce, is it?" Lola began as she stood to her feet, green fire flashing in her eyes. "I will say this only once. Tell me what happened or my vines will crush you."

"Nasir cannot take Mōsa from Sole while she possesses magick. But there is a way to take her magick if he obtains one of the Shadowforge Arsenal. With the Champion's Choice, he can...he can kill Sole and acquire her magick in the process."

"Your sister sent us because she believes that if Nasir succeeds at taking her magick, he will come for you next. But she knows that together, you can defeat Nasir," Rory explained.

"I still find it so hard to believe that Nasir is capable of harming Sole," Lola whispered to Rory.

The room grew quiet once more and Lola's gut tightened. Rory and Kia wouldn't make eye contact with Lola. It was Luce who locked eyes with her. He was an asshole, but she could tell he would be honest with her. Even if he was from Sundom.

Lola stood from her seat, closed the gap between them, and asked, "What does the new King of Sundom have to say about this?" She didn't want to react without careful consideration.

"After slaying Nisa and gravely injuring our comrade Zari, Nasir made an attempt on the life of High King Rill. We managed to conceal him, but not before Nasir abducted Prince Rivian. Since then, High King Rill's sole objective has been to rescue his brother and safeguard the realms."

"Forgive me if I find it hard to believe that the king of Sundom is aligned with the people of Mōsa. How convenient that now that a Sundom prince has been accosted, Sundonians want to work together?"

"What did you say?" Kia's tone warned Lola that she may have crossed a line.

Lola's eyes flashed.

Placing a gentle hand on her shoulder, Kingsley whispered, "Lola, maybe you should sit back down?"

Jerking away from his touch, she made her way to Rory.

She'd had enough loss. Enough pain. Enough grief. She wanted her sister. She needed her now. "Sole...she needs me," she told Rory. "I must go to her at once."

"We promised your sister that we would bring you to her and that is what we will do," Luce cut between them. "However, we cannot go until we do one more thing."

"You will take me to her now!" Lola demanded of Luce.

"Lala," Rory gently said. "We must stay two moonrises before we head back." She placed a fallen braid behind Lola's ear. "First, we have traveled a long way and need rest, as do our soldiers, and second, this is not only a retrieval mission. We are here to secure allies as well."

"King Heath tells us that all the people of the Western Isles will be here for tonight's festivities. It is imperative we are all at the ball to represent Queen Sole," Kia said.

"Your sister is aware that you have hidden your true identity for safety reasons. Tonight, we are to introduce you as her diplomat and the next in line to inherit the Western Isles, should something happen to her."

"What are you saying?" Lola demanded.

"You are the only living heir to Mōsa, but since Sole has no children you, Lola, are the heir to the Western Isles."

A hush fell over the room once more. All Lola had ever wanted was to be a warrior. Now she might be a queen. She wanted a war, not a kingdom. Laughing like a mad woman, Lola's green gaze fell on Kingsley and, for the first time, she understood how he had felt when his dreams had been taken from him in that one instant.

Pulling Lola's focus back, Rory continued, "We need you to be a diplomat tonight."

These people had no idea what they were asking her. A panic began to consume her. She was no diplomat.

She was the sister destined to be a warrior. These people couldn't understand what they were asking of her. As much as she hated to admit it, Kingsley was the only person in this room that could understand.

Turning to face King, she was surprised to see that he was standing just a couple of feet away from her. "What would you do if you were me?" she asked as tears filled her eyes.

"There is no one in Transea that can do this for her. You are the heir. There is no other." Closing the gap between them, Kingsley whispered, "After all, you are your mother's daughter. The warrior queen."

Hearing Kingsley's words, Lola couldn't help but shed tears. He knew what she was giving up. All of her dreams were gone. In that moment, she realized no one understood her more than Kingsley.

CHAPTER 14

The road to home

For the first time since waking in the woods, Lola didn't feel so alone. It wasn't that Kingsley, Sirena, and their family weren't kind to her. They just weren't her people. She had become distracted by their riches, fine balls, and King's honey eyes. Those damn eyes.

Waking up to find Rory sleeping beside her felt like a dream. They had stayed up most of the night talking about Sole's new love, and how he had been taken by Nasir. Lola told Rory of King, and what happened with the dire wolf, but decided to leave out the part about kissing him. When Lola told Rory about being held captive, she immediately demanded to know who had done it so that she could cut his balls right off.

A knock at the door jolted Lola up from her pillow. Jumping off her bed and quickly wrapping herself in her navy robe, Lola hurried to the door.

She opened the door to reveal Sirena, standing outside with a tray full of delicious kinds of breads, cheeses, and jams. Stepping into the room, Sirena said, "Mother insisted I make sure you ladies have enough nourishment before tonight's ball."

"Thank you, Sirena," Lola said with a smile still heavy with sleep, taking the tray and placing it on the table beside the door. Sirena nodded and turned to head back down the hallway.

As Lola went to close the door, a black-slippered foot blocked the door from shutting. Cracking the door open, Melia waved

and said, "Good morning, Lola!"

"Good morning, Melia," Lola said, rolling her eyes.

"I hope you slept well?" she asked.

"Yes. I did."

"The queen wanted me to remind you that as is tradition, my cousin will escort you to tonight's ball."

Lola caught her breath. The last thing she needed was Kingsley distracting her from connecting with potential allies.

"I'm Melia, Kingsley's cousin," she peered into the room at Rory, who was fixing her hair in front of the window.

"Yes, I believe we met yesterday," Rory said shortly, smoothing her robe around her hips and forcing a blank expression across her face as she turned to Melia.

Lola instantly regretted telling Rory about her encounters with Melia. She surely would not let Melia's behavior go unchecked.

"I believe you are the one who approached Lola about taking advantage of your cousin Kingsley." Well fuck—she went right for the jugular.

Smiling as if having found a new toy, Melia replied, "Yes, one must always protect their family."

Standing close to Lola, Rory continued, " Then it's a good thing I am here."

"Why is that?" Melia asked as a sardonic smile reached her lips.

"Because I will break the teeth of any bitch that tries to tell Lola who to be. You will find that Mōsian women bring all parts of them wherever they go. That means that what Kingsley admires in Lola is all of her. And if he doesn't, then he and anyone else who has a problem with Lola, can eat shit."

"Rory!" Lola clipped.

Tense silence settled between the women. "It's fine, Princess Lola," Melia finally said. "She's right. I'm glad to see that you have allies. Because after tonight's ball we will all need allies."

"If you three are done pulling each other's hair," Sirena interrupted, pushing the door open with her foot and entering with the pot of tea to accompany the breads.

"I'd love to discuss my plan."

She poured hot tea into a teacup for herself and set the

pot back down on the tray.

"What plan, Sirena?" Lola questioned.

"The plan to gain allies for Queen Sole. I haven't been the princess of House Do'Ramos all these years and not learned who the important players are in the room." Pulling a note out of her cleavage, Sirena sipped her tea and began plotting.

"First, we must make sure you look like a queen when you step into that ballroom tonight. Melia is in charge of your gown."

"What? Wait, No!"

"Listen," Melia reasoned. "I am here to help. If you want to look like the queen's regent, I can make that happen. If not, I can leave."

"Fine, stay, but I have to agree on what I wear."

"Lola, I have something for you to wear tonight as well. It's from your sister," Rory interjected.

Opening her travel sack, Rory pulled out something wrapped in black burlap. She unwrapped it to reveal a mirrored crown. Lola knew that crown anywhere. It had belonged to her father. But something was different. At the center of the crown sat a small, oval-shaped, golden mirror. Her mother's gilded mirror.

"Your sister sent her crown to you along with this note."

Opening the note with shaky hands, Lola recognized that handwriting.

Hi Lo (Lola) - I have missed you. I have much to share with you when we meet. For now, that will have to wait. I know you never wanted this crown. Neither did I. It was meant for Luna, not for us, and still here we are. There is much I need to tell you. For now know this, I ask that you adorn yourself with this crown tonight. It is the crown of Mōsa and you, my dear, are Mōsa. You are everything brave, true and beautiful. I would trust no one to rally armies more than you.

If you could convince Papi to take you fishing during the coldest moonrise of the year, you can do this.

One last thing. I have also sent you something special to wear with the crown. Something very royal…which you will absolutely hate."

Lola smiled at her sister's ability to know her so well, even after all of this time.

Tonight, you will be the hand of Mōsa. Remember that you are not alone. You still have me and the 50 Sunguards I sent to ensure your safety.

Here, now, before and after,

Your sister,

Sole-

High Queen of the Western Isles

Squeezing the small note tight in her palm, Lola couldn't stop the tears that streamed down her face, wetting the note she had read at least six times. Her heart ached as if it were breaking. Lola knew she missed her family, but the knots in her belly revealed how painful the loss had truly been for her. She hadn't realized how desperately she missed her big sister until now.

Knowing Sole was depending on her was a strange feeling.

She wasn't alone.

But she still feared facing everyone tonight.

"Why me?" she asked no one in particular.

Gently touching her shoulders Rory asked, "Are you a Misa Warrior?"

"What?" Lola's brows furrowed.

"Don't make me ask it again, warmaiden. Are you a Misa Warrior?"

"Yes. Yes I am Misa," she said with more confidence than she had felt in a long while.

"And Misa were built for what? "

"War!"

"Louder warmaiden, I can't hear you!" Rory shouted.

"We were made for WAR!" she shouted as tears streamed down her face and her lips trembled.

"Tonight you will go to war. It will just be a different kind of battlefield. You can do this."

Embracing, the two women walked into Lola's dressing room, where a large black box leaned against the settee.

"You're going to war, so I wanted to make sure you had the best armor."

Lola opened the box. Nestled within was a gown that seemed to radiate its own light, shimmering like molten gold. As Lola lifted it from the box, the gown cascaded in graceful folds, promising to drape her in elegance and make her the center of attention wherever she went.

Piercing green eyes met Rory's as Lola whispered, "Holy shit, let's prepare for war."

***

Standing at the threshold of the great hall, Lola caught her breath. Tonight was critical to Sole's victory. She had to do everything in her power to secure allies for Mōsa. But Lola was dreading seeing Kingsley. She couldn't help but look his way, even though he hadn't noticed her yet.

He looked stunning in his smoke-colored suit, the perfect balance between light and dark. That's what made King dangerous. She thought she could trust him but the minute he didn't get his way, he betrayed her. He kissed Mya. He threw insults just to bring her down. Yet now, she couldn't really remember what she was so mad about.

She had seen him in suits before, but this one...this one had all the girls staring and she didn't blame them. It fit him just right, tightening just enough around his strong arms and amazing ass. His molten eyes glimmered more than usual, begging her to get lost in them. His hair had been freshly cut, but he fashioned a light, scruffy beard. All Lola wanted to do was run to him and have him hold her face in his hands—to face this room of vipers together. The realization that he might very well be one of the vipers twisted her stomach. No. He was a distraction she could not risk. Especially not tonight.

Her stomach tightened and her golden bangles chimed as she clasped her hands in front of her golden skirt. Whispering to herself, Lola murmured, "I hope you know what you are doing, Sole. I am no diplomat; I am a warrior. Here goes nothing."

She raised her arms and the bangles rattled to the rhythm of her royal movements. Only her emerald eyes were visible above the transpicuous material draped loosely about her head and across the lower half of her face.

The bioluminescent jewelry laid delicately on her neck shimmered ever so gently as she entered the room. The gleaming corset bodice with a sweetheart neckline certainly stood out, but it was the long, shimmering skirt with a thigh-high slit and court train that sparked the attention of her hushed, black-uniformed courtesans. Ebony braids swished at her flowing hips—hips that invited every man's attention.

That's when she saw those honey eyes land on her. His

eyes. For a beat, there was nothing but the two of them. Then, the crier announced her entrance. Lola flinched at the volume of his voice.

"Lola Sirena Porte of Mōsa, third daughter of Porte house, survivor of the Darkness and yielder of life-bending magick, Mighty Misa Warmaiden of the Sirena Sea and sister to the High Queen of the Western Isles."

The crowd grew silent as the esteemed Princess of Mōsa entered with ten Sundom Sungards at her back and Rory by her side. As if directed to do so, the room gasped in unison. Lola felt smaller than ever before. But his eyes. His eyes kept her steady as she made her way to her friends. Hands clasped at her front and each step feeling firmer than the last, Lola stepped into power.

She joined the group, but it felt as though only she and Kingsley were the only two people in the room.

"Maestro, play the Medina concerto please," Kingsley demanded. Turning to face his guests, Kingsley urged, "Let us feast and dance. The night is young." The crowd heard him loud and clear and scattered to the dance floor or to their assigned tables. But none of them stopped staring.

As Kingsley made his way back to her, Lola could feel their energy colliding. She couldn't tell if her stomach was twisting because of his stare or the attention of the crowd. When the people began to dance, he whispered "Are you alright?" His voice was soft and soothing.

"Me? I'm great, perfect even," she replied sardonically. Though her words were stern, her voice cracked a little. She hated that.

King narrowed his eyes. "Liar."

Much to her embarrassment, she snorted in response, revealing that her nerves had already gotten the better of her.

When the corner or King's mouth twitched with amusement, her stomach flipped. Her worry and her desire fogged up her mind; she couldn't decide whether she wanted to get closer to him or retreat back to where Rory was standing with her guards.

It was a bad idea to be this close to him. She knew that. All eyes were on her and she hated it. Taking a deep breath, Lola wanted just one second where she wasn't planning her next move. She just wanted to be in the moment. "May I escort you to the garden?" King asked her with those kind, molten eyes.

She nodded, slid her arm into the crux of his, and left everyone behind.

***

In the garden, serene snowdrops cascaded to the ground as a gentle breeze shimmied them from the evergreen needles. They glistened as they fell, illuminated by the glowing lights along the garden path.

After what seemed like a long, deafening silence, he whispered, "Lola, I must apologize for what happened the other night. I was incredibly drunk and..."

She raised one hand to him and said firmly, "I don't want to talk about that night. It's none of my business if you and your betrothed—"

"She is not my betrothed!" he blurted out in defense, turning the heads of the stray partygoers by the entrance and a few just inside.

Looking up at him with wide eyes, Lola whispered, "Well, now everyone else knows that, too."

A soft laugh—as refreshing as a swim in the Sirena Sea—ripples out of him.

"I noticed," he replied echoing the conversation they had before, when it had just been the two of them in the woods. Things were simpler then. In two strides, he closed the gap between them. Lola took a nervous step back and slipped on the wet snow. Without faltering, he caught her. With his arms around her, secure, Lola felt as if he could catch her for an eternity and never let go. A pang of desperation through her heart and she swallowed the lump in her throat. What is wrong with you? She thought to herself. Get it together.

"You caught me," she said while catching her breath. The space of unspoken questions lingered between them for what seemed like forever. Tipping his chin down, topaz gaze enveloping Lola like a soft blanket, he said, "I'll do that anytime you need me to, snowdrop."

Turning as cold as the icicles dangling on the trees, she warned, "Don't call me that. You forget yourself, Prince."

"Oh I heard your title. It's an impressive one, if you ask me. Even more ridiculous than mine."

That last part made them both smile and they continued their stroll through the gardens.

"Snow—Princess" King said, correcting himself quickly, "Since I met you in the woods, you have consumed my every thought. Seeing you now in this dress I fear I will not sleep for a hundred years. Just like your title, your attire is fit for a queen."

She peeled her gaze away from his chest. "Shit," she said, realizing she had to get back to the ball—back to work. He had distracted her again. "I must go," she said abruptly. Kingsley reached for her once more, but she yanked herself away and exclaimed, "You shouldn't touch me!"

His face went unreadable and his shoulders stiffened at her next words. "This will only end in ruin."

Walking slowly back where they came from, he says, "Fuck it! Why shouldn't you touch you? Does it bother you? Do you hate it?"

"Because I am leaving, King," she stated, more like a plea than a fact. Turning to face him, she told him the truth.

"You are a distraction I cannot afford! Just look at where I am now. Here with you. Doing the Holy Mother knows what. I have duties to attend to, and you are not one of them."

Far too flustered, she pushed her way past King walking and rushed to the entrance of the great hall. Grabbing her by the arm, he pushed her up against the maze wall where they would have a few more minutes of privacy.

"What do you think you are doing? Let me go!"

"No."

How could she emotionally distance herself when he wouldn't physically let go of her?

"No. I have been attempting to speak to you for what seems like an eternity," He spat.

"What do you want from me!?"

"I don't fucking know what I want!" He raised his voice. "All I know is that since I found you that day in the woods, all I can do is think about you. You have bewitched me. It is you who haunts my dreams, my mind…and other parts." He ended with a devilish smile.

Her stomach fluttered. She stood, unblinking, in a state of surprise. How she wished that things were different. That they weren't facing war on the horizon, that the Darkness wasn't still out there, and that it wasn't up to her—with her new royal status—to stop both.

Sounding entirely too pleased, he said, "Come here."

Kingsley stood closer, letting her drink him in.

She swallowed the lump in her throat as she looked down at the bulge rising in his trousers. She didn't say a word as he lazily looked at her. Lola took a shaky breath.

When she says, "Holy Mother, you are beautiful," his surprised smirk reminds her of the day he found her in the woods.

There was no holding back. Not anymore. He completely devoured her mouth the way he had wanted to since he first saw her. This kiss was a demand. It took all his willpower not to undress her on the spot as she leaned against the wall of greenery. Running his fingers through her braided locs, he pulled her head back to open her mouth wider for him as Lola ground her pelvis on him.

The muffled echo of laughter and string music quickly reminded him of where they were. There was a hall full of royals and dignitaries just inside. If he wasn't careful, he would surely take the Princess of Mōsa right here on the ground. In the bitter cold, she was warm, and King didn't know how he could ever let her go.

The sight of her made an animalistic drive to claim her as his own rise within him. "You are a fucking perfection, Lola," he growled.

Her heat rose once more as they tangled in a web that they had no business navigating. Two kingdoms hung in the balance. She wanted him. She let a low noise come out in her voice as she said, "King please, we must stop."

Looking down at her, he couldn't bear to part, though he knew she was right—that they were too close to each other.

He withdrew from her embrace, leaving Lola feeling cold, like she'd been robbed again. Robbed of her family, robbed of her calling, and now robbed of whatever this thing with King could have been. A knot tightened in her throat and no matter what she did, she couldn't swallow it down.

"I can't—I won't do this with you," Lola corrected.

They hadn't spoken since the previous ball, and having his warm breath so close to her ear sent goosebumps down her entire body. Kingsley plucked Lola off the hedge, his grip different. Like he'd already mentally separated from her. She didn't know how she could continue to stand this constant push and pull between them. But it had to end, and she had to be the one to do it.

His words and his touch left her just as lost as she was when he found her in that forest. Kingsley was nothing like the others—the ones who suffocated her with their stares, bitter words, and demands. Part of her wished to stay with him. But that wasn't written in the stars for them. Tonight was about bringing her best royal presence to a room full of her enemies.

"I won't do this with you," she repeated, pulling herself together and removing as much emotion from her voice as she could. "You have life here and a beautiful royal bride waiting inside for you."

"And what do you have Lola?" he spat.

Tear-filled eyes told him everything he needed to know. Lola was born for war. She would always choose her people over anything. Including him.

Perhaps that's the excuse she would always use to keep her distance from Kingsley.

"Let me go...please."

She didn't mean physically; he'd already taken his hands off her. Running his fingers through his hair, he couldn't bring himself to make eye contact. He knew he would be ruined if he did.

Lola did the only thing she could do. Straightening her dress and wiping the lipstick she'd smudged, she walked away.

"Lola." His voice sounded harsher than he would have liked.

"King." She stopped and turned to look at him across the garden. "We can't keep doing this. I need to go."

"Your eyes," he insisted. "They are glowing."

Shrugging her shoulders, Lola said, "We just announced to all of the Western Isles that I have magick. It's about time they see what I can do." Her voice softened. "While I grieve what I have lost."

The walk back through the gardens was bitter and quiet, though the air was thick with many words left unsaid between them.

Now was not the time for her to grieve. She had to hold it together. And she was tired of grieving. Tonight was bigger than her and she would make sure she did not fail her duties.

Leaving King behind, Lola made her way inside and headed for Rory, who was casually pacing from one part of the great hall to the other, eyes scanning the crowd. Handing Lola a drink, Rory noted, "From the looks of it, that didn't go well."

Lola downed her entire glass of honey wine before saying, "I don't want to talk about it. He is insufferable."

"Be careful, Princess, or I might think he may be your mate."

"Mate? What? No. That is not—nor will it ever…oh just give me another drink, will you?"

Before Rory could protest, a voice said, "May I have this dance, Princess of Mōsa?" Turning, Lola found the dashing Lord Sebes promising to take her away from all the politics in the room.

"Lord Sebes, It's lovely to see you."

"May I introduce you to my dearest friend and leader of my entourage, Aurora Gamble of Mōsa, the bravest warmaiden I know. Rory, this is Sebastian Krauss, Captain of the Sanctum Guards."

"It is a pleasure to meet your acquaintance," Sebes said as he reached for Rory's hand.

Rory withheld her hand, for in Mōsa it was forbidden for anyone apart from one's betrothed to kiss their hand.

Realizing his error, Sebes quickly adjusted, but Lola didn't miss his jaw tightening. "My apologies Lady Aurora. I may be behind on my Mōsian customs, I'm afraid."

"Princess Lola, may I say how surprised I was to learn of your true identity," he continued.

There was something about the way he said the last part that made Lola uneasy. Sebes had always been kind to her, and a great escape when she didn't want to think about King. Tonight, he seemed on edge and frustrated.

"Forgive me for my discretion. My sister, the Queen, insisted my identity be kept quiet until my entourage arrived."

"Surely you could have told me. I thought we were close," he said with a kind smile and sharp eyes.

Stepping between them, Rory responded firmly, "The Queen of the Western Isles will be pleased to hear how well the Sanctum took the news of Princess Lola's true identity."

Lola felt his presence before she saw him. Kingsley was standing behind her with Thad. As the handsome pair joined their group, tensions rose. After King elbowed him, Thad said "Princess Lola, I want to introduce you to Lady Athea and Lord Ezra Sarlee. Lord Sarlee is the House Master of the Sanctum. Their relationships will be essential in gaining support for your sister." Placing his charming elbow in front of Lola, she took it and pivoted abruptly, seizing the opportunity to escape. Leaning into Thad's ear, she whispered, "Thank you."

With a wink, he patted her hand. "I'm always here to save a beautiful princess in distress."

"Was that distress?"

"Yes. Princess, watching my cousin watch you with Lord Sebes was distress."

Not knowing what to say to that, Lola smiled and they both made their way to the den of vipers.

Luce Dragonmore

CHAPTER 15

The price of trust

Time was running out, but Lola was a natural diplomat. It didn't hurt that the charming and hot Thad was accompanying her. Having Thad by her side made for an exciting evening. Lola observed his ease and meticulous engagement, always careful to not say the wrong thing. Even when the obnoxious Lord Humfry made a joke in poor taste, suggesting that Thad should have taken Kingseley's place as heir to the throne, he simply replied, "Then who would be here to escort lovely women like the Princess of Mōsa?" But it was the way he weaved in and out of critical conversations like a spider ensaring its prey that revealed his pragmatic approach to diplomacy.

Lola wasn't sure if it was his ability to hold complex conversations or if it was his golden eyes that drew people in. His chestnut locks were coiffed to perfection. His eyes had the same startling clarity as a mountain stream at sunrise. Although it was the Solstice, his skin appeared as if painted on by the sun. She swore his mountain peak cheekbones had been chiseled into shape by the Holy Mother herself. How was it that he didn't have a woman on his arm? Thad was loyal, handsome and well respected. And although their harmless flirting pissed King off to no end, Thad had become one of the people she trusted most.

The two Sunguards at her back looked tired of the revelry and niceties. It was obvious they were not accustomed to standing around idly while others did the work. "Typical Sundoinians," she muttered a little louder than necessary.

"What?" Thad asked with brows furrowed.

Changing the subject, she asked, "Do you have a special someone?"

"Why are you asking? Are you interested?" he said with that cherubic grin.

"I'm serious, Thad!" Something in his eyes hinted at a bit of sadness but he quickly brushed it away, saying,

"That is a conversation for another day, Princess. Tonight, you have one last dignitary to impress." He was right. She made a point to pick up this conversation later.

Of all the diplomats he introduced her to, Thad whispered, "the most important people in this room, aside from King and Queen Do'Ramos, are Ezra and Athea Saree."

"Mya's parents? You mentioned them before."

"Yes. You will have to win over the High Priest of the Sanctum and his wife. He gestured his chin to the left. "Athea inherited the largest troops in the Western Isles when her father died. They say her wealth runs as deep as King Rill of Sundom's."

"Surley, Mya has told her mother about me. She will hate me if she doesn't already," Lola sighed.

"She will be lucky to know you," he assured her, lifting her chin to face his cosmic smile. "She is not as conniving as her daughter, but she is a viper so watch your words. Securing her army is critical to the pending war."

Lola's stomach tightened in knots as she realized that all the allies she secured tonight—the guests cupping honey wine and peacefully swaying to the rhythm of the string quartet—were ready to go to war. "I've always said I was ready for war," she said, swallowing. "But now that it is right at our door I want to find a way to avoid it. Not for me"—she looked across the gilded hall at Rory—"but for my people and for those who have already lost so much. For all of the people in the Western Isle."

Her emerald eyes sparkled when Thad whispered, "War comes when we least expect it. The best way to face it is to be prepared and remember what is at stake. That's how Kingsley and I know you can do this." Something about the way he said Kingsley's name assured her that maybe she could hear him out before she left in the morning. First, she needed to connect with the Sarlees, and then she would make her way to Kingsley. Taking one final gulp of honey wine, Lola straightened her skirt and made her way to the

High Priest and his bride.

She placed her small bangled hand in the crux of Thad's arm as he encouraged, "Now, come on. Let's build your sister's army."

It was Athea's steely gaze that landed on Lola first. The Princess of Mōsa reflected it right back. She had witnessed her mother do this when she was just a child, when they still had some dealings with the people of Sundom, before Mōsa broke all ties. Reminding herself that she was not alone, she whispered, "Here now, before and after," as she made her way to greet Mya's parents.

"Father Saree," Thad said, extending an arm to the high Priest of the Sanctum. "Glory, pride, and honor," said the two men as they locked arms in their greeting.

"Ah, Sir Martin," chimed the short, raven-haired beauty with the same, sparkling green eyes as her daughter. There was no way she could be Mya's mother. They could have passed for sisters. Her mother was beautiful and beguiling.

"May I introduce you to the Princess of Mōsa, Lola of Porte House," Thad said as he gestured.

Lola was instantly taken aback when they both bowed low before her. This was a tremendous show of respect that Lola did not want to overlook.

"You highness," Lady Saree graciously said.

"It is a pleasure to meet you both."

After some light-hearted banter about the melodic music

and the foibles of the newer, more youthful musicians, drinks arrived.

Athea closed the gap between herself and Lola. "Forgive us, Princess Lola, we have never engaged with the people of Mōsa. I fear that we have grown to believe that the women of Mōsa were too busy running barefoot on the beaches of the Sirena Sea and waving swords," Athea said absently as joyful dancing commenced around them. Swallowing a string of profanities, Lola reminded herself how crucial this conversation was to the future of Mōsa.

Refusing to segue to a different topic, Lola replied, "I can assure you that the women of Mōsa are both regal intellects and savage with a sword." Her tone was stiff and surly as she refrained from adding, "You fucking bitch."

In the irritatingly unhurried voice that royals reserved for the people of Mōsa, Ezra said, " We cannot tell you how shocked we all were this evening to learn of your true identity. In the Reef, we believe that honesty builds trust. It may be helpful for the queen to remember that in her future negotiations." Every word he uttered was charged with authority.

In a calm steady voice, Lola said, "The decision of the High Queen of the Western Isles is one to be admired, don't you think Lady Saree? After all, a woman ruling the Western Isles was unheard of until now. Surely a woman of your stature can respect a woman who sacrifices her love, land, and even her freedom for her people."

Narrow hazel eyes intently washed over Lola's emerald glow. With her rosy lips turning up a fraction, Lady Athea said to Thad, "I like this one. Any man would be lucky and crazy to get entwined with the Princess of Mōsa. Now tell me, Princess, what plans can we assist Queen Sole with?"

"Let us not be hasty, my dear," Ezra said with a voice that hardened as he spoke. Taking a deep breath, Lola organized her thoughts on how to proceed with the High Priest.

"My mother was devout to the Holy Mother," she began. "And every night at moonrise she would come into our room and have us recite the same prayer. Let me see how it goes? Oh yes…something like:

Holy Mother, guardian of souls, in our time of need we come to you. Kindle our fire so we may go forth and face the enemy in your name. Strengthen us with your infinite flame that we may bring glory, pride, and honor to your holy name.

Did I get it right, Father?"

Ezra's wide eyes told her everything she needed to know. He wasn't going to support Sole. He was used to power—to control. In the war to come, he would choose the side that secured that position of power. Lola knew Sole wouldn't support the Sanctum functioning as it has for generations. Her reign threatened to usurp that power.

"Yes Princess Lola, your prayer was perfect," he said civilly. "We hope to see you at the temple this seventh day for the moonrise vigil service?"

Lola wanted to say, " My mother taught me to be cautious with men who use the Holy Mother as a way to enslave women and make them feel small." But she didn't.

"I fear I will already be on my journey to my sister. Perhaps when I return to Kingsguard, I will take you up on that offer."

"It would be our pleasure," Lady Athea chimed in.

"Now my dear," she said eagerly to Lola. "Let us go off and have a chat." Walking out to the terrace, the two women spoke in hushed tones.

"I will be honest with you my dear. My daughter told me you are not to be trusted. You must understand her position. Mya is our only daughter. She had high hopes that the Darkness stole from her. It has left her jaded with the future. And you my dear are just that. The future."

Her voice soft and measured Lola said, "You mean women are the future. At least that is what the women of Mōsa were taught. Women like you Lady Athea are the very reason why my sister can sit on the throne. However, it might be dark."

Eyes wide, Athea lowered her voice and said, "Tell our queen that should she call on The Wolven Saints, we will stand with her." Lola wasn't quite sure what to say.

"Although I am honored, Lady Athea, I fear your husband will not agree to this arrangement."

"Let me worry about my husband. Besides, we have an agreement. I don't tell him how to run his Sanctum and he doesn't tell me what to do with my army," she said with a wink.

"Now, tell me. Is he going to keep staring at you like that all night?"

"I'm sorry?" Lola asked.

"Prince Kingsley. He seems a bit desperate for your attention."

Sure enough, when Lola glanced over her shoulder, following Athea's field of view, Kingsley was watching them with a tight smile on his face. Lola knew his expressions well enough by now to tell he was masking a cocky grin.

"May I give you some advice?" Athea continued. "Choose whom you love carefully. It can change you, or even change the world."

Lola nodded. Athea was right, regardless of how much Lola wished she wasn't.

"On behalf of my sister and my people, I thank you."

"Remember my dear, these are now your people, too. It's important that you figure out where we will all fit in this new world you are creating."

With that, Athea dipped her head respectfully and returned to the great hall, leaving Lola to ponder her words in the chilly evening breeze. This is bigger than you, she reminded herself, taking a deep inhale before turning on her heel and following in Athea's steps.

Passing Kingsley without so much as a glance, Lola returned to the warmth of the ballroom where Rory and Luce awaited her. Her two guards were positioned closely by her side, a proximity that made Lola roll her eyes.

"Don't worry, you'll get used to them," Rory remarked, trying to lighten the mood.

"I fear I'll never grow accustomed to being surrounded by Sunguards," Lola replied, her frustration evident.

Impatiently, Luce asked, "Are you ready to go to your rooms?"

But before Lola could answer, Thad abruptly seized her elbow, spinning her around to face him. The Sunguards instinctively drew their blades, causing the room to fall into a tense silence.

"All is well! All is well!" Lola reassured, the threatening intensity of her gaze fixed on Luce. He knew she was capable of crushing him where he stands.

"Tell them to sheathe their swords! I'll be in the garden with my friends," Lola declared, turning away and guiding Thad and Sebes out of the hall.

"You must take your guards with you!" Luce demanded.

Facing him with a mixture of contempt and fury, Lola stepped closer, her voice a venomous whisper. "Let me be perfectly clear, Sundonian. I am the Princess of Mōsa, and I take no orders from you."

With that, Lola, Thad, and Sebes departed, leaving the quartet to resume playing at King Heath's request.

As Lola stood in the garden with her two friends, she couldn't help but reflect on the events not long ago when she had shared an intimate moment with Kingsley in this very spot, shielded from prying eyes. Now, she sought solace with her loyal companions, needing their support more than ever. She didn't care if Luce disapproved; she was determined to bid her friends a proper farewell before her departure in the morning.

She shook the thoughts of Kingsley and Luce from her mind and looked up at Thad and Sebes, who were staring at her as if awaiting an answer to a question she hadn't heard.

"Sorry, did you say something?" Lola asked as her eyes danced between Thad and Sebes.

"I asked if you were ready to go?"

"I'll be ready to go to my rooms soon."

"No, that's not what I meant," Thad said. Lola furrowed her brow.

"What do you mean?"

He brushed a loose braid behind her ear and leaned in close, very close, to her ear.

"I wanted to know if you were ready to go with Lord

Sebes back to the hole you came from?"

Lola's blood ran cold.

"What...?" she breathed.

Lola suddenly realized she was alone with Sebes and Thad. As their eyes went shadowy, a hollow feeling in the pit of her stomach told Lola she never should have told Luce to stay behind.

"Thad? Please tell me what this is all about?" she said through clenched teeth, slowly backing away from him and Sebes.

At least she carried the Champion's Choice, though she hoped she wouldn't have to use it.

Thad responded, "For years, I have watched my cousin waste his privilege. He and Avenn treated me like shit. I was relieved to learn that Avenn died alone, surrounded by his own excrement and vomit. A death fit for a prince, if you ask me. I was sure Kingsley would screw this all up, and our families would be left with no choice but to appoint me heir to the throne. But Kingsley rose to the occasion, didn't he? Not even his own father expected that. So, as a final attempt to break my cousin, I suggested to my uncle that Kingsley should not marry a second-born daughter. That would definitely seal the deal."

"How could you do that to your cousin? He loves you!" Lola asked, voice cracking.

He kept talking as if she hadn't said a word, his shadowy

figure towering over her as he inched closer and closer.

"But, he would never give up Mya. And yet somehow, my fucking cousin moved on…and then you came."

Thad's beautiful face had been rained on by the sinister look in his eyes. He sneered, the taste on his tongue now clear contempt.

"Did you know I was out that day looking for you?"

"What day?" Lola asked.

"Then I saw you at the gate with him, and my plans were thwarted. When I saw King falling hard for you, I knew this would be our only chance to make things right. We would use you to get Kingsley out of the way. So, I decided to do everything I could to ensure you were both alone. But I must tell you, that the kiss in the woods was really something to witness. I heard my brother shouting for Kingsley that night. Once again, I stepped in and saved you."

"Saved me?"

What on earth was he talking about?

"Dear Sebastian had a brilliant idea to win your trust so that even when your entourage arrived, you would still be comfortable when left alone with me. Like you are right now."

A fire took over Lola as her magick began to rise.

"Ahhh ah ahh, I wouldn't do that if I were you. Please don't put it past me to kill my favorite cousin tonight."

Taking one more step, he crowded her and concealed

them both from prying eyes.

"Tell me, Lola, did you ever think of kissing me all those moments we were alone? Did you ever think, maybe I should be with Thad?"

Lola's stomach twisted as her rage simmered.

"Speed this up, Thad. We must make haste," Sebes said, irritated.

"I hope you enjoyed your time with him in the garden tonight. You were definitely closer than I had ever seen you. I was really hoping he would fuck you and get it over with. Before he'd never have the chance, again..."

As he rubbed his cold hand across her jaw, Lola could see Sebes becoming more irritated as he stepped closer to them.

"Don't you fucking touch her!"

"There you go again, Sebes," Thad sighed. "Falling for the wrong girl. You did it in the Sanctum, so why wouldn't you do here?"

Breaking from his languid gaze over her body, Thad faced Sebes.

"When do you plan to tell her?"

"Tell me what?" Lola demanded as her emerald eyes flashed brightly.

"Now, take a moment to calm yourself. Don't let your little abilities rule your head. If I don't return to the great hall in one piece, Rory, Kingsley, and all the others will be slaughtered this very night. Is that what you would like?"

Lola gritted her teeth. "Tell me what?" she spat out, bitter but quieter than before.

Clasping his hand behind his back, Thad began to pace.

"It was Sebes who held you prisoner. It was he who, night after night, allowed his guards to beat you, strip you and do The Mother knows what to you. Yet, somehow, this fool fell for you. I don't blame him, really."

Thad stopped his pacing and looked over his shoulder at Lola with an animalistic grin.

"I have always wanted to have my cock deep inside a Mosian woman," he said. "I've heard it is delightful. You are very lucky, Sebes. To have dipped your wick in that wax."

Lola whirled around to face Sebastian. She was barely able to hold back her magick.

"Is that true? Did you?"

He couldn't meet her eyes.

"While you were playing around with her," Thad continued, "I ensured that the king didn't know we were hiding her right under his nose. Fortunately for Sebes, the master told us we were not to kill you. But, unfortunately, for you, he didn't say we couldn't touch you in other ways."

Lola's whole body was numb. She remembered it now.

Their cold hands breaking her bones, stripping her of her soiled garments…and his voice. That haunting voice had been Sebes all along.

She knew there was no way she could use her magick here. The lives of Kingsley, Rory, Sirena—and everyone in that castle—depended on it. She would have to be compliant until she could defend herself.

"Who is your master?" Lola asked Sebes.

"Should we tell her?" Sebes asked Thad.

"I see no harm in it."

"Listen closely, sweet Lola. It was just over a year ago when Prince Nasir came to the Sanctum, seeking refuge. When he arrived, the priest refused to meet with him, so it fell to me to welcome him. As soon as our eyes met, his magick called out to me, taking hold of my senses and enveloping me in its power. A swirling vortex of darkness and light consumed me, revealing secrets and truths that had long been hidden," Sebes said, his silver eyes piercing.

"It was then that I told him of our possession of one of the Porte sisters, and I saw the hunger in his eyes. That very night, as the moons cast its ethereal glow over the tower, Prince Nasir crept in and observed you as you slept."

Lola's heart pounded.

"I watched Nasir kneel down next to you," Sebes continued. "I heard him recite the prophecy."

The wind rustled through the garden as Sebes lowered his voice and took another step towards Lola, unblinking as he spoke, "When the dark throne rises, the three shall bring forth an era of magick and sorrow."

A chill ran down Lola's spine and she held her breath as he stared at her.

"And then he left," Sebes said plainly. "He told us to keep you safe until he returned with his army. But you didn't wait for that, did you?"

Lola hated him. She hated all of them. But more than anything, she hated how after all this time, she could still barely piece together her memories.

"Later that night, you somehow got enough strength to free yourself and kill good soldiers along the way," Sebes finished firmly.

"I told you we needed to increase the potency of the Nova Dust we gave her," Thad scolded.

Nova Dust? Lola had heard her mother mention it before. It was some sort of sedative—one that, if given in large amounts, could cause amnesia or even death.

Lola's blood boiled. Panicking wouldn't help her; she had to stay alert.

"Don't fret, brother, I have perfected it this time," Sebes said as he suddenly whipped a crimson cloth over Lolas' face.

She struggled and scratched his hands as her magick rose, green eyes flaming until her eyelids felt too heavy. Blackness engulfed her, and as she felt her legs give way, she bit out her final words. "I will see you all dead."

CHAPTER 16

Trail of treachery

"Have you seen Lola?" Queen Alina asked Kingsley as he stood on the terrace, warming his hand by the fire there. He couldn't tell if they were shaking from the frigid air or if he was still in shock after what had happened in the maze with Lola. Icy wind slashed at his face as heavy flurries danced around his head.

Turning away from the fire, his molten eyes landed on the one person who knew him best, his mother. One look at Kingsley and his mother knew that things had gone badly.

"Tell me," Alina said, coming to stand close to Kingsley so that no one would overhear their discord.

"I don't want to talk about it."

"You will and you must talk about it. Contrary to what you might believe, your love life is not private. Not when you are heir to the throne and definitely not when the woman you are talking about is the only living relative of the High Queen. Now out with it." His mother had a way of making his problems her problems. In this case—as with many others—she was right.

Stowing his hands in his pockets, Kingsley leaned back on his heels. Looking up at the moons, he took a deep breath. A white blanket of snow began to cover the ground, and he wished that it would just as easily cover the disaster of how things had turned out. He told his mother about the garden. How they had made up and kissed and how, just as quickly, they had fought.

Standing in her white mink fur, Alina took in the garden and the stars. "Did I ever tell you about the time your father asked if he could court me and I said no?"

"Wait, what?"

"I was nine and ten and he had just turned twenty and one. We had been spending a great deal of time together, reading and horseback riding, but your father was quite unsure of what he wanted to do."

"What do you mean?'

"I was not a royal, but the daughter of a lord. I was not considered the best-suited mate for a future king. His parents and courtesans insisted that he keep his options open. So he did just that. While spending time with me in secret, he openly courted another. He conveniently found times to bump into me at the market or to show up where he knew I would be with my ladies."

"So, he finally saw the light and asked you anyway?"

"He did," she confirmed as a coy smile reached her lips.

"And you said no?"

"Yes. I said no."

"Why? I mean...he chose you."

"I said no because your father has always been a rebel."

"My father, the king, a rebel?" Kingsley asked with wide eyes. Alina chuckled and nodded. "Honestly," she said. "It's one of the many things I love about him."

"Is there a reason why you told him no?"

"Yes. I didn't want to be his rebellion or his second choice. I wanted to be the only choice." Turning to face her son, she fixed the color of his tunic and whispered, "No woman wants to be a consolation prize. I wonder if that is exactly how Princess Lola feels."

Kingsley let out a breath. He'd been an ass. He hadn't let her in. Always questioned her motives and her intentions, even when all she had ever been was kind. Yes, she was incredibly frustrating, determined, and isolating, but he saw that as a challenge. She was different from Mya. Lola was fierce, soft, and she knew who she was. There was no comparing the two. Kingsley saw himself as her hero—her protector—but in actuality, she had found him. She had saved him. An urgency came over him. He needed to tell her that right now.

His heart beat so hard he was sure it would come out of his chest. He knew he would never be well again, not until he spoke to her and made it right.

"Thank you, Mother, I must go."

Heading towards the great hall, Kingsley was stopped by a rather large fist in his face.

Hitting the ground hard, Kingsley looked up to find Luce and his guards surrounding him.

"What the fuck did you do to her? Where is Princess Lola?" Luce shouted through gritted teeth.

Kia and Rory stepped between the two men as Bishop jumped in beside his cousin with a firm grip on the pommel of his sword.

"Prince Do'Ramos," Rory said, calmer but with the same sense of urgency. "Lola was last seen with your cousin Thaddeus."

"Where is your cousin?" Kia demanded, gripping her gloves as if ready for war.

"If she is with Thad, then there is nothing to fear," Bishop said. "My brother would never let any harm come to the princess."

King Heath's voice boomed as he approached surrounded by his wolven warriors. "What is the meaning of this?"

Everyone froze except for Kingsley, who rubbed his jaw. "I will only ask once more," Heath said. "And then I will have you all sent to the dungeons."

"Forgive our haste, King Heath," Luce said as he adjusted his jacket and ran his fingers through his hair. "Princess

Lola has gone missing."

Heath immediately motioned for his guards to ease.

"The last I saw her," Luce continued. "She was with Lord Thaddeus and Lord Sebes. They stepped out into the gardens, and that was five sonnets ago. When I came out here, I found this."

He gestured to Kia, who handed Kingsley a familiar blade. "She told us you gave her this blade, Prince Do'Ramos."

"King," his mother gasped, turning to face her son. "You gave her your grandfather's blade?"

"Mother, that is not important now." Facing Rory, he explained, "Yes, I gave her that for her protection. It has never left her side since."

King's stomach tightened when he realized something must have gone terribly wrong for her to lose it.

"Kia, tell me again, where did you search for her?"

"We went the the garden, the maze, her rooms, and even checked the stables"

"She isn't here."

"No shit, asshole. That's what we have been trying to tell you."

Eyes wide Kingsley pointed to two guards. "Go find Thad and tell him the princess is gone. Don't return until you have found him."

Pointing to two other guards, he commanded them to search the great hall. When the guards cleared out,

Kingsley turned to Luce.

Fist balled tightly and his tone stiff and surly, he said, "I know you care for her. So I will let this incident pass. But let this be the last fucking time you question my loyalty to Lola."

With a voice that could cut glass, Luce said, "How informally you address the Princess of Mōsa." Taking a step closer to Kingsley so that they were mere inches away from each other, Luce continued, "Careful, Prince, your feelings are showing."

ACT II

CHAPTER 17

Betrayal unveiled

In the serene stillness of the night, the dual moons' ethereal white glow seeped through the intricately-designed stained glass windows of the grand study, casting a mesmerizing dance of light and shadows across the room. Rory stood amidst the enchanting radiance, a silent observer of the emotions that played out before her.

She felt as if she had lost Lola all over again. And this time, everyone in the room was to blame.

Kingsley paced back and forth with restless determination. Rory could see why Lola had fallen for this man, even if she hadn't yet admitted that. He was steady in a crisis. When the guards returned with the news that she was nowhere to be found, Kingsley's heart broke in two.

When he was told that Lord Sebes was in the Sanctum but that no one could locate Thaddeus, Kingsley's gaze fell on Bishop. His cousins resented his newfound freedoms; he was sure of it. But before he could demand his cousin to speak, a small voice from across the room silenced the group.

"It was the Sanctum."

Princess Sirena sat on the settee in the corner of the room with her head hung.

"What?" Kia asked sharply.

Sirena's skirt ruffled as she stood and made her way to the king. "Father," she said. "Did you not tell us, just three moonrises ago, that the Sanctum has been capturing mages because they believe it to be their responsibility to rid the world of magick?"

The room fell quiet at the revelation. King Heath did not need to confirm his daughter's suspicions.

"We must leave at once!" Kingsley demanded, balling his fists by his sides.

"Wait!" King Heath shouted for order. "If you go there now, it will be seen as treason. We can not risk war with our neighbor. Not now, not while the Darkness ravages our kingdom."

"Fa...Your Highness, if the Sactumn does in fact have Lola, then they have already declared war."

King Heath saw something in Kingsley's eyes—despair behind his conviction. As if seeing his son as a leader for the first time, he swallowed and said evenly, "I know you and princess Lola have grown to be close friends."

"She is more than my friend," Kingsley corrected, louder than he wanted to.

All eyes went to him as a sea of silence fell upon the room.

"I made her a promise. And I intend to keep it."

"My order is final. We will wait until we know more and then—"

"With all due respect, King Heath," Luce interrupted the father and son dispute. "I do not fucking answer to you. High Queen Sole made it clear to me that I was to bring her sister home, unharmed, and that is exactly what I will do."

Flat and steady, the King continued, "We cannot proceed without proof. We must send someone who can verify that the princess is there."

"I will go," Bishop said. The room turned its attention to him. "I know I haven't been the friendliest to Lola—I mean Princess Lola, but I never wished her harm. And if my brother"—he turned to Melia—"if our brother has done this, then it is our duty to make things right."

"No!" Luce shouted. "None of you get a say in this. She is my responsibility. She will be safe or I will burn this whole place to the ground."

Kia placed a hand on Luce's shoulder. "Brother, I fear you may have gone too far," she whispered.

"Kia, I won't do this again, I won't let them take her, too."

His voice cracked. "I will see her safe!" With that, Luce fled the room. Kia sighed and turned to the group. "You must understand that what we have lost…it's more than we can bear. Lola is the last hope of this world. Her and Sole. Without them, the prophecy will not come to pass. It is their fate to save Transea, to save us all," she said. "It is written in the prophecy. When the dark throne rises, the three shall bring forth an era of magick and sorrow."

As hot tears streamed down Kia's face, Queen Alina closed the distance between them. She took Kia's hand in hers and softly said, "We will find her and bring her home. Give us til the next moonrise to locate her exact position and we will join you in the search."

Noddin, Kia exited the study.

Turning to face the queen, Rory muttered, "Once she is found we will leave with the princess. Make sure your young prince understands that."

CHAPTER 18

A promise unveiled

Kingsley couldn't bring himself to look his father in the eye. He had given her his grandfather's blade. He stood in the study, feeling the weight of his parents' expectations heavy upon his shoulders. He wished he could simply slip away and join the search party for Lola, but he knew better than to even entertain that idea.

His voice was barely above a whisper. "Yes, I gave her the blade."

His mother's voice cut through the tension in the room. "Do you understand what that means, Kingsley?"

Kingsley knew exactly what it meant. The Champion's Choice was a symbol of great power and responsibility. It was meant to be wielded by only the most skilled and honorable of warriors.

But that was not what his mother had asked. He knew what giving that blade to Lola meant to his family and to his kingdom. What it meant to Kingsley. But that conversation would have to wait until his return. He felt a bead of sweat roll down his forehead as his mother forced him to meet her gaze.

"Yes, Mother," he said, voice trembling. "I understand."

Queen Alina let out a heavy sigh and turned to face her husband. Kingsley felt his father's eyes upon him and tried to steel himself against the judgment he knew was coming.

"It's settled then," Alina said firmly. "Kingsley must go and save the Princess of Mōsa. He has no choice."

Kingsley's heart leapt at his mother's words. He felt his father's hands on his shoulders and he turned to meet his gaze. "Go. Find the princess and bring her home," his father said. "We'll be waiting for you here."

With a resolute nod, Kingsley pushed aside the fear and doubt that threatened to surface. As the war governor, he had faced countless battles before without flinching, but Lola had changed everything. She had opened his heart to feelings he had never known before.

"The revelation dawns on me that Lola and my duty to our kingdom are inseparable threads of my destiny; by serving both, I become the king Kingsguard Reef deserves."

As Kingsley's father drew him close, he whispered, "Now our enemies find rest." And Kingsley, with a newfound sense of purpose, echoed back, "Now our enemies find rest."

CHAPTER 19

A descent into madness

The warm waves crawled gently to the shore, kissing her wet toes. The water reflected the rose petal-pink glow and string of neon green and purple from the canopy of stars scattered in the night sky.

A salty, humid breeze caressed Lola's copper-brown skin. Oh, that breeze.

She was home. She was in Mōsa.

Behind her, she heard the cheerful chatter of her sisters.

"Lola, come join us and tell us about Gavin. Didn't you mention you were going to ask him out for a stroll on the beach tonight?" her sister Luna called out.

Lola pondered for a moment, a slight blush creeping up her cheeks. "I might have," she admitted. Though she enjoyed Gavin's company, being with her sisters was what truly made her happy.

"I wouldn't want to be anywhere else but with my sisters," Lola declared. "Besides, he smells of fish and sand. I love fishing, but I don't want to smell like one."

Her sisters burst into laughter, their joy infectious as they playfully ran up and down the seashore. The bond they shared was unbreakable, and Lola cherished every moment spent with them. She couldn't recall why this moment was making her so sad.

"Sole, let's go for a swim!" Lola suggested, eyeing the moonshine on the water.

The three sisters laughed loudly as they ran up and down the seashore.

"Sole, let's go swim!" Lola asked again.

"No. You know I can't swim."

Lola's face lit up with determination. "I can teach you!" she exclaimed. "We'll start slowly, and you'll see how much fun it can be."

"Just hold on," Lola says, "and put some trust in me, Princess Sole Porte, first of her name." She winked. "Others have done so and not been badly disappointed."

"I'd rather not die, thanks. Besides, it's dark out and the storm is coming..." Sole replied apprehensively as the last words of her sentence trailed off into the air.

"The storm is coming!" Luna shouted from ahead, her voice carrying a dark rage that sent shivers down Lola's spine. As Luna's anger intensified, her eyes underwent a startling transformation, no longer brown, but now a mesmerizing combination of azure and silver that seemed to pierce through Lola's soul.

"When the dark throne rises, the three shall bring forth an era of magick and sorrow."

The sisters repeated the prophecy as the wind consumed them. Lola couldn't see. As she pushed through the dark wind to reach for her sisters, she felt tethered to something.

It pulled her back.

A panic gripped Lola's heart. Please don't take me from them.

But the tether pulled. It demanded she return to the dark.

"Take me with you, don't leave me alone!" The wind stopped abruptly. The dark beach was void of laughter, joy.

"Sole…Luna…"

She waited for them to answer, but the echoes of her own hoarse voice were all that she heard. Her sisters were gone, and she was alone.

And then, as the tether pulled her further into the near black of the sea, she felt Sole grab her hand one last time.

"Lo, you must stay alive. Without you the world will be consumed by the Darkness. Live…"

She was gone, and the waves pulled Lola under.

But it felt more like someone was holding her down in the water rather than pulling her from beneath. She couldn't move her feet. Clarity swept over her in an instant.

Someone was actually holding her under water. Strong, rough hands—familiar hands—lifted her out of the basin in the dungeon.

A dungeon.

She was never in Mōsa. When the huge hands pulled her out of the water, she coughed and shivered as she tried to make sense of her surroundings. She was tied and bound in the Sanctum again.

Large torches lit the area above, where she saw a bridge extending from the upper floor from left to right, supported by pillars. Ahead at the end of the chamber was a large double door, opened to reveal stairs leading upward. Shallow water and piss covered the entire floor where Lola stood barefoot.

The water dripped from the ceiling into her hair, and she could barely move on the uneven floor. Algae and plants sprouted up from the cracks, and small fish swam about in the flood. She shivered in the bitter cold, and her breath clouded as it escaped her lips.

That's when she saw him standing against the open door.

Sebes's silver eyes drank her in, and she looked down at her body.

Her gown was gone, and all she wore was her white underdress, which was so soaking wet that it left her completely exposed.

Eyes set on ripping Sebes apart, Lola whispered through chattering teeth, "I will see you dead."

***

The study was empty after Lola's escorts left the room. Especially Luce, who unapologetically took up so much space. Kingsley thought hard about Luce and the comments he'd made about Lola.

It took everything for Kingsley not to lose his temper. Luce seemed to think he had a chance with Lola, and that Kingsley was just going to roll over and take it. King put on a tough face, as if what happened hadn't bothered him, but he was exhausted.

Storming past his father, King lifted Bishop off the ground.

"You! You will tell me everything you know about your brother and what he has done with Lola!" Kingsley shouted in his face.

He tossed Bishop onto the wooden floor with a hard thump that had Melia running to his side.

Bishop seized in his breath and shook on his hands and knees before getting his bearings and standing to his feet.

Kingsley couldn't control himself. Why the fuck was he even reacting this way?

The only woman that had ever made him feel crazy was Mya, but this wasn't like that.

This was madness.

Lola had made him greedy for her time, for her attention. Lola had changed him. She had changed everything.

Before her, he had felt like a lost little boy.

But with her by his side, he really could rule this kingdom.

Together, they could save Transea.

But first, he wanted nothing more than to beat the shit out of Bishop.

His fist collided with Bishop's gut before the Wolven guards were called in to hold him back.

"What the Fuck, King!?" Melia shouted as she ran to shield her brother from him.

Ignoring her, King shot forward to seize Bishop once more before he crashed into a wall of guards.

Dragging himself to his feet once more as he adjusted his jacket, Bishop put one arm up to Melia.

"I am fine, sis."

"No you fucking aren't," she spat.

Looking past his sister, Bishop said, "King, I know you are hurt—"

"I'm not hurt," he sputtered. "I am irate! When I find Thad...I will—"

"You will what?" Queen Alina demanded.

Everyone turned to face her.

Alina was many things: kind, loving, and demanding. Her children and her nieces and nephews adored and revered her. The queen very rarely raised her voice, so when she did, her family listened. Stepping out from behind her tall, Alina took her regal stance before her kin.

"Have you all forgotten we are family? I will not sit back and watch us shrivel and die, following suit with the world around us."

She raised a hand in command.

Everyone took their seats. "We will sort this out as we always have—as a family."

Melia, Bishop, and Kingsley did as they were told. Even King Heath sat at his wife's command.

Kingsley smirked every time he saw his father bend a knee to his mother. If anyone in the royal court knew about betrayal, it was Alina. Becoming Queen meant she would be second to no one ever again.

Her commitment to her husband had resonated with the people and over time, the people became committed to her.

Now Kinglsey was committed to Lola. He'd learned from the best.

Reluctantly, King sat down on the crimson settee, arms propped on his knees as stared Bishop down with daggers in his eyes.

"King," his father said. "I ask that we listen to Bishop before we act, and that is an order."

"Bishop, tell us what you know so that we can save Lola and Thad," Queen Alina requested.

"Auntie, I'm not quite sure where to begin," Bishop replied, voice cracking.

"Start at the beginning, fucker," Kingsley demanded. Bishop shot up from his seat. "King, if you weren't so far up Lola's skirts maybe you would have noticed it too!" he shouted.

"Fuck you!" King shouted back as he rose to his feet. The guards stationed by the door made their way to him in an instant, shoving their weapons in his face and forcing him to sit back down. His father had obviously made it clear to his guards that their duty was to restrain his son.

"Let me explain, King!" Bishop pleaded, his gaze intense and unwavering. He shifted from foot to foot, his restlessness reflecting the weight of what he had to say.

"I thought he might have been going through something after the Darkness," Bishop continued, his voice softer. "You know, the aftermath of what happened to Avenn. It changed him, and I couldn't help but worry about the toll it took on him."

"I remember asking him about it and he told me he had seen the truth," Melia said to no one in particular as she tucked her hair behind her ear. "I joked that he had fallen for someone in the Sanctum. But he just fucking laughed."

"Right," Bishop said. "So, that's when I started to keep a close eye on him. I mean...our father would kill him if he became a priest or something. Thad was built to lead."

A hushed silence settled in the group as they absorbed Bishop's revelations. The pieces of the puzzle began to fall into place, yet they were still left with more questions than answers.

Through gritted teeth, Kingsley asked the one question

everyone was surely thinking.

"What do you mean he changed?"

"At first it was subtle. He was spending more time with Lord Sebes, playing card games and such. Things that were easy to overlook. Then he was coming to his rooms less and less. By the time Lola arrived, he'd already told me that he wanted to challenge King Heath to be next in line for the throne."

Everyone turned to face King Heath. They all held their breath, awaiting his response.

The King cleared his throat.

"Thad did come to see me," he revealed. "He didn't ask to be next in line, but he did share his...his..."

"His what?" Kingsley spat out.

"He shared his frustrations about your inability to move beyond what you lost and open your eyes to what you had gained. A kingdom." The King spoke without looking his son in the eyes.

"Heath," Alina said, turning to her husband with a flat expression. "Did you entertain such talk?"

"I thought the boy needed guidance," Heath reasoned. "That he just wanted to make his frustrations known. But I realized something was off."

Stepping from behind his desk, Heath closed the distance between him and Kingsley.

"Son, the last time he came to me, I urged him to aid you

in your role as war governor and future king. He became upset and said you would lead our kingdom to ruin. I asked him to leave and he hasn't come back to talk with me since. Knowing what I know now, I wish the poor boy would have come back."

Bishop took a wary step toward his cousin. "Kingsley, I…I think my brother didn't only want the throne."

Kingsley whipped his head to Bishop and flared his nostrils. Bishop swallowed.

"He…had mentioned how he and Lola were getting closer."

Bishop paused as if expecting Kingsley to do something—to blow up or to throw his chair through the window. Stepping into the light, Bishop holds his hands out. "My brother has been sick for a long time.

"Son," King Heath said. "You must tell us everything. He hurt our family. The High Queen's sister has been kidnapped. This will be a declaration of war if we don't do everything we can to make this right."

Heath strode over to his nephew, the hard demeanor he'd worn before now softened into a subtle smile. Kingsley studied him as he did when he was a child. His father was always mesmerizing as a leader. Eloquent. A backbone of steel.

"Several months ago," Bishop began, "my brother joined the Sanctum on a pilgrimage. I was the one first asked to go, but you know Thad…he knew I would hate it and so he went in my stead. High Priest Martin said it would be a diplomatic trip. So Thad accompanied Lord Sebes and High Priest Martin to Sundom."

Bishop exhaled and continued.

"After all, Sundom built its wealth from war. They are known for the best steel. We laughed about how we would finally stand a chance against you in training, King."

Kingsley remembered his favorite cousin then. Thad had been the first to greet him when he was brought home from the Sanctum. Thad always knew what to say to ease the tension. Kingsley always thought he would have made a great king if the tables were turned.

But that was before his cousin had betrayed him, his family, their kingdom, and most importantly, Lola.

That shit was unforgivable; Bishop could read it in his steely gaze.

"I didn't know where he had gone until last night. My brother and I are very different, but that doesn't mean we aren't close. You know that Melia and Thad are just as important to me as Sirena is to you. When Thad told me last night that he was in trouble and would have to go away for a while, he never mentioned Lola. Had he, I would have come straight to you, King Heath. But he didn't."

"What did he tell you, son?" King Heath asked.

Kingsley hated his father's use of the word 'son' when

referring to his cousin. It never bothered as much as it did now.

At that moment, he was a step away from spiraling out of control. But he knew that if he did, his father's guards would be on him sooner than he could move, and he'd never be allowed near Lola's search and rescue mission.

Bishop's eyes darted between the king and queen. Kingsley recognized that look. It was the look Bishop had whenever he'd been caught screwing up.

It was the look he saw when his mother caught him and Thad sneaking out to climb one of the Lycos Towers facing the Sirena Sea. Each tower housed twelve soldiers of the Reef. Their one task: protect the island at all cost.

As young lads, they were mesmerized by the enormous fortitude of the towers and what they represented: preservation of their freedom.

Being the second-born son, Kingsley knew that he was never meant to be king, which was fine by him. His dream—his heart—was to one day be War Governor of Kingsguard Reef. Although his brother and his cousins loved the thrill of climbing the towers at night, none of them felt the same as King did.

He knew that one day he would be responsible for protecting the Reef.

His stomach dropped at the realization that now he was the governor, and he'd failed to keep Lola, a royal guest in the simplest description, protected.

Focusing on the crisis at hand, Kingsley listened intently as Bishop continued.

"Thad told me that when he went on the pilgrimage, he met a stranger who introduced himself as the King of Mōsa. He said his name was Nasir."

Kingsley looked at his father without a word.

Summoning the two Wolven Guards that stood at the door, King Heath commanded, "Send for the Mōsian entourage at once. Have two guards escort them to the war room. We must inform the High Queen that Nasir has infiltrated Kingsguard Reef."

CHAPTER 20

Echoes of regret

"We have all failed Lola…" The echo of Aurora Gambles' words haunted Kingsley. Standing in the great hall, he placed his black leather satchel on the table. Without her in it, this space felt incredibly empty.

The room's candlelit glow reminded him of the first time he saw Lola walk through the ornate doors. Her eyes were captivated by the history that consumed the walls with pomp and circumstance. Until she mentioned it, he had never considered the reality that Mōsa suffered most during the Great War.

According to his grandfather, the Mōsians were brave enough to stand up against the tyrannical king of Sundom. Being that brave came with a cost. Their family history was literally burned out of the scrolls, and many of their women that couldn't make it onto the last ships were raped and enslaved. They said the men were the first to lose their magick. Their heads were found on a spikes in front of the House of Alacor and Avireal.

His grandfather told him that the house of Do'Ramos fled without notice to their allies, leaving the Mōsian people to fend for themselves. For a long time, the Mōsians felt abandoned by their allies. "We fled like thieves in the night, and our Mōsian brothers and sisters were left holding the blame and the loss. Cowards are what we were," his grandfather had told him before he died.

"There you are." Sirena called to Kingsley in relief.

"Do you want to wake the entire house?" He nearly yelled.

"Did you think I would let you leave on your own?"

"What are you talking about?" King said, looking everywhere but at his sister's face. At twenty years old, she was only a year younger than King, but a force to be reckoned with.

"I know that look. It's the same look you had when Jauqin pushed me into the berry bush after I refused to kiss him."

"That fucker didn't know I was there until I pushed him back."

"You also waited til no one was watching and kicked his ass alone."

"Yea, what of it?"

Sirena sighed and continued, " You are brave, loyal, and the noblest man I know. And you are my last brother." Her voice cracked. "That's why...wherever you go, I go."

Kingsley didn't know how he had missed his sister

wearing her black riding suit and boots.

Joaquin was always a little shit. He was obsessed with Sirena. As he grew and matured, he and Sirena became good friends. When he died from the darkness, it hit Sirena hard. Losing their brother in the same horrid way made them closer. But that didn't mean he would risk her life so easily.

"Who said I was going anywhere?"

"Because we have the same travel satchel," she said as she plopped her bag on the ornate table beside him. "So don't treat me like I am fragile, King. You know I fucking hate that!"

"You. Can't. Come," he said, eyes steely.

"Fine." She snatched her bag off the table. Her boots thudded on the worn stone floor as she yelled over her shoulder, "I will just go and inform our father of your ridiculous plan to go save the princess alone."

"Wait," he said with a sigh as he grabbed Sirena's arm, turning her to face him. The smirk tugging on her lips infuriated him, but he knew she was right.

"Sirena, this will not be easy."

"Well then, it's a good thing I am my mother's daughter. I'm pretty fierce with a bow. When do we leave?"

"Ris," King said, using the name he called her when she was a girl, "If you get hurt, I'll never forgive myself."

Her eyes filled with tears. Shakily, she whispered to her

brother, "And if you get hurt…if I lose another brother, I will not forgive myself either."

Crossing her arms in defiance, she continued, "I'm going with you and that's final."

Seeing the determined spark in her eyes staring back at him, Kingsley knew there was no talking her out of it. "We leave tonight," he said.

"So that settles it," Sirena said. "We are going to the Sanctum. But how will we know where to find her?"

"I can show you the way." A man's voice said from behind them. Melia and Bishop stepped out of the shadows of the dark corridor. The brother and sister donned their matching navy travel attire, dark leather satchels hanging off their sides.

"The fuck you are!" Kingsly shouted as he headed to Bishop, intent on socking him in the face.

"The fuck we are not!" Bishop spat out.

Melia and Sirena stood in between their brothers, arms out, demanding their patience. "King!" Sirena warned firmly, her jaw tight. "I am sure we can sort this out, but now is not the time. If Bishop knows where she might be held, let him take us to her."

"Bishop," Melia began, "I swear to the Holy Mother if you tell one more fucking lie, it won't be Kingsley you should fear. I promise I will kill you myself." She narrowed her eyes at him. "Now, let's get on with it. We will have to be back before everyone notices we are gone."

Eyes like molten lava, King looked at Bishop. "This will be the last time I will trust you. If you betray us at the Sanctum, I will run you through."

"Let's be clear!" Bishop put his hands up diplomatically. "I know I have amends to make, of that I am certain. Helping find Lola alive is our first priority. But I am also going for my brother. I need to see if there is anything left worth saving." Hot tears filled his eyes. "I thought everyone would understand what it means to want to save your brother."

His cousin's words rocked Kingsley. They pierced his heart, and he couldn't help but remember what his mother had said. "It will take me time to forgive you," he said with a steady breath out his nose. "But we are family, and we must stay united during this mission, or the house of Do'Ramos will surely perish if we all do." Bishop nodded with a firm smile. "Now, let's make the circle."

Forming a circle, the four cousins pondered the risk of marching on the Sanctum, the representative of the Holy Mother throughout all of Transea. If they were caught, they would surely be killed. And yet, none of them looked afraid. Fear wasn't in their blood. Their family knew what it meant to be ostracized and forgotten. Kingsguard Reef had once been a mighty nation with an army that could be heard marching from miles around. By legend, their ancestors were wolven. Now, from this den, the wolves were emerging, and may the Holy Mother help anyone who stepped in their way. Melia with her staff, Sirena with her bow, and King and Bishop with their swords—the familial mercenaries had one goal in mind: save Lola and bring her home.

Placing one hand in the center of the circle, King's cousins followed his gesture. Together, they recited their family battle cry three times. "Now our enemies rest. Now our enemies rest. Now our enemies rest."

CHAPTER 21

Rising from the ashes

The shivers wracking her body almost stopped Lola from breathing. She went stiff. How many days had she been here? Five? Six? She'd lost count after Sebes visited her two nights ago—the worst night Lola had spent in captivity. It wasn't the slaps or punches Sebes gave her that made her stomach tighten; it was how he apologized as he cleaned the blood. The blood he tore from her body. She was sure he'd knocked one of her molars loose with his last punch; a metallic taste had lingered on her tongue since.

The worst part wasn't the beatings; it was the savage cutting of her hair. Lowering his head to her ear, he whispered, "High Priest Srabas was told by the Holy Mother that the only way to release you of your sinful magick is to cut your beautiful locs off. I have to say, at first I did think it was a bit extreme." He pressed his hands to her cheeks, jerked her hair back, and raised his dagger. Tears stung in Lola's eyes and dripped onto the wet floor beneath her bare feet.

Since that awful night, Lola had been in a petrifying state of shock. How had she ended up back here? The sound of water usually soothed Lola, but the white noise of the rushing waterfall outside had her on edge in the darkness of the dungeon. That sound would never be her refuge again.

She was desperate. Since the cutting of her hair, Lola struggled to bring her magick to the surface. Maybe the High Priest had been right. Maybe they had killed her magick. The thought of that ringing true broke her heart. The only thing the Darkness had given her after killing her parents and her sisters was magick. Now that too was gone.

Resting her head against the cold stone wall, Lola found it harder and harder to keep her eyes open. She had to get out of the Sanctum, with or without her magick. Drained of her strength and her magick, she would have to find a way to dig deep and kill Sebes this very night.

She opened her eyes to see Sebes, white-blonde hair catching her glassy gaze. The reminder of what he'd taken from her made her want to pierce him with her magick. Panic and rage flickered in her eyes, causing tears to well up. This was a familiar reaction whenever he entered the room.

She didn't know how long he'd been watching her sleep, but the way he was drinking her in with his eyes warned her that tonight would be a bloody night. As much as she hated Thad, she knew he could calm the rage in Sebes. But Thad wasn't here, which meant this was the time to fight or die. She couldn't remember the last time she'd seen Thad. The coward was nowhere to be found since the first night he dropped her in this cell. She did overhear the tall, lanky Holy Guard say that Thad was having a change of heart and that he'd asked to consult the High Priest after learning that they'd cut Lola's hair.

As a smirk rose on Sebes's thin lips, Lola wanted to vomit. Seeing him turned her stomach and brought out a fight within her that she hadn't felt in a long time. Seeing Sebes here alone stirred her magick into a frenzy; it bubbled in her veins screamed to be let out. And she would do just that if she could.

Setting his sword and shield against the stone wall, Sebes made his way to the princess, stopping just inches from where her ankle was chained to the ground. The slip she wore was brown and ragged now, torn where he'd cut her and stained where she'd bled.

"What the fuck do you want?" she spat in his direction.

"You know after all this time, I never get tired of that beautiful face and that fucking mouth." Crossing his arms, he continued, "I wonder…if the Darkness had never come, would we have met at some point? Would we have made a life together?"

Bile rose in Lola's stomach.

"We could have been so good together."

"You are one sick bastard!" Lola snapped at him. "You know that?" She struggled to stand on her aching feet.

"Where is your man boy, huh? Where's Thad? I'm surprised you can even speak without his permission."

Sebes tsked and shook his head in amusement.

"Don't you worry about Thad. I knew when he first told us he found the Princess of Mōsa that he was a little too fond of you—my pet. I don't blame him, really. But see, I have a problem with him and the second-born prince touching you. You are mine."

"Yours? Huh! Do you treat all your women this way? That would explain a lot."

For that, she earned a backhand to her jaw that knocked her back on her ass, metal chain clanking as she fell. Slowly and painfully, she forced herself to her feet once more, smiling because it was worth it—to show him that he could never knock her down for good.

Spitting out the blood filling her mouth, she continued, "Typical of a man with privilege to take and take and take but never ask permission. I can't be yours if I don't agree to it. And here's something you should know…" Spit and blood dripped down her chin as she gritted her teeth and took a defiant step towards him. "Taking my body will never make me yours. It only makes you a thief and a small man," she ground out as she inched even closer.

Smack!

Lola recoiled for only a heartbeat before reaching forward and smacking him back. The bastard smiled.

The more Sebes spoke, the hotter Lola's magick began to boil in her veins. Her magick knew that she was in danger; she could feel it as a wave of energy rose from within her blood. A tendril of green magick snaked around the rusty metal chain at her ankle and tugged her free so quietly that Sebes never heard a thing.

"That beautiful mouth is always spewing out venom. But I have a remedy for that," he said as he drew closer to her.

Lola's magick whipped out in front of her in an emerald pulse that glowed brighter and brighter until a beam of jade light shot straight from her palm and towards Sebes. He dodged it quickly, rolling away and reaching for his shield. The gleaming dragon scales on it absorbed the magickal blast, and as he lowered it and stared Lola in her emerald eyes, the shield began to pulse an eerie aquamarine. She bared her teeth at him and sent a larger blast his way, but once again, he raised his shield just in time.

Sebes was a warrior; Lola had no doubt about that. Although he didn't possess magick, he knew his way around a battlefield. He caught one blast, then another, dodging a third, before his shield cracked down the middle.

Lola's magick rose as an emerald fireball swirled in her palm, swelling in size. She hurled it and it sizzled through the air towards Sebes, who swept to the side and lunged for his gilded sword. As the fireball exploded near his feet, Lola launched another, hitting him square in the face. He stumbled backward, smacking the ends of his singed hair as he tightened his jaw and tried to regain his composure. Holding his sword with both hands, a small smile crept on his face. Lounging forward, Sebes punched her in her stomach once, twice…and as something warm dripped down her belly, Lola realized they weren't punches at all. He'd stabbed her. A cold wind swept over her at the sight of her crimson blood dripping onto the dark, wet floor. This is it, Lola thought. This is where I will truly die.

Taking one last breath, Lola collapsed onto the blood-stained floor.

Dropping his sword to the ground, Sebes knelt beside the bleeding princess. "Look what you made me do," Sebes said as his voice cracked.

Closing her eyes one last time, she was overcome with relief. This nightmare…all of it would soon be over. But her magick wouldn't let her die. It poured onto the dungeon floor like mist, calling on the life of nature—of the nearby trees, plants and vines—to save her.

Lola shot him a look that told him she was no weakling; she was a warrior princess and a Misa warrior with magick. With one pulse, Lola threw Sebes clear across the room. Grabbing his heavy gilded sword, she stabbed it into the ground as the magick left her body, passed through the sword, and settled in the ground under her feet.

Her magick controlled her like a marionette, spreading her hands at her side, palms up. Emerald flames rose around her. Her lifeblood was done with men using her, breaking her will, and taking what she did not freely give. Her magick had come to collect a debt. It would ravage everything around if Lola didn't control it. Her power needed to listen to her. She had to protect her sister and her kingdom. But her magic fought. It didn't want to be controlled.

Sebes stood a good distance from her. Tilting her head as if seeing through him, Lola's power raged. Holding it down was like trying to stop a hurricane with her bare hands. Her pulse struck him once more like a battering ram, shoving him face first against the stone wall.

Sebastian stumbled to his feet and charged forward, red with fury. But Lola, her hand raised and her power feeling lighter than air, met his advance with a swift flick of her wrist. Fire erupted around Sebes, engulfing him in a fierce inferno.

As the flames consumed him, Sebastian's guttural screams of agony echoed through the chamber, slowly dying as he did. Lola's gaze remained fixed on the spectacle, the dancing flames reflecting in her green eyes, the intensity of the moment etched into her memory. Then, his screams silenced, leaving only the sound of the crackling fire.

With a controlled breath, Lola closed her palm, drawing back her green magick before it could consume the entire dungeon and its unfortunate prisoners. As the emerald fire subsided, Sebastian's body collapsed, melting into the ground beneath him, merging with the filth and shit of the dungeon floor—a fitting end for a man who belonged in the depths of depravity.

Lola felt someone in the shadows behind her. She swung her palm in their direction before even turning her head.

Kingsley stepped into the light with his hands up. "Lola, it's me," he said. She blinked him into focus, her out-stretched hand softening and falling to her side.

"You came for me?" she whispered, looking through him.

"Of course I came," he breathed, face falling as he swept his eyes over her body, her clothes, her hair… "I'm here to take you home." He stepped closer, still and cautious as if approaching a wounded animal.

"We came to save you."

Slowly, Sirena stepped out of the shadows behind her brother, shiny tears welling in her horror-struck eyes. Lola's knees shivered, knocking her off balance. Trembling hands reached for King, who closed the gap between them in two quick strides, his strong arms catching her before she collapsed to the filthy ground. Hot tears smeared down her face, and Kingsley couldn't help but think that, even in this broken and fragile state, she was still the most beautiful thing he had ever seen.

"I'm sorry," he whispered, voice cracking as he caressed her chopped hair. "Her locs…who fucking did this?" Sirena asked no one in particular.

Surveying Lola's disheveled appearance, King's heart sank. "I'm sorry I couldn't get to you sooner, Tesoro," he murmured, his eyes taking in her tangled, cropped locs, evidence of the ordeal she had endured.

Voice trembling, King whispered into Lola's ear, "I'm sorry I didn't come save you in time."

Touching his cheek with her weak, small hand, the Princess of Mōsa whispered, "I never needed saving, I just needed you."

Lola didn't hear what he said next before she fell to darkness.

CHAPTER 22

Into the clutches of darkness

Lola awoke in a cold sweat under a heap of furry, warm blankets. Unable to recall how she got into the bed, she stretched, removing the heavy blankets. Someone had left a glass and a porcelain jug of water by her bedside table. A freshly tended-to fire lit the room with a warm glow in the blackness of night. Now that she had slept, her mind was clear. Everything came back to her.

Thad and Sebes had kidnapped her under the order of High Priest Sarlee. Mya's father…Somehow Sarlee was aligned with Nasir. "But how?" Nasir had vowed to take over Mōsa and the whole of Transea. Nasir, my sister's enemy, Lola thought. My enemy. Together, Nasir and Sarlee had imprisoned and slaughtered mages whose power rose from the Darkness. She couldn't escape her imagination and the thoughts of how the others had been treated. Shivering, she wondered if she would ever escape the stench of rotting corpses, blood, and shit. Even here, it lingered in her memory.

Touching her cracked lips, her thoughts dragged her back to the dungeon. How many moonrises had it been since her magick had melted Sebes to a pile of black wax at her feet? Black just like his soul. How would she learn to control magick that could kill someone like that—that could burn whole cities down?

Lola felt her heartbeat quicken and she reached for the water, drinking directly from the jug. Flashes of Kingsley raced into her mind alongside brief memories of how she had ended up in her room. But was it her room? It didn't feel familiar. Lola looked around, blinking, and realized she was in Kingsley's quarters. He must have brought her here after returning home.

Kingsley had done the honorable thing. He came for her. He was a good man, but he was also a liar who treated women like second-class citizens. He wasn't a man who took his lots and kept moving forward. No, King was a man broken. A man stuck in the past. Stuck in the past with a love for Mya. Did Mya know of her father's treachery? And if so, did Kingsley? After all, it was his own cousin who had kidnapped her and allowed Sebes and his guards to beat her, stab her, and cut off her hair.

Standing to her feet far too quickly, the room spun and Lola fell back on top of the blankets. Pace yourself, Lola.

"What is your plan, Lola Porte?" her mother would have asked. Mama…If her mother were here, she could help her figure that out. Warm tears cascaded down Lola's gaunt cheekbones. She hadn't always been one to cry so easily, but since waking after the Darkness, she was different. Under the weight of all she had lost sat a little girl waiting for her mother to come to save her.

The only way to stop Nasir and The Sanctum was to reunite with Sole and raise an army of Transeans and mages alike. She would reclaim the Western Isles for her people, her sister, and for herself. That was her plan, and though it wasn't much, it was a good place to start.

She slowly rose from the bed and took a glance at herself in Kingsley's full-length mirror. She was a woman of deep caramel complexion, but today her face appeared pale, almost as if a thin veil of moonlight had washed over her features. Dark circles beneath her eyes, blood smeared on her hands and face. Gone were her long locs. Tears of rage pierced her emerald eyes as they pulsed with the one thing she knew she could count on: her magick.

She looked like a corpse. The new plan: look less like a corpse and more like the Princess of Mōsa, then destroy her enemies.

Lola opened the armoire and found at least two dozen beautiful dresses all in her new favorite shade of hunter green. Most of them were designed in the style of

Kingsguard Reef—beautiful and regal—but the version of Lola that would have worn such attire was dead now. Searching for something more suitable, Lola's emerald eyes flashed as they fell upon her Misa armor. Rory must have put it there amongst the sea of beautiful gowns. She was done dressing like them. She was a Mōsian and Lola knew exactly how she wanted to be seen when she exited this tomb. Trading her soiled nightdress for her Misa armor, she felt proud that it fit like a glove. She scrubbed her face as best she could with the little water that remained in the jug. Opening the bedside table, she found a small golden comb. Her mother's comb. Untangling her short, coiled locs took time, but she managed to tug the knots out. Taking one final glance at the new version of herself in the mirror, she went to the door.

***

"Don't fucking tell me what I need to do!" Kingsley shouted to Luce. "Or have you forgotten that I am the future king in this realm?"

He and Bishop stood outside Kingsley's rooms, face-to-face with Luce and his guards.

"Future king doesn't mean shit where I come from," Luce retorted.

"Do you want to go there again? Seven fucking days you

have come by these rooms demanding the same thing. For the last fucking time, the princess does not want to see you." Anger rippled the air.

"I will wait here until Lola comes and tells me herself," Kingsley said, folding his arms over his chest and scowling at Luce and the whole lot of them as if they had stolen something precious of his. "You expect me to trust you? A freaking Sundoinan?" King continued, his sardonic laugh echoing off the stone walls.

Luce tried to breathe and calm his anger. Voice low and measured, he said, " Have you ever thought that the reason she is in there and not out here with you is because you failed? You failed at protecting her, at being her friend." The room went cold. "I mean for fuck's sake, your own cousin kidnapped her while your fiance helped him plan it! And now you stand here asking me to grant you entrance to the last living princess of Mōsa. Over my fucking dead body!" Luce shouted as he signaled the Sunguards to configure the moon crest stance in front of Lola's doors.

Kingsley's eyes lit up like twin flames. "Tell me that again and see what happens." A small smile crept up Bishop's face. He knew happened when King made that demand. Standing closer to his cousin, Bishop prepared to pounce.

"Enough!" A woman shouted from behind the Sunguards. Lola pushed her way through the ridiculous men who believed they had the right to speak for her. All men

262

had ever done was use her body, her might. Other men felt it was their place to tell her where she could and couldn't go. But she was her mother's daughter: the warrior queen of Mōsa. Lola was tired of not taking charge of her life and this fucking situation.

Looking up at Kingsley's beautiful, desperate face, all Lola wanted was to strangle him for not being there when she needed him most, for getting inside her heart, for making her think that she was special and that he and his family could be trusted. Lola wanted to hit him over and over.

Locking her flashing emerald eyes with his molten gaze, she politely asked everyone to clear the room. When no one moved, she shouted, "NOW!"

Her eyes never fell from his, not even after several minutes had passed. Unable to control herself any longer, Lola rushed forward and shoved him square in the chest with a bit of magic that sent him into a shelf. Antique relics toppled and rolled onto the ground, shattering and sending shards of glass skidding across the stone floor.

Kingsley's eyes lit up. "We are not going to do this right now. Hit me later if you must but for now I ask for just five minutes to speak with you," he pleaded.

"I will honor your request for five—no, four minutes, so talk fast."

Lola was tired of his beautiful presence, how she cared

for him more than she would ever say.

"I hate you."

Lola hated his privilege, his brokenness, and how all she ever wanted was to save him from himself. Most of all she hated his lies.

Kingsley stilled and smiled. He stepped over the shards of porcelain on the ground and said, "Let's go."

"What the fuck," she said. "I said you could talk, not that I would go anywhere with you. Now you have three minutes."

He didn't respond, only clicked his boots down the hall as he began walking away, then turned back and offered his hand out to her. She refused it but joined him regardless.

When they arrived at the maze, Kingsley stopped mid stride at the very spot where he had last kissed her. He turned to face Lola's beautiful gaze. She was thinner now, but the color had returned to her face. The glow of her piercing eyes outshined the dark circles that remained. Holy Mother, she was beautiful. Even now with her hair chopped off, no one could deny that Lola was a sight that could take any man's breath away.

"I am not staying here any longer. It's cold."

"Would you prefer to go to the stables? We could ride?"

Remembering their last rise into the Ventane Woods, Lola took a shaky breath.

"I would prefer to leave this place and make my way to my sister."

"Holy fuck, Lola," Kingsley burst out. "Why can't you just believe that I had nothing to do with Thad and Mya's plans? You think if I knew I wouldn't have fucking stopped them?"

King stepped forward, stopping when his boots met hers. Her rage glowed in her eyes, but it was the rage in her heart that she couldn't quell. Kingsely leaned close as the heat of his minty breath caressed her face.

King's eyes darkened with sorrow as he spoke, his voice heavy with regret. "My cousin was captured the night we found you," he said, his words tinged with a hint of bitterness. "And Mya…" His voice trailed off, the weight of her betrayal evident in his pained expression. "Mya, she did collaborate with the enemy."

When Lola said nothing, King continued, "He's in the dungeons. I thought you and I could interrogate him and find out why he did this?"

Lola swallowed and said nothing, clearly riddled with anxiety at the thought of facing Thad again.

"Every fucking bone in my body tells me to leave Thad to rot," King continued. "But I wonder if he knows more, more that you could learn for the sake of your sister before… before you leave."

"Why would you do this? He is your family and you owe me nothing, Prince."

"Why do you think I came to your fucking door night after night for 7 moonrisies? Why do you think I stayed at the Sanctum until every mage had been set free? Why do you think I am standing here in the fucking cold with you now? I'm here because you would never forgive me if I couldn't make this right."

Wrapping her arms around herself, desperate to ward off the truth that lingered in his eyes, which were all too close to hers.

"I will ask one last time. Why would you do this for me?" Lola demanded.

Drawing up and tugging on the collar of his black tunic, King continued, "Lo, I am doing this because from the moment I saw you in those woods, the moment I saw those eyes, I knew two things. The first," he whispered, "I was found that day; the second, I could never be where you are not. I have never saved you Lola. You saved me. But I will do whatever it takes to be close to you. I will leave my kingdom, abandon the throne—my family and all of it—to be with the one person who saved me. You. You are mine."

"I am no one's treasure," Lola countered. "I am my own woman. I make my own decisions, I will rule my own king-dom and I am in no need of a king. I also know that I cannot trust you. So, no I am not yours."

"You are right. You are fiercely independent and will make a great queen warrior just like your mother, and I have broken your trust in more ways than one. None of that makes you any less mine," he whispered.

Her wobbly legs gave out as her head spun and she began to stumble to the floor. Kingsley caught her in his strong arms, smiling that crooked smile. "Help me stand."

Straightening her tunic, Lola steadied herself.

"Let's go visit your cousin," she said, "I have a ship to catch in the morn."

He stared at her as she walked away. She could feel his eyes as they penetrated her back. "Are you coming, Prince? "

As if waking from a dream, King whispered, "Yes, my princess."

CHAPTER 23

Whispers of betrayal

Six days had passed since he had betrayed those he loved.

Sitting in the damp, dark dungeon of his uncle's castle, Thad stared into the darkness, not understanding how he'd gotten there. The warm crimson liquid dripping down his right leg was Kingsley's doing, but he couldn't remember why or how it had happened. He struggled to recall the events that brought him to the dungeon, but a dense fog shrouded his thoughts. All he could grasp was the memory of his room, and then an abrupt plunge into this bleak, frigid abyss. His feeble attempt to rise was thwarted by weakened legs. He slumped back down, shutting his eyes tight as he attempted to piece together the puzzle of his confinement.

What the fuck is going on? He clawed at his tousled brown curls and shoved them out of his face.

Flashes of memories consumed him in this darkness, but they were jumbled. He took a breath and started from the beginning. He saw his childhood home, his parents' faces, his brother laughing, and his little sister playing.

Bishop and Melia—where were they? Thad remembered his first kiss and his first mission. He saw the good times, but it was the bad times that fucking wrecked him.

In the dimly lit dungeon, where the cold stone walls kept out all traces of hope, a solitary moment unfolded. Lola's emerald eyes flashed through the bleak space in his mind. They shimmered like precious gemstones in the surrounding darkness. He wasn't sure why, but her eyes brought him inescapable sadness.

Hunched and disheveled, he occupied a small corner of the dungeon. His eyes, once vibrant and full of life, now mirrored the despair around him. As he mumbled to himself, his voice trembling with self-doubt and remorse, he created a haunting melody that resonated through the damp air.

"Now our enemies rest," he repeated over and over again as the madness that intruded in his mind refused to let him go.

The garden of his memories was vividly painted by Lola's angry, terrified eyes.

"I will see you all dead." Her words were laced with magick and rage at the person she trusted most.

Her last words to him.

Once again, flashes of her green orbs flickered with a spectral glow, igniting the shadows that cloaked Thad's thoughts.

"I couldn't have betrayed her...not Lola. I brought them

right to her. Right to her!"

His voice wavered as he continued whispering to himself, unable to escape the torment of his actions.

"Will she ever forgive me?" Thad's voice echoed softly through the dungeon, his words hanging heavy in the air like an unanswered plea, the image of Lola's eyes still piercing the darkness.

The room was shrouded in an unsettling gloom, swirling with maddening chaos, and Thad, disoriented and dizzy, found himself surrendering to its relentless whims. Desperation etched into his every move as he fully collapsed onto the frigid concrete floor, his body unable to defy the overpowering force that seized his senses. The room's cruel, relentless spin intensified, leaving him at the mercy of its disorienting dance.

The rats, ruthless in their scavenging, clawed and scuttled ominously, their presence a chilling reminder of his dire predicament.

Thad's thoughts took a dark turn. He knew he would surely die in this wretched place, the weight of his actions closing in on him like a vice. It was a reckoning he believed he deserved—a punishment befitting the depths of his perceived sins. The cold, unforgiving stone beneath him mirrored the cold, unforgiving truth he accepted.

The room, bathed in an eerie, sickly light, continued to spin, Thad's heart racing. He struggled to maintain his balance but found himself surrendering to the merciless forces at play.

He started to pray to the Holy Mother for mercy of death when heard a faint sound in the chamber.

An unmistakable creak warned him that someone was approaching. Perhaps the Sungards again—the ones he had once commanded. But no. A shift in the air told him that the visitor was his cousin.

Kingsley had finally come to do him in.

Summoning all his remaining strength, Thad rose to his feet with excruciating effort. He knew that this conversation, fraught with tension and uncertainty, could not be had crumpled on the ground. The room continued its dizzying waltz as he clung to the bars of his cell with a white-knuckled grip. It was a silent testament to his resilience, a symbol of his unwavering will to face whatever awaited him, no matter how unsteady the ground beneath him had become.

Seeing Kingsley round the dark corner of the passage before him, he pleaded, "Brother, I promise you, whatever you think I've done, it was not me. I only wish to protect you and our family." His voice was desperate and his eyes reflected profound remorse.

"Thad!" Kingsley roared to the cousin he'd once thought of as a brother, his voice thick with anger and heartache. "You're exactly what I need protection from."

"Brother, please, let me explain," Thad implored.

"Thad, I'm giving you a single warning," Kingsley ground out. "Don't call me your brother."

Tears welled up in Thad's eyes as he persisted, "You are my brother! We've endured the Sanctum, the Darkness, and countless battles together. You are my brother!" His voice quivers with earnestness in a desperate plea to reclaim the bond that was slipping right through his fingers.

"I AM NOT YOUR FUCKING BROTHER!" King's voice boomed through the chamber. His chestnut hair fell out of place, and he straightened his tunic in one quick motion.

"You have to believe me, King! I don't know what happened or how I got here. You have to help me!" Thad begged, eyes wide with vulnerability and fear.

Rage glistened in King's eyes, a tempest of emotions swirling within.

Lola, hidden behind King, finally stepped forward. She looked at the man in the cell with disbelief and sorrow. This wasn't the charming, confident Thad she'd once called her friend. The man before her was fragile, emaciated, and consumed by fear. The weight of the situation hung heavy in the air.

Something was terribly wrong here.

"Lola, finally, you've come to see me. Please, help me." Thad's voice trembled.

"Tell him I had nothing to do with kidnapping you. Please, he loves you, he will believe you."

Thad's words about Kingsley's love for Lola struck her like a hammer to the heart. She refused to be overwhelmed by another emotional hurdle Kingsley had thrown her way. She had to uncover the truth, and she had to do it immediately.

In a hushed whisper, Lola turned to face King and murmured, "Something is terribly wrong; he's not himself. Tell me where you found him...how you found him. This isn't the same Thad I met when I first arrived at Kingsguard Reef. It's not the same Thad who kidnapped me. This is a broken man, desperate and afraid. What have they done?"

Rage smoldered in King's molten eyes and his anger simmered. He didn't give a shit about Thad's plight.

Facing his cousin, Kingsley bitterly declared, "The Darkness took my life from me. It took my brother, and now it's taking you. You will tell us what you know, or I will cut you where you stand."

"Kingsley, I am your FAMILY! Or was that all a lie too?" Thad choked on his plea for understanding.

Stepping between Kingsley and Thad, Lola's green gaze remained fixed on Thad. "Thad, what is the last thing you remember before waking up in this cell?"

"I...I remember Kingsley and Bishop finding me near Velo Falls."

Lola sensed something amiss in Thad's words and pressed on. "You see King," she said. "Something isn't right with him."

273

"He's fucking lying!" King's fury finally bubbled over.

"He's not!" Lola insisted, her magick flashing with otherworldly intensity.

"Tell me what you remember before then," she said to Thad.

Eyes darting from one end of the cell to Lola's face, Thad stammered, "I remember…I remember meeting you the day Kingsley found you in the woods."

"After that?" Lola hovered closer to the cell, struggling to keep her voice even. She knew what it was like—to not remember and be trapped.

"I…I remember going with High Priest Sarlee towards… towards the Dark Wilds," Thad said. "Before we arrived, something—no, someone grabbed hold of us."

With an abrupt crash, Thad collapsed to the floor, clutching his hair in desperation. "My fucking head is going to explode, ahh. Help me cousin!"

King's knuckles tightened around the rusty cage that held his cousin. Beneath the resentment, there was a profound love between them. What if Lola was right? What if Thad had been controlled in some insidious way?

Lola's fierce green eyes locked onto King's as she whispered, "Something is incredibly wrong here."

Thad's wails pierced through the dungeon. "Guard, unlock the cell!" Kingsley ordered.

Pushing past King, Lola moved to rush toward Thad

before King seized her elbow to stop her.

"Let go of me!" Lola demanded.

"Absolutely fucking not," King responded firmly.

"You of all people should know that I can take care of myself," Lola retorted.

He didn't want to admit that her words stung, but King acknowledged the truth in them. He knew he made numerous foolish mistakes, ones he would never be able to forgive himself for, and now was not the time for self-recrimination.

He released her arm, saying, "I'll go first. The last thing I need is Luce, the mighty, wanting revenge for letting the enemy get his hands on you again."

Waving her hand toward the cell, Lola conceded. "Fine, go on then."

***

Was that remorse flickering in the prince's eyes? Lola knows her words were brutal, but she couldn't bring herself to care anymore. Her journey wasn't about him; it was about her sister. She'd leave in the morning, and he'd move on with his life.

Yet, as she watched Kingsley kneel before his cousin, it broke her heart. After a few moments, Thad began to calm, and Lola took in the scene: the lost princess, the broken prince, and the court jester who longed to be king.

They were a far cry from the regal image of the royals they once represented.

"Thad, what happened to you?" King asked.

Tears welled up in Thad's honey eyes as he replied in a detached tone, "I don't know. Parts of my memories... they're gone."

Kingsley furrowed his brow in bewilderment. "How can this be?"

Lola, her eyes briefly darting skyward, pressed on with uncertainty. "Could it be possible that Nasir's black magick wields the power to manipulate others? Didn't you once confide in me that this is precisely how Rivian, the second prince of Sundom, managed to betray his own people? Consider the notion that Sarlee might not have taken them on a pilgrimage after all, but rather led them straight into Nasir's grasp. What if..."

A firm hand suddenly clamped onto Lola's arm, pulling her nearer to Thad's once-beautiful face. Those hazel eyes lacked something now. They were void of the love and fear they had brimmed with just moments before. In their stead, a smoldering rage blazed.

"I will not hesitate to kill you where you stand, Thad. Do not make me do this," she cried out.

"Hi, Sissy."

A shiver ran down Lola's spine. The familiar refrain was only ever spoken by one man—Nasir.

Nasir had been a brother to Lola in the same way Thad was to Kingsley. Even now, standing in this cell, she wasn't entirely sure if she could believe the rumors about Nasir being a murderer.

"Nasir?" Lola breathed in shock.

"Yes, Sissy," came his reply. Nasir's words from Thad's mouth. The air around them was stiff, as if Nasir had paused time itself. Lola knew Kingsley was behind her, but he felt far away, disconnected from her and Nasir.

"How is this possible? How are you here, inside Thad?"

"We don't have much time," Nasir said urgently. "So I'll be quick. Tell your sister that I wait for all of you in Mōsa. There, we will see if the prophecy rings true."

Lola attempted to unleash her power, but Nasir tightened his grip, pressing dark magick around her arms and into her chest until she found it difficult to breathe. Lola unsheathed the blade Kingsley had gifted her. If only she could free her arms long enough to stab Nasir—or rather, Thad. But with everything that had happened between them, could she muster the courage to kill her friend?

The black mist of Nasir's magick coiled and solidified, forming an impenetrable barrier around the inside of the cell. Kingsley and the guards couldn't get in, and Lola couldn't get out. Her heart sank as she realized there was no escape from this dire confinement. She had to either end Thad's life, or lend her ear to Nasir's cryptic words.

"What prophecy?" Lola asked.

"When the darkness returns, the three will be reborn, bringing forth an era of magick and sorrow," Nasir explained. "Tell Queen Sole I await her in her father's throne room. Tell her to come for me if she dares."

Thad crashed to the ground as fragile as glass as the mist receded to reveal Lola standing above him, holding the bioluminescent Champion's Choice as its glow illuminated the dark cell. Nasir's presence dissolved, and King finally broke into the cell.

He wrapped his arms around Lola, who allowed it.

"What did he say?" King asked.

Looking up at King, Lola whispered, "I must speak to Luce at once. He will know what to do."

Jealousy ignited in Kingsley's eyes.

"It's not what you think," Lola said. "Not that I have to explain that to you." She pushed away from Kingsley's hug. "Thad was possessed by Nasir. When he takes someone over, he can give them his power. That's how Thad was able to isolate us with the mist."

Lola moved swiftly, setting off towards the exit and towards her entourage of warriors.

"Will you wait a moment?" King demanded, frustrated.

Turning to face him, Lola yelled, "What do you want? Don't you understand, Nasir is in Mōsa, awaiting my sister? He spoke of the prophecy. He plans to kill Sole!"

Sliding his hands in his pockets, King said, "Surely he wouldn't do that. He must have loved her at some point. After all, he was her husband."

"If the Darkness has taught me anything," Lola huffed. "It's that it is not a respecter of persons, and it cares not about love. It takes and destroys. Nasir will not take my sister as he has taken his own. I must leave at once." The gravity of her words pressed on Kingsley's broken heart as she sped away, leaving him alone with Thad in the dark recesses of the dungeon.

CHAPTER 24

*Promises made
in the dark*

After making plans with Luce and Rory, Lola met with King Heath and Queen Alina. The decision was final. Now, it was time to tell Kingsley of her decision.

Lola stood before the wooden door, nervous but determined, her delicate hand raised and her fingers curled into a gentle fist. She hesitated and then tapped lightly, the sound echoing through the quiet corridor.

Her other hand instinctively smoothed the fabric of her tunic. Her eyes remained fixed on the door as she listened intently for Kingsley on the other side.

Sirena had told Lola that Kingsley was furious that his father would not let him into the throne room for the discussion of Lola's next move. "He stormed out like a banshee," Sirena had said. "Ran off towards his rooms."

Time stretched on as Lola lingered, caught in the moment. The silence amplified the rapid beating of her heart in her chest. She didn't know how she would tell him that...she was leaving without him.

Suddenly, the door swung open to reveal Kingsley's tall frame. His eyes were on fire as he drank her in. Lola couldn't tell if he was enraged or lusting for her. Both made her nervous.

"May I come in?"

"You seem to do whatever you want, Princess. Don't let me stop you now," Kingsley said as he went back to sitting behind his desk and focusing on the book he was pretending to read.

"Will you please do me the honor of looking at me?" Lola said with a sigh.

Lurching to his feet in a sudden movement, Kingsley stood inches from her beautiful face.

"Why the hell are you here, Lola?" His words dripped with bitterness, each syllable a sting. She braced herself, knowing this encounter wouldn't be gentle.

With a roll of her eyes, she pressed on. "I came to express my gratitude for—"

"Don't you dare thank me for simply doing what we always do," he interrupted. "Caring for each other." His words slashed through the air like shards of glass. "Don't you dare, Lola," he spat. "I will ask it one more time. Why are you here?"

Looking up at him, she continued, "What do you want

me to say? That this matters?" She motioned between the two of them. "It doesn't because you are not mine and I am not yours." She shrugged.

"We still haven't processed everything that happened before...you were taken."

"What do we still have to process?"

"Everything! Especially the shit with Mya."

Lola paused as a growl escaped her lips. "King, that doesn't matter! You are allowed to do whatever you want with whomever you want. I am leaving."

"Lola!" he blurted. "We have played this game long enough, don't you think?" He reached for her arm and drew her body close to his, spinning her around like he once had on the ballroom floor. With one hand on the small of her back and the other around her neck, he gently pulled her in until they were close—too close. His body yearned for hers. He could smell the

scent of her hair and feel the heat of her skin beneath his fingertips. He longed for the familiar taste of her full lips.

She tilted her head up, and her broken heart felt restored, beating faster when his gaze fell upon her. She knew she was the only person in all of Transea that he desired.

"Are you going to kiss me or what?" she demanded. His eyes darkened.

"I have been dying to kiss you, Tesoro," he whispered, his breath warm against her skin.

"Then do it, King," she murmured, her voice soft and inviting.

His lips crashed against hers with a heat that surged through her body. It was as if he wanted this kiss to wipe away every horrible pain she had experienced in that cell. Time disappeared as he lifted her off the ground. Within the embrace of his kiss, her magick surged to life, pulsing with the same fervor as their entwined souls. In that fleeting moment, nothing else mattered except the electric connection they shared. He bit her lips as if he owned them.

Kingsley held onto her like a lifeline, unwilling to let even a moment pass without her close. He kissed her with a desperate hunger, as though she held the key to his existence. In that embrace, his intensity enveloped her entirely, a heady mix of exhilaration and fear coursing through her veins. She couldn't deny the thrill of it all, knowing that this was just the beginning.

Kingsley bent down and brushed his lips over hers. Lola felt something pulling inside that she just couldn't stop. Her hands gripped the front of his tunic as she held him closer. He pulled away just long enough to look into her eyes before he kissed her deeply. He could see the fire in her emerald gaze, feel her drawing from the power within her. Her pulsing energy intensified with every movement of his hands.

Kingsley ran his fingers down her soft neck, pulling her

towards him and feeling her shiver. She didn't resist. She opened her lips, tasting his own as they fed on each other in this moment of desperation. His hand slipped under her tunic, touching the skin he has desired for so long. Goosebumps prickled from her shoulders down her torso, and then at the delicate curvature of her lower back as he grazed his fingertips over her body. Her heart beat faster as he parted her full lips with his tongue.

"You are mine. Do you understand that?"

Lola nodded.

"If you want me to stop, tell me now," he said half-heartedly.

Resting his hands on either side of her face, insisting she look at him, he repeated his question.

"Lola if you want me to stop, you must tell me now, because I fear that once I take these off of you"—he motioned to her garments—"I will not be able to stop."

"King, I have been waiting for this since the moment I saw you in the woods. I want you...I need you inside me."

Stepping back with a graceful motion, Lola unbuttoned her riding pants, revealing a glimpse of delicate brown skin beneath. The fabric slipped from her waist and past her toned thighs, pooling in what was soon to be a growing pile of discarded garments on the floor.

She reached to untie the side laces of her tunic, her small hands gently tugging the ribbons free. They loosened around her waist and she raised her top up and over her shoulders, gracefully releasing it from her hand. It fell gently to the floor.

Her breasts, freed from their confinement, settled into their natural, full figure, embraced by only the chilled air around her. Her dark nipples responded in kind.

"Holy fuck, Tesoro," King breathed out in a hushed tone, utterly captivated. He found himself unable to resist the urge to continue kissing her relentlessly.

"Has kissing anyone else ever felt this good?" she murmured, barely audible, against his swollen lips. He responded only by deepening the kiss until she abruptly pulled away with a smirk.

"Take them off," she said, pointing to his dark trousers. His fingers moved with practiced ease as he unfastened the clasp of his pants, sliding them down until they joined her clothes on the floor.

His tunic fell away, revealing the deep V-shape at his waist. The lines of his body accentuated the confidence radiating from his crooked smile. "Do you like what you see, Princess?"

Taking a small step back, Lola drank in the sight of his perfectly sculpted physique, her heart racing. She was uncertain how exactly they had arrived at this moment, but there was no turning back now.

***

Lola defied Kingsley's expectations.

Releasing her only to walk her to his bed, he placed her tenderly onto the dark, silk sheets. He'd never experienced such intensity before. She was both gentle and powerful, and he would claim her this very night.

"Are you ready?" he growled, his cock pulsing.

"Are you?" she challenged, defiant but excited.

He kissed her deeply once more. Although it should have, the deep feeling within his chest didn't scare him.

She is my home, he thought.

He sat on the bed beside her as she lay back, putting her full, toned body on display. Kingsley was pretty sure he stopped breathing at some point. As if waking from a dream, he moved slowly, leaning back to join her.

The tiny minx straddled him, suspending her warm, wet pussy narrowly above his cock. He couldn't take it anymore. He flipped her over and she landed with a startled laugh on the mattress.

"If I let you continue, Princess, this will be over before it's begun."

Kissing her again, he started at her lips, slowing making his way to her chocolate-colored nipples and then to her stomach. He slid his warm tongue around her belly button, determined to taste and explore every inch of the Mōsian princess. When he finally reached her pussy, he admired her. "Lola, you are fucking perfect," he groaned.

"I am sure there have been many that you thought were perfect," she said.

Cupping her face, he said, "You, Lola Sirena Porte, are the most magnificent woman I have ever looked upon. When I found you in the Ventane Woods, I knew…there is no other for me. Do you understand?"

Nodding, she pulled him in close and gently kissed his perfect face.

"You also have the most perfect pussy, Tesoro," he said as he lowered his mouth and gave her clit a lick with his warm tongue.

She instantly grabbed his hair as her hips bucked. Kingsley never liked for women to touch his hair, but Lola…Lola was different. He feared that, after tonight, he would let her do or say whatever she wanted. He dipped a little lower, giving a hard lick to her folds. He devoured her pussy and, just as she approached her release, he stopped.

"What the—"

"Now, now, Princess, if I continue to lick this perfect pussy, I will never know how good it feels to slide my cock inside you." Grabbing her legs and dragging her to the edge of the bed, Kingsley slid deep inside her.

"Oh…fuuuuck," were the only words that fell from Lola's lips.

"Language, Princess," he whispered as a dirty smile crept up his perfect face.

The second he thrust his hips, she couldn't help but be lost in him. The idea of where he began and she ended was lost on her. All she knew was that his huge cock was breaking away all of her fears with every thrust, leaving her breathless.

"Relax, Tesoro," he whispered. "Take a deep breath. Tonight I am taking what is mine." He groaned in her ear as if he was in physical pain, releasing a long, warm breath before filling her once more.

His fingers twisted into her short hair, bringing her closer so her nose touched the tip of his, holding her in place. As golden as his eyes were, there was a dark desire in them.

"You have no idea what you have just done, Tesoro," he whispered as he moved inside her. "You are so fucking tight."

Their chests heaved together in lust. Lola wasn't sure what warning King was trying to give her. His cock stopped moving and sat twitching inside of her, feeling heavenly, but she wanted his throbbing heat to move.

"I need you to move, King!"

She didn't know if it was the heat between her legs, the look in his golden eyes, or the sheer disbelief of finally having him inside her, but she whispered in his ear, "Fuck me like I am yours, Kingsley. Make me forget what those monsters did to me."

His fingertips dug into the toned flesh of her thighs and

ass, nostrils flaring for a second when he pulled out. Then in a roar, he slammed back inside her.

"Kingsley," she screamed as he thrust so deeply it hurt—in the best way.

"More!" she panted.

Kingsley pounded into her as if possessed. Dipping his face into the crook of her neck, he dragged her head to the side and pressed his teeth into her skin. Lola didn't realize he had drawn blood until she tasted the copper on his lips. It was dirty, wild, and fucking amazing. She knew it would be good; she didn't know it would be this good.

"I'm cumming, King," she screamed.

"I am too, Tesoro."

They tensed as their bodies collided. Lola's magic surged forth, enveloping the room in undulating waves of vibrant emerald green. Mesmerized, they gazed upon the ethereal spectacle above his bed, a breathtaking display of their intertwined energies.

"Well, that's new!" Kingsley proclaimed.

"What is?" she asked.

"I never made a girl cum as her magick rose to light up my entire bedchamber." Lola laughed. Kingsley held her close to his chest as he tugged the dark covers over their glistening bodies.

In the embrace of the magickal glow, they surrendered to each other, finding solace and fulfillment as sleep claimed them. In that moment of serene tranquility, Kingsley believed that their love bound them together in a union as timeless as the stars themselves.

CHAPTER 25

Love's betrayal

Kingsley's eyes snapped open, a jolt of unease coursing through his veins as he became aware of the void beside him where Lola had been just hours before. Emptiness filled the air, stirring restlessness in his heart. With a racing pulse, he sat up in bed, scanning the room until he saw the solitary piece of parchment resting on his desk, its presence both ominous and foreboding.

He rose from the bed, each step heavy as if he was wading through the Sirena Sea. His hands trembled as he reached for the note, fingers tracing the delicate creases. Time hung suspended as he swiftly devoured the words on the page, each syllable etching a deeper wound on his soul. The contents of the note sliced through him.

In the dim light, Kingsley's features contorted into anguish and disbelief. The words on the page danced before his eyes, taunting him with their finality.

"I have gone in search of my sister. Please do not come

Princess Lola Porte

after me—I must do this alone. I will send word with Luce if I should fail."

A storm raged within him, unleashing a torrent of questions and regrets that assaulted his every thought. He clutched the note tightly, as if hoping to crush the words that shattered his world.

His mind raced with questions, heart heavy with the echoes of their love, now lost.

"Lola, I will not let you do this alone. My kingdom be damned."

Determined to find his missing princess, Kingsley quickly donned his black leather armor and grabbed his satchel and sword. His cloak was nowhere to be found.

He searched the castle grounds, asking everyone he met if they had seen Lola, but no one had any information to offer. As he wandered through the castle halls, he replayed the events of the previous night in his mind, trying to understand what had gone wrong.

Fury consumed him. Had they not promised each other last moonrise that they would face this together?

Did she too not whisper, "I love you?" Had he dreamt it? Kingsley walked down the dimly lit stone hallway, his black leather armor feeling tighter with each step. The weight of his despair pressed down on him. As he turned the corner toward the great hall, he spotted Bishop and Sirena near a stained-glass window, the soft, colored light illuminating their silhouettes.

Bishop leaned nonchalantly against the wall, his dark brown hair falling over his forehead. He grinned at Kingsley as he approached with heavy steps.

"Lola's gone," he said in a low voice, his eyes searching theirs, begging one of them to tell him where she was.

Bishop's smile faltered and he straightened.

"Gone? What do you mean, gone? Did you two have a fight?" he asked, a hint of mischief in his voice.

Kingsley shook his head, his jaw clenched. "No, she just left. Without telling me anything."

Sirena covered her mouth.

"Did she not tell you?"

Before Kingsley could utter a word, the great hall doors swung open with a thunderous force and Melia burst into the corridor, gravity etched upon her face. Her every step resounded with determination as she made her way over to them. Her eyes locked with Kingsley and, in that instant, the depth of Kingsley's pain lay bare before her. He stood there, vulnerable and exposed in front of Melia, who understood the magnitude of the storm raging within him.

Melia strode forward with urgency, eyes alight with fierce determination. With a deep breath, Kingsley braced himself for her news. He steeled himself as Melia met his eyes.

"Lola came to me early this sunrise," she announced.

Her words landed like a hammer, striking the very core of Kingsley's being. His heart sunk even further.

Melia's gaze remained steadfast, her honey eyes narrowing ever so slightly, undeterred by his state of shock. "If I thought telling you would have made a difference, I would have," she retorted, undeterred by his shock. "But she's made up her mind. If she wanted to stay, she would still be here."

"When did she go? Is she alone?" he asked frantically.

Melia's words, like a dagger to the heart, struck with unyielding precision. "She left with Luce, Kia, and Rory, with her Sunguards at her back" she revealed, her voice solemn.

Bishop, who has been silent up until then, cleared his throat.

"We'll fuck that! Do you love her?"

"What? I...I...yes, I love her!" Kingsley said.

"Then go get your Princess!" Bishop declared.

"I will go with you!" Sirena jumped in eagerly.

"As will I," Bishop added.

Sighing, Melia crossed her arms over her ample chest.

"I thought you would say that. So I went to King Heath earlier and told him we would go to Grimerg Rise to assist the High Queen of the Western Isle in securing Mōsa. It took much convincing, but the queen came to my aide and convinced the king to release you."

Smirking, she continued. "We must make haste, the king and queen await us at the stables."

Eyes brimming with tears that threaten to spill over, Kingsley clutched Melia tightly around the waist, lifting her off the ground in a desperate, impassioned embrace. The world whirled around them as he spun her, a moment of shared gratitude and solace in the midst of turmoil. Gently, he set her back down, steadying her with trembling hands. In a gesture of heartfelt appreciation, he pressed a tender kiss upon Melia's cheek.

"Thank you, cousin. I owe you one," Kingsley whispered.

"Don't thank me yet," she advised. Their journey was far from over.

Confusion and concern knit Kingsley's brow as he sought clarification. "What do you mean?" he implored, a flicker of worry dancing in his eyes.

"My brother must come with us. Mya too."

"I already said I was going," Bishop interjected. Melia shook her head.

"I didn't mean you," she said, swallowing hard. Kingsley gritted his teeth. No. No way was Thad accompanying them—not after everything he'd done to Lola.

"Thad must atone for his betrayal," Melia reasoned. "And the king believes this is a way for Thad and Mya to repay the throne."

A pregnant silence hung heavy in the air

"Brother, fuck that!" Sirena's vehement proclamation shattered the silence. Everyone was surprised at her use of profanity. "Alright. If they must, they can come," Sirena declared. "But I promise"—her voice lowered and her eyes narrowed—"if Thad or Mya even blink when they're not supposed to, I will run them through."

She would do whatever it took to protect her brother.

Kingsley locked eyes with his sister. In a low, solemn whisper, he conceded, "Fine. But just keep him away from me. I will go see about Mya."

Sirena placed a comforting hand on his arm, giving him a sympathetic look. "We'll help you find Lola, brother," she said softly.

Kingsley nodded, grateful for their support. He knew he couldn't let Lola go without at least trying to find her first. With a heavy heart, he turned to head down the hall in search of Mya.

***

Mya's sleek black bob framed her face in the dimly lit dungeon, her bright green eyes shining in the glow of the torch on the wall. Despite the bleak surroundings, she remained a striking beauty, though her features were marred with weariness and sorrow. As Kingsley approached, memories of their past as inseparable friends in the Sanctum flooded his mind.

Standing before Mya, Kingsley felt a number of things—disappointment at her betrayal, mainly, but a glimmer of hope lingered in his eyes. "Mya," he began, suppressing the anger in his voice. "I never thought it would come to this. You were once my friend, my lover, and I owe you for helping me survive those difficult years in the Sanctum."

Mya's eyes softened for a brief moment before raising her guard again. "Things have changed, Kingsley," she retorted, her voice laced with bitterness. "You chose Lola over everything, even our history."

"This isn't solely about Lola, and you know it," Kingsley asserted firmly.

"Everything is about her!" Mya insisted, her jaw tense.

"You and I both know that our issues began long before Lola," Kingsley countered. "Your father's ambitions for you were never something I wanted to be part of. The pressure of being the High Priest's daughter took its toll on you, especially at the Sanctum. I remember how violent the others were to you."

"And you saved me from it all. You always found a way to save me," Mya acknowledged.

"I'm afraid I can't save you this time. This time you will have to do it on your own," Kingsley admitted with a heavy heart. But there is a chance for redemption. Help me get to Grimerg Rise so that together we can help the queen of the Western Isles."

Mya's emotions conflict as she looks at him, and the weight of their shared history weighs upon her. "Why would you do that for me?" she asks, genuinely puzzled.

"Because I remember a time when we dreamt of making Kingsguard Reef a better place. That is one dream they can't take away from us," Kingsley replied with sincerity.

After a moment of silence, Mya finally conceded, "All right, I'll do it." Her eyes remained locked on him, torn, but willing to take the chance at redemption.

Kingsley turned to the guard behind him and instructed, "Please make sure Lady Sarlee has warm clothes, a satchel, and sustenance for our journey. It will be a long one."

***

Gathering their supplies, Kingsley and his small entourage converged at the stables, their steps echoing with purpose. In the midst of their preparations, they found Kingsley's parents patiently awaiting their arrival. The weight of their presence commanded attention, so they bowed before their king and queen.

"Rise, and approach," King Heath commanded.

Kingsley approached his father with trepidation. The king, with his graying brown beard and weathered countenance, locked eyes with his son, conveying a silent understanding. The queen, radiating grace and strength, stood beside him, eyes filled with love and concern.

The King's voice, deep and commanding, resonated through the stables as he addressed his son. "Kingsley, my son, know that the path you tread is fraught with uncertainty. But within you beats the heart of a king, and it is in times like these that you will be tested."

Queen Alina, her voice gentle yet resolute, joined her husband's words of wisdom. "Remember, my boy, that love is a guiding force that can fuel both light and darkness. Stay true to your heart and let your love for Lola be the beacon that guides you through the shadows."

Kingsley nodded, absorbing their guidance, his eyes filled with gratitude and determination. "I will, Mother. I will find Lola and bring her back, no matter the obstacles that lie ahead."

The king placed a firm hand on his son's shoulder, proud but concerned. "Do not underestimate the challenges that await, my son. The path to true love is rarely smooth, but it is a journey worth undertaking. We have faith in your strength and resilience. When you return, it is you who shall sit on this throne. My prayer to the Holy Mother is that Princess Lola is with you."

The Queen stepped forward, her voice laced with maternal warmth. "Remember, Kingsley, that you are not alone.

Take care of your sister and bring her home safe. Lean on your family, trust in their abilities, and draw strength from the bonds that unite you."

His sense of purpose renewed, Kingsley took a deep breath. "Thank you, Mother, Father. I will carry your words with me wherever I go."

The king and queen exchanged a knowing glance, a silent understanding passing between them. "Go now," the king said, his voice filled with love. "Now our enemies find rest."

With a final embrace, Kingsley, accompanied by Mya, Melia, Bishop, Sirena, and Thad, set forth on their journey. The tension between Kingsley and Thad hung thick in the air; their bond had been deeply scarred by the betrayal. Thad remained eerily silent, but his presence was still a constant reminder of the wounds that had been inflicted upon their family.

Before their departure from the stable, Kingsley turned to face his traitorous cousin, his voice resolute and firm.

"Remember this, Thad," Kingsley warned, eyes unwavering as he locked onto Thad's. "If you so much as breathe wrong in Lola's direction, I will be the one to personally deliver you to the Holy Mother herself."

The stable fell silent. Despite their shared blood, loyalty and justice could not be compromised. Trust must be earned, and Thad's actions had consequences.

The group embarked on their journey, each step forward bringing them closer to helping Lola. The fate of their loved ones hung in the balance.

As the group made their way through the Ventane Woods, the snowfall grew heavier and the trees became taller and darker. The forest swallowed them whole as they trekked through the thick blanket of snow, boots crunching in the snow and whispers hushed. Kingsley led the way, his eyes scanning the woods.

The wind picked up as they reached the base of Grimerg Rise, the mountain looming over them like a dark sentinel. The climb was treacherous and they had to tread carefully as the snow and ice threatened to send them sliding down the mountain. Kingsley and Thad argued as they climbed, their voices raised in anger as they relitigated the past.

As they climbed higher, the snowfall intensified and the wind picked up even more. The group huddled together, their bodies pressed tightly against each other for warmth as they pushed forward.

The snowflakes were huge, blocking their view as they climbed the mountain.

Suddenly, Thad slipped on a patch of ice. Kingsley's heart leaped into his throat as his cousin started to slide down the mountain. For one terrible moment, Kingsley hesitated. He thought of letting Thad go, of letting him fall to his death. But then he heard Melia's scream, pleading with him to save her brother.

Kingsley lunged forward, arm outstretched. His hand closed around Thad's wrist just as he was about to disappear over the edge. Thad's weight pulled him forward and Kingsley lost his grip altogether, the two of them tumbling together in a tangle of limbs until they landed hard on a ledge. Kingsley gasped for breath, looking to find Thad beside him, eyes filled with fear. The others scrambled down, their faces etched with concern. Kingsley looked at Thad with anger and hurt flashing in his eyes.

"Thad," Kingsley said, his voice wavering with genuine worry, "Are you okay?" Despite his fury, which was mostly directed at Nasir, Kingsley didn't wish for his cousin to die.

As he helped Thad to his feet, memories flooded Kingsley's mind of him, Avenn, and Thad climbing the towers together when they were young and thick as thieves. Avenn was dead, and Thad's betrayal was gutting, but Kingsley couldn't help but be reminded of all they had lost since the Darkness had descended upon them.

"Thanks for saving my life," Thad said.

"I think we need to set up camp soon," Melia called from above them, her voice firm. "We're wasting time staring at each other. Let's keep moving. It is fucking cold."

Kingsley nodded, eyes still fixed on Thad. "We need to talk later," he said.

Thad nodded back, still refusing to look his cousin in

the eye.

"I'd like that."

ACT III

CHAPTER 26

Ascending the frozen summit

Wearing King's long black cloak, Lola trudged her way up the snow-covered path. She wasn't on her own, but even surrounded by her golden entourage, she still felt incredibly alone.

In a short time, Lola had come back from the dead, fallen for the broken prince, and been kidnapped all over again, all while trying to understand the magick that was coursing through her veins.

If not for Sole, Lola would have little to live for now. Her heart grew heavy as she slowly made her way up the steep terrain to the top of Grimerg Rise.

From her perspective, the journey to the summit had begun the night the Darkness came to Mōsa. In the note Rory had given her alongside Queen Lygia's dress, there was one piece of information Sole had asked her not to share with anyone.

"Did you want more stew?" A frigid Rory asked as she made her way to the Princess. Mōsians were not accustomed to bitter winter nights. Mōsa stayed warm year-round for the most part. It was on cold nights like these, the wind biting at the back of her neck, when Lola missed her hair most of all.

The luxuriously soft, gray stoles cocooned Lola, shielding her from the biting cold that sent shivers down her spine.

"No thanks. I just want to sleep."

Glancing up at the ink-blue sky, Rory said, "He should know by now that you left him behind."

Face tight, Lola stared into the fire, "I don't want to talk about him."

Bumping her knee, Rory affectionately exclaimed, "Lola Sirena Porte! We've been inseparable since our childhood days, and I can sense it in my bones when you have a crush on someone."

"Is that what you call what King and I have…a crush? If that's the case he has a funny way of showing it. He kissed his ex-fiance in front of me the third night we met. Oh and let's not forget that his cousin kidnapped me. I'd hate to see how he treats someone when he loves them."

"I guess if he loved you, he might do anything to save you, even arrest his cousin, go searching for you against the king's orders, and carry your fragile body on his horse, demanding you be healed at any cost. He came to your door for seven moonrises before his guards were commanded by the king that he rest."

In the face of such revelations, Lola's world shattered, exposing the vulnerability she thought she had carefully concealed. Tears welled up in her green eyes as she softly uttered, "Love? No, he doesn't…"

Feeling the weight of Lola's pain, Rory swiftly gathered a stack of soft pelts and reclined on the weathered stump they shared. "I wouldn't wish for anyone to love me in such a manner," she confessed.

Lola's heart raced with a newfound urgency. She couldn't believe what she was hearing.

In a voice tinged with shock, she demanded, "What? What did he do? Why didn't he tell me?"

Rory leaned closer, drawing Lola into her comforting presence. In a hushed tone, she said,

"You made it clear that discussing him is off limits, that it is none of our business. So we respect your boundaries, even if it means withholding painful truths. Luce endured numerous confrontations from Kingsley, though he may never admit it."

Sensing Lola's apprehension and fear, Rory's voice carried a rare severity as she said, "Lola, my dear friend, we will face this battle together. We will find a way forward, but first, we must confront the truth."

Heartbroken, Lola laid back under the pelts and let the

wintry gusts lull her into a fitful slumber, hoping that sleep would bring a temporary relief from the ache in her chest.

***

The climb was exhausting, evident from the faces of the Sunguards and friends at Lola's side. The atmosphere was thick with ash and snow, but they pressed on, unwavering resolve leading them to their long-awaited destination.

Standing before the imposing stone arch at the entrance of Grimerg Rise, Lola was confronted with a sight she had never fathomed witnessing. The sheer presence of it commanded her attention, stirring a kaleidoscope of emotions within her.

The mountains of Grimerg Rise loomed above Transea like a curse, their jagged peaks and deep valleys shrouded in a perpetual white mist that whispered secrets to those brave enough to venture within. Few dared to traverse the treacherous pass; legend told that spirits of the dead haunted the rocky crags and dark magick lurked in the shadows, waiting to claim souls.

Lola was not afraid, but she was on high alert.

She stood tall, her spirit fortified by the triumph over the Darkness. Propelled by the fixed purpose to aid Sole in reclaiming her usurped throne, Lola felt a fire burn within her that blazed with a fierce determination to right the wrongs inflicted upon her people by Nasir's thieving grasp. With each step forward, Lola moved closer to seizing back their stolen legacy and restoring honor to her bloodline.

The harsh environment left Lola and her companions breathless. Enveloped in a realm of towering heights, swirling soot, and eternal fires, the very air itself became a challenge to inhale. Covering her face with Kingsley's black cloak, Lola entered the city, her ability to draw a breath becoming a testament to her endurance and resilience. Every inhalation was an act of defiance.

Grabbing her arm, Luce said, "Let them go before you."

Lola's eyes widened in astonishment as she witnessed people bustling about in Grimerg Rise. Her whole life, she had been told that this land was a desolate, uninhabited wasteland. The sight of life flourishing there challenged everything she had been taught.

He ushered the golden guards to enter the kingdom. "Why did you not tell me?" Lola asked.

"Tell you what?" Luce said, eyes inquisitive.

"She wants to know why we didn't tell her that people inhabit Grimerg Rise," Kia chimed in, her pink bangs falling out of her covering. Soot and rose-colored strands flowed across her pale, tattooed face.

With a somber expression, Luce stood before Lola, delicately adjusting her cape to conceal more of her features.

"Your sister made it clear that we must keep the existence

of the people of Grimerg Rise a secret, even from you. It was a difficult decision, but we had to ensure their safety and their willingness to provide refuge to Sole, your family, and others in need. Revealing their existence to the outside world would have jeopardized their sanctuary and the crucial support they offer in these troubled times."

Lola nodded, understanding the decision. If she were in Sole's position, she'd have done the same. She caught Luce's eyes and said, "We must make haste. The queen is waiting."

Inserting themselves amongst the Sunguards, Lola, Luce, Kia and Rory entered Grimerg Rise and were suddenly surrounded by its people. Their voices dwindled to hushed murmurs, their curiosity giving rise to an air of quiet anticipation. Every step Lola took was met with focused attention, as if the entire kingdom held its breath, waiting to discern the nature of this new presence in their midst.

Eyes scanning the new environment, Lola asked Luce, "Who are they?"

Without breaking his stride, Luce replied, "The people of Grimerg Rise are a hardy and stoic race, forged by the harsh and unforgiving environment of their igneous mountain home. Like the people of Mōsa, they are a proud people, fiercely independent and fiercely loyal to their own."

The walk up the hill to what seemed like the makeshift war room revealed that the people lived in small, tight-knit communities scattered throughout the mountain, each one built around a central hearth fire where they gathered to share stories and offer thanks to the spirits of their ancestors.

"You will love this kingdom, Princess," Rory told her. "These people are warriors just like the Misa. They are skilled hunters, and are known for their proficiency in the use of crossbows and spears."

Lola's gaze met a sea of unyielding, hard eyes that stared back at her, their intensity cutting through the air like shards of ice. As she walked alongside Luce, unease settled in her stomach.

Her magick rose.

The collective scrutiny pressed upon her, stirring a disconcerting realization. Apprehensively, Lola confided in Luce, "I fear they are not filled with excitement at our presence here." Luce nodded. "I remember feeling the same when we first arrived," he admitted.

"The people here, known as Caciques Children, are deeply rooted in their land and fiercely protective of their resources. They hold a profound belief in the importance of knowing one's heart before exchanging even a single word." Lola was impressed by Luce's extended knowledge of the cultural intricacies that governed this kingdom. "In this place, trust and honor are not freely given; they must be earned." At his words, a newfound resolve blossomed within Lola. She was ready to bridge the divide and earn the trust of the Caciques Children, one heart at a time. She only worried that there might not be enough time.

"I wish some of the royals in Sundom were more like the Caciques Children," Kia said to the group.

"Much like our people of Mōsa," Rory intervened, "the Caciques Children hold a deep reverence for the spirits of the land and their ancestors." She gestured to a group of people circling a bonfire, each of them holding something to toss in. "Offerings of food, weapons, and other goods are frequently made to appease the spirits, a ritual that embodies their deep-rooted connection to the spiritual realm. They hold an unwavering belief in the power of magick, harnessing it to ward off the Darkness." Her words painted a vivid picture of a realm where magick was intertwined into the fabric of everyday life. A flock of birds circling a tent caught Lola's eye as they gracefully glided through the air, the faint flicker of glowing embers emanating from within their bellies, casting an otherworldly glow against the backdrop of their ebony plumage. Their eyes, like twin orbs of smoldering coals, pierced through the shadows with an intense and mesmerizing brilliance. "Those birds are magnificent. What are they?" she asked.

"They are called ember crows. Much like our fireflies, these birds are said to carry the souls of their fallen. They are sacred and are never to be scavenged for food or

313

feathers," Rory explained.

"Holy Mother, they are beautiful," Lola praised. "Tell me more about the people." Luce gave Lola an inquisitive look before sighing.

"From what we have gathered, the people of Grimerg Rise come from different realms, brought together by fate in these volcanic mountains," he explained as Lola stumbled on ashen rocks.

"Right before the great war, they fled Sundom in search of a place where they could be secure. People from all over the realm were forced to flee their homes in search of freedom to worship the Holy Mother and not be separated from those they loved. Many of them found themselves wandering the treacherous mountains with nowhere else to go." A sense of displacement and longing lingered in his words. Lola wondered if he, too, was thinking about the similarities with her and her sister—the hardships they'd endured and the things they'd lost. "Lost and wandering, many of them found themselves navigating the treacherous mountains," Luce continued. Lola's perplexity deepened as she continued to grapple with the enigmatic nature of the Sundonians and their capacity for compassion. She wondered if Sole had anything to do with that.

"In their desperate search for sanctuary, these resilient souls arrived at the refuge of Grimerg Rise," Luce explained. "It became a beacon of hope, a haven where they could rebuild their lives and honor their beliefs without fear of persecution. As they journeyed, they encountered scattered survivors who had also sought refuge in the mountains. Together, they pooled their skills and resources to survive. Farmers cultivated the rocky land, creating terraces. Trades people set up shops and markets for bartering, while hunters and fishers provided food."

"So, they built it hidden in plain sight?" Lola questioned.

"Yes. Out of despair and love, the city of Grimerg Rise was born," Luce finished.

"So if people from all realms gathered here, how is it that they have not killed each other?" Lola asked as they continued to trudge up the path.

"We asked them the same thing when we first arrived," Kia said. "They told us that despite their diverse backgrounds and cultures, the people of Grimerg Rise found common ground in their shared struggle to survive. They worked together to build shelters and fortifications to protect themselves from the harsh elements and potential raiders. When they discovered the magick that stirred in this palace, they knew it was something to protect."

Lola marveled at the diverse faces that surrounded her, each bearing a unique blend of features reminiscent of different lineages. "It's fascinating," she remarked, "how many of them exhibit this captivating mix of different heritages."

Luce nodded, understanding Lola's observation. "In

Grimerg Rise, your identity is defined not by your appearance, but by the essence of your magick," he explained. "Over the course of five generations, this extraordinary community has thrived and evolved. They embraced the challenges of these unforgiving mountains, refusing to succumb to adversity, and forged a vibrant life for themselves here."

Lola's eyes widened with intrigue.

Abruptly, the rhythmic footsteps of the Sunguards came to a halt, and a hushed stillness to envelop the gathered crowd. The air itself seemed to hold its breath in anticipation of what was to come. Luce leaned in and spoke in a barely audible voice, "Your sister awaits."

Trepidation coursed through Lola's veins. This was the moment she had been preparing for. With a nod, she mustered the courage to step forward.

Rory voiced their collective decision. "We will wait here," she assured Lola.

In the expectant silence, Lola's heart raced. She drew strength from the presence of her companions and the knowledge that her sister, after all this time apart, awaited her just a few steps away.

Her dark cloak dragged on the ashen rocks as she made her way to the only family she had left. Heart beating out of her chest, palms sweaty, she suddenly thought about how much she had changed since she had last seen her big sister. What if everything was different now?

Ducking under the flap of the tent as ember crows circled overhead, Lola entered.

***

The crimson tent had elements of ruggedness and grandeur. The walls were made of thick, blood-red canvas, stretched tight over a sturdy wooden frame. The high ceiling allowed for plenty of headroom and was adorned with intricate patterns of ash-black and fiery orange depictions of volcanoes. Thick furs and woven mats covered the floor and atop them, in the center of the tent, was a large, circular table adorned with metal studs and intricate carvings.

A short woman stood with her back to the door, leaning over the table and studying a map of Transea. Her mahogany skin was smooth as selenite in the dancing firelight, her two braids plunging over her shoulders in elegant waves of copper.

"Sole?" Lola breathed.

The woman turned around, and Lola was met by the breathtaking presence of the most captivating pair of eyes she'd ever seen—deep violet and delicate lavender, shimmering like a twilight sky kissed by magick.

Delicate vertical lines of gold graced her high cheekbones, and a single golden vertical line adorned the center of her full, crimson lips, which turned upward at the sight of Lola.

"Lola..." Sole whispered as tears threatened to escape her shining eyes.

Tension gripped Lola's belly as she laid eyes upon her older sister, her once radiant and joyous demeanor now overshadowed by an unyielding hardness. Donned in the traditional war gear of Mōsa, the dark bronze glow of the Mōsian lunar markings adorned her serene visage. Though her regal presence remained intact, there had been a distinct transformation in her countenance. Lola's heart sank as she recognized the subtle changes etched upon her sister's face.

Tears fell as Sole and Lola collided in an embrace that was long overdue.

"It's ok, I'm here now," Lola whispered as she brought her sister in tighter. "It's gonna be okay. We're alive and we are together, that is what matters now." As Sole looked at Lola, she gasped with delight at the sight of her baby sister's emerald eyes.

"Your eyes sparkle, just like you," whispered Sole as she held her sister's face in the palms of her hands. "Green looks good on you!"

"There you go again, getting sentimental" Lola grinned as she rolled her teary eyes.

"What? A sister can't praise her sister's new look?" Sole

frowned as she studied Lola. "You don't look too shabby either!"

"How have they treated you in Kingsguard Reef?" Sole asked as she motioned for Lola to sit on the satin pillows. "They—well…we have much to discuss. Maybe you should start first, Sole. Tell me about Sundom. Tell me about the Second Prince of Sundom. Tell me everything."

Lola listened as Sole talked about her journey to Sundom, her captivity, her newfound love, and how together, she and Rivian had defeated Nasir. Tears streamed down Sole's face as she recollected how Nasir used his dark magick to control Rivian in the hopes that he would kill her. When Sole told Lola that Rivian almost succeeded, Lola's eyes flashed green.

"How can you ever trust him again?" Lola asked her sister.

Holding her hand, Sole told Lola of Rivian's last words to Zari: "Protect her."

Tears filling her eyes, Lola held her sister's hands as she whispered, "Sole, I am truly sorry that you have suffered so much on your own. Had I known, nothing would have stopped me from making my way to you sooner. Nothing."

"I wasn't alone. Nisa and Rory were with me." Holding back tears, Sole said, "I have lost much, but the betrayal has been just as hard to navigate. All of these losses have changed me. It has been awful to lose Nasir twice and to have brought Rivian into this mayhem. I never meant to…" Sole's voice cracked.

Regaining her composure, Sole inquired, "Tell me about your time since waking from the Darkness." Lola observed a shift in her sister's demeanor. No longer shy, Sole was now more reserved when it came to opening up and expressing her emotions.

As Lola exhaled a deep, shaky breath, she recounted her harrowing experiences of captivity: meeting Kingsley, losing him tragically, and enduring another kidnapping. She poured out the tale of Queen Alina and King Heath's remarkable kindness along with Thad's shocking betrayal.

"It seems that Thad and Rivian were both under Nasir's control. Blaming Thad for something beyond his control may not be fair," Sole said. "You need to find it in your heart to forgive him and seek a way to save your friend."

"I don't plan on ever seeing them again, so there is nothing to forgive."

"Reality has shown us that our family has experienced its fair share of betrayals, hasn't it?" Sole whispered softly while gently caressing her little sister's cheek. Her voice trembled as she added, "If you don't think you know what that feels like, then just look at our father's migration from Sundom. Betrayal has been part of our family's story since before we were born. I fear betrayal will remain part of our story long after we are gone."

Lola's tears flowed like rivers, for their future seemed bleak and their past long lost. But there was a ray of light shining through the cloudless sky. "Nasir ruling Mōsa is not an option," Sole declared. "I will crush him and take back what our father built."

While it unsettled Lola to hear Sole speak so openly about killing her husband, she couldn't ignore the fact that every moment since emerging from the Darkness had been filled with disturbing experiences. With determination, Lola brushed off her black cloak and said, "I'm ready to crush some heads. What do you need me to do?"

"The journey ahead promises many trials and more betrayals," Sole told her. "But we are our mother's daughters and we will overcome this."

Time seemed to stretch, an invisible thread woven between the sisters as they stood in captivated silence, absorbing the changes that had befallen them both. The glow in their eyes mirrored the subtle shifts within their souls, changes that would unravel and reveal themselves with the passage of time.

Sole beckoned her sister forward with a nod, urging them both to focus on the task that lay before them: reclaiming her throne. Sole returned to her desk and took her position behind it with a quiet strength. It was time to get to work.

"I have been reading the scrolls of Grimerg Rise. These people were the first to flee Sundom nearly five generations ago. Before they arrived, many died on the perilous journey. Still, they say they were blessed by the Holy Mother."

"What do you mean blessed?"

"They were given magick."

"How can that be? Father told us magick died generations ago. Our tomes told us that the Holy Mother did away with magick because it was evil."

"Yes, that is what we were made to believe. It's what our father was made to believe. It is not true. I am learning that people with power and privilege will always rewrite the narrative to erase their atrocities. But that stops now; it ends with us."

"Let me show you what I have learned," Sole continued. "Grimerg Rise, being a mountainous volcanic expanse, is a very unique and powerful realm. The volcano holds a great amount of energy and power, and the people have always had a deep connection to it. They call it Zemi's Favor."

"What is Zemi?" Lola asked, her emerald eyes wide.

"The people believe the Zemi has the power to control the weather and magick and protect them from harm."

"So, the people of this realm can pull their magick from this Zemi?"

"Yes. and I believe they have learned to harness the magick held within Grimerg Rise."

"But how have they passed it on from generation to generation when the rest of Transea was depleted of all magick until the Darkness?"

"I have been in conversation with King Ashok and Queen Indira, the rulers of this realm. They believe that it is this connection to Zemi's Favor that has allowed them to retain their magick when the rest of Transea lost it."

Sole went on to tell Lola that, for generations, the people of Grimerg Rise had been practicing mages, skilled in the art of harnessing the power of the volcano and channeling it into their magick. "These mages have passed down their knowledge and skills through the generations, ensuring that the people of Grimerg Rise always have access to the power of the volcano", Sole said.

She also told Lola that the people of Grimerg Rise had always held deep respect and reverence for the volcano, and it was that respect, they believed, that allowed them to maintain their connection to Zemi's Favor. They believed that by living in harmony with the volcano and respecting its power, they were able to access the magick within it.

"I am having a hard time believing that the very people who stared me down with such alarm as I entered their city would be open to sharing their secrets with you," Lola stated.

"Trust me, that was no easy feat, but I won over the favor of their war general, Rayven. He is King Ashok and Queen Indira's first son and a guard of the Night Walkers, the protectors of this land."

"Rayven? How did you do that? Is he hot?" Lola couldn't help herself. "Holy Mother, no!" Sole emphatically stated. "He and I realized we were determined to protect the one thing we both loved most."

"Which is what?" Lola asked.

"I promise to tell you more about that shortly." Sole's lavender eyes smiled. Lola would have to get used to her sister's new hue.

"The culture and traditions of these people are deeply intertwined with the volcano. Their spiritual beliefs are closely connected to it. They take immense pride in their heritage, firmly believing that their bond to their culture and traditions is bestowed upon them by the Holy Mother."

Sifting through the numerous scrolls and books strewn across her desk, Sole retrieved a magnificent golden tome, its ornate cover shimmering in the light.

With the utmost care, she opened it to a specific page, pointing to a picture. "I firmly believe that these three items hold the key to our victory over Nasir," Sole said.

Lola followed Sole's outstretched finger to the depiction of three formidable weapons with a profound inscription above them:

THE ARSENAL OF GUARDIANS.
"These weapons were fashioned to aid those who defend against the Darkness," Sole revealed. "It is believed that

*the Arsenal of Guardians is meant to defend and protect
the innocent from the dangers of dark magick."*

Lola's eyes widened as she beheld the images of the
dagger, the bow, and the sword. She blinked several times,
narrowing her eyes on the dagger.

Could it be?

Gathering her thoughts, Lola turned to Sole. "Sole…" she
began hesitantly. "I believe I possess one of these weapons." Taking the blade King had given her many moons ago,
Lola carefully placed it atop the book beside the depiction
of the dagger.

"This is the Champion's Choice. Kingsley gave it to me
in hopes that I would protect myself should I ever be kidnapped again." Sole noticed how her sister's voice trembled.

"Kingsley gave you this?"

"Yes," Lola said. "Right after the dire attack. He wanted
me to be safe. He said it once belonged to his grandfather."

Sole's violet eyes widened and Lola furrowed her brow.
What was so significant about Kingsley's involvement?
What did Sole know? Sole tightened her jaw and said
nothing. Drawing her sword, she placed it on top of the
ornate desk. "Rivian and I found the sword in the Dark
Wilds," she said. "It's called the Life Drinker."

"Wait, you fucking went to the Dark Wilds without me?"
Lola gasped. "I always wanted to go and you got to do it?"

"I think you are missing the point, Lola," Sole chastised.

"Rivian and I went there in search of the Life Drinker."

"Why?" Lola questioned.

"To revive Nasir," Sole said simply. "But instead, the journey to the caves ultimately drew me closer."

Lola saw pain hiding behind her sister's eyes.

Sole paced and bit her thumbnail. "We have located two of the three weapons. That confirms the prophecy. We are the three."

"The three?" Lola asked, brows furrowed.

Sole ignored her sister's question. "I believe the third weapon is at the base of the volcano and that it will require the magick of the three to release it."

"What do you mean the magick of three?"

"Remember the Mōsian prophecy?" Sole asked as she halted and turned to Lola, violet eyes flashing. "The one father told me about?"

"Once the three are reborn, the bond shall bring forth an era of magick and sorrow," Lola recited. "Of course I remember it, but what does that have to do with us?"

"Three weapons, and three who are reborn," Sole whispered to her sister.

"Are you saying you and I are two of those three?"

"Yes!" Sole exclaimed.

Arms crossed and thoughts racing, Lola paced in front of the ornate desk.

"Let's assume what you've uncovered is true," she began, locking eyes with Sole over the open book. "We are only two."

Sole's voice grew quiet, and the air stilled around them when she said, "Lo, I need you to sit down."

Both sisters settled in silence as Sole looked deeply into her young sister's emerald eyes.

"We...we are the three," she whispered.

Lola swallowed a lump in her throat, her bottom lip trembling. "What do you mean we are three?"

"That's what I needed to tell you," Sole whispered with a tearful smile as she held Lola's hands in hers.

"Luna is alive," she said. "She is here in Grimerg Rise."

CHAPTER 27

Awakening Ashen

"Luna?" Lola felt her magick surge as disbelief flickered in her eyes. "What…what did you just say?"

She couldn't make direct eye contact with Sole, the shock stunning her to her core.

"Our sister lives," Sole repeated slowly, her words resonating deep in Lola's chest. Sole held her composure as she cautiously explained what had happened to Luna in their absence.

"Luna was taken from Kingsguard Reef. Mõsa had been overrun by the dead during the worst of the Darkness. It was decided that the Western Isles would assist in disposing of the Mõsian dead. Everyone except the Sanctum followed our burial rites. "

Through gritted teeth and eyes glowing green, Lola asked, "Where is she?"

"Lola, Lola." Sole urgently attempted to calm her sister. "I will take you to her now."

Tremors of anticipation and dread rippled through Sole

as she swiftly rose to her feet. Sole couldn't bear to keep Luna away from Lola any longer. They were bound by something deeper than blood; their souls were intertwined at birth.The three of them belonged together, a trio destined to navigate life's journey as one.

As Sole and Lola entered the dimly lit tent, their footsteps softened by the thick fur rugs beneath them, a heavy silence hung in the air. Luna lay in the center, nestled atop an array of blankets, her once vibrant braids now a tangled mess and her skin pallid against the warm, obsidian interior. Still, Luna's ethereal beauty shone through, casting a melancholic glow in the flickering firelight.

A pang of sorrow twisted through Lola's chest at the sight of her sister. Her eyes glistened with unshed tears as she knelt down and reached out to tenderly caress Luna's cheek.

Sole and Lola sat by Luna's side, their tears falling simultaneously. The Darkness had ravaged their family so much already, taking their parents, splitting them apart. Now, it threatened to take Luna again.

"We must do something about her hair," Lola said, a small smile twitching at the corner of her mouth. "If she wakes up looking like this, she will have our hides."

"What was it that she would say?" Sole asked.

"We must always look our best. We never know when we might fall in love," the sisters recited in unison, laughing at the memory.

"She looks so fragile." Lola's voice quivered. "How did it come to this?"

"Rayven found her in the crypt, where she was thought to have perished," Sole explained. "When he discovered her, she was covered in mud, soot, and ash."

"Who is this Rayven and why does he hold such sway over Luna's fate?" Lola's voice wavered with a mix of curiosity and concern, her gaze still fixed on her sister.

Sole paused, grappling with the weight of her words. "He is a fierce warrior just like you," she said. "He believes that Luna's magick called out to him." Her tone was laced with uncertainty. "He brought her to Grimerg Rise, for he believed the power of the volcano would heal her. And miraculously, thirty moons later, she awoke."

"Why does he care so deeply for Luna? Can we trust him with her life?" Lola couldn't help her apprehension; she'd become far too familiar with betrayal.

Sole saw the fear and doubt clouding Lola's eyes and tenderly took Lola's trembling hands in hers. "I cannot explain Rayven's motives," she confessed softly. "But I sense love for Luna in his eyes. Love that echoes the depth of Rivian's gaze upon me. He has remained steadfast by her side since the moment he found her."

Lola can't help but notice the profound transformation that had taken hold of Sole. She was different now—older and more insightful than she'd been.

"We can't lose her," Lola whispered, her voice bubbling with emotion. "We've already lost too much."

Sole nodded, her own tears falling freely. She sniffled and pulled herself together quickly. "We'll find a way to break the curse of the darkness and restore her to health. But, Lola, it is imperative that you adhere to my plan, for any deviation could place Luna's life and all of Transea in peril."

Lola opened her mouth to respond but silenced herself at the soft sound of Luna's labored breathing. Sole leaned down to press a gentle kiss to her sister's forehead, her heart heavy with grief and worry.

"Luna, our sweet firefly," Lola whispered. "We will fight for you. Now It is time that you fight too."

Sole took a deep breath, reciting, "Here before, now and after."

Lola held Sole's hand tightly as she repeated her sister's words. "Here before, now and after."

As if on cue, a gust of wind billowed through the tent, carrying with it the scent of ash. In its wake stood a man with striking blue eyes, his presence commanding attention as he regarded Lola. This had to be Rayven.

Long, dark hair that framed his sharp features gathered in a tightly wound bun at the back of his head. As he crossed his muscular arms over his chest, Lola noticed intricate, bioluminescent tattoos enhance his captivating allure.

"Holy shit, Sole, you didn't tell me he was a god," Lola whispered.

Smiling, Sole muttered, "Our dear sister seems to have enamored him in her sleep. Isn't that just like Luna?"

"Yes. She…is the best of us isn't she?" Lola smiled. "What's with all the tattoos?" Rayven cautiously approached them.

"Each bioluminescent symbol tells a story of his past, marking his body with the trials and tribulations he had faced on his journey in Grimerg Rise, and even the Darkness."

Despite his formidable exterior, there was a vulnerability in Rayven's eyes that hinted at a hidden pain—perhaps a longing for something he could not have. Lola has seen that very same look before in Kingsley's eyes.

Bowing before Queen Sole, Rayven's voice resonated with solemn reverence. "My queen, I bring news."

With a nod from Sole, Rayven rose to his full height, his gaze never leaving Lola's. "This is my sister, Lola," Sole introduced. Lola couldn't help but note the caution in her voice.

Rayven's vibrant gaze softened as he regarded Lola, a flicker of recognition dancing in his eyes. "The daughters of Mōsa. It's an honor, Princess Lola," he said with a well-mannered nod.

Lola, worn out from placing her trust in strangers,

remained stoic. Sensing her wariness, Rayven stepped closer. "Rest easy, Princess Lola," he told her with sincerity. "You are not alone in this. We will do everything in our power to safeguard Luna, ensuring her safety and well-being as if she were our own."

Lola's breath caught in her throat, a glimmer of hope flickering within her weary heart.

"Rayven, You said you have news?" Sole asked hopefully.

"Yes, High Queen. We've found what we believe is the exact location of the Ember's Edge bow on Mount Ayuwoki," Rayven stated. He reached into the bag on his shoulder and retrieved a weathered tome, flipping to a marked page.

"May I have a look at that?" Lola inquired, glancing up at Rayven for approval as she reached for the book. He nodded and handed it over to Lola, who began reading aloud. "Let's see, okay here…" she began, tracing a passage with her index finger. "The arrows are forged from the bones of the fallen—talk about viciousness! And guess what? They're sharpened to a fine point and come with a deadly poison. Impressive!" Leaning closer to the text, Lola grinned mischievously at Rayven and added, "The fletching on each arrow is made of feathers from an ember crow, supposedly imbued with the power of fire itself. So, not only will you be killing your enemies, but you'll be doing it in style."

Then, Lola's tone turned serious. "And when an arrow

from Ember's Edge whistles through the air like a deadly storm, guided by some unseen force, it strikes with impeccable accuracy, leaving wounds that refuse to heal. Oh, and did I mention the slow and agonizing death caused by the poison? Even the toughest warriors are said to crumble before the might of Ember's Edge." Closing the tome and handing it back to Rayven, Lola said, "Now that, Prince Rayven, is a weapon worth talking about."

Turning back a the page, Rayven began to read aloud.

"In a fiery realm, whispers echo deep, Where unseen forces make arrows weep. Bravery, respect, and unwavering might,

Unlock Ember's Edge in the heat's fierce light."

Rayven, his bright azul eyes narrowing, skimmed through the pages intently until a spark of excitement lit his expression. "Here it is," he said. "This is the part that tells us where the weapon is exactly."

He stepped towards Sole and Lola, the three of them looking down at the book as he spoke.

"According to this, the Ember's Edge could be hidden within the depths of Mount Ayuwoki, where the ancient flames burn brightest. It's a treacherous journey, but if we're willing to face the challenges that lie ahead, we might just have a chance at laying our hands on this legendary bow."

Sole looked back at Luna on the blankets, then turned to Lola. Letting out a breath, she nodded. The three daughters of Mōsa were together again, something that had seemed so impossible at the height of her darkest times. They'd braved their separate journeys and had not only survived, but made their way back to each other again. Not even the most treacherous volcano could compare to the challenges they'd already faced.

CHAPTER 28

A Warmaiden's call

Sole and Lola exited Luna's tent to find their five Misa warriors standing in crescent formation, the standard formation for shielding the royals of Mōsa. Lola wants to run to and embrace each warrior, her sisters in arms. Her emerald eyes filled with pride as she stared into the eyes of Sierra, Assane, Talora, Natara, and Rory.

Each of these women had trained from the tender age of ten to become one of the most skilled and dangerous warriors in all the land. Lola had begged her parents to let her train with the Misa when she was ten, but they refused. She was finally allowed to train at the age of ten and three.

The training had been grueling and intense. From dawn to dusk, they repeated rigorous combat and weapons training, learning how to adapt, learning discipline, focus, and mental fortitude. They were drilled on strategy, tactics, and how to read their opponents. Stealth and infiltration in any terrain, efficiency—all were skills that were deeply ingrained into the Misa way of life, but none were more important

than the values of honor and duty. The Misa were not just warriors, but protectors of their people and their land.

These five girls in front of Lola had grown physically skilled and mentally strong to take their place among the ranks of the Misa War Maidens. They were a fearsome force, feared by their enemies and respected by their allies. The War Maidens stood in rose-gold armor provided by King Rill of Sundom that glinted in the dim light of the volcanic city, moving gracefully despite the weight of the protective plates. The metal shone as if enchanted, and Lola suspected that Sole had imbued it with her magic.

The crest of Mōsa was emblazoned upon each warrior's chest plate, and the shoulder guards were shaped like the wings of a dragon. The armor was not only a symbol of Mōsian strength and skill, but also a warning to any who dared to challenge them. "Don't worry, I think we have a spare suit for you, Lola," Sole whispered to her sister.

Beyond the War Maidens, Lola's eyes fell on Luce and Kia talking to a few guards of Grimerg Rise. As the Misa shouted the Mōsa war cry to their queen, the people stood as if frozen in time. As Sole began her regal descent, Lola felt strangely proud of her sister. Though neither one of them was meant to bear the responsibility of the crown, Sole looked fit for royalty.

Turning to face her, Sole said, "Lola, are you coming? There is one last thing I must show you."

Taking three strides, Lola reached for Sole's hand as they walked together through the soot-covered terrain. As the seven women of Mōsa stood in all their glory, the people of Grimerg Rise stared—some in awe, others in fear. The Misa led them through many turns to a ravine at the peak of the mountain, where a black tent stood tall. In the distance, she could hear people chanting. Lola felt like she was dreaming.

"Kilthar, azenoth, arakor!"

As they approached the cliff, the chant grew louder.

Lola felt her magick beginning to rise as something in the chant spoke to her.

"Sole, what are they saying?" she asked.

"They are saying Kil-thar, ah-zen-oth, ah-ra-kor!" Sole explained. "It means to 'strike down before and after.' When chanted together in battle, the phrase inspires warriors to strike down their enemies both before and after the battle."

Eyes full of tears, Lola reached for her sister's hand. She feared she would fall if she didn't seek her support.

"Sole, how is this possible?" she asked, voice cracking. "Kilthar, azenoth, arakor!" Sole began to chant in unison with the others. The words echoed across the land and into Lola's heart. Pulling her sister close, Sole continued.

"When I arrived at Grimerg Rise, Queen Indira and King Ashok insisted I meet with them."

Arriving at the peak with their five Misa beside them,

Lola's gaze swept across the panoramic view, but her attention was immediately captured by an ebony-skinned woman standing at the top, her fierce, royal blue cape fluttering in the wind. Lola's eyes widened and she froze in her tracks. Queen Indira of Grimerg Rise stood before her.

Sole, sensing Lola's astonishment, whispered, "It is uncanny how they look alike, isn't it? Come, I will introduce you."

Sole guided Lola closer.

"Your Highness," Sole greeted, dipping her chin to the queen. "May I introduce my sister, "Princess Lola Sirena Porte of Mōsa, third daughter of Porte house, First of her Name, survivor of the Darkness and the yielder of Life Bending magick, Mighty Misa Warmaiden and sister to the Queen of the Western Isle."

Lola's heart raced, for Indira bore such a striking resemblance to Queen Lygia that she had to fight the impulse to run toward her. As much as she wanted her to be, this woman was not her mother.

Indira's lustrous hair cascaded down her shoulders in a voluminous crown of natural, dark strands streaked with silver—a testament to the wisdom and experiences etched upon her. Her eyes, deep pools of gold, held an alluring universe of emotions within, and her captivating smile brightened the world around her with a seemingly magnetic force.

Lola found her voice as Indira gently said, "Lola, it is an honor to finally meet you. May our refuge be your refuge."

In the distance, the chanting grew louder and more fierce, signaling a gathering force.

Grasping Lola's hand firmly, Sole's voice filled with excitement as she exclaimed, "We have so much to catch up on, dear sister. But first, allow me to introduce you to some truly extraordinary individuals."

Ten paces later, Lola couldn't believe her eyes. Below them was a sea of Misa warriors—as far as the eye could see—each wearing black golden armor and golden warpaint. But their eyes—could it be? Every single set of them glowed with magick. With one calm raise of her hand, the High Queen instantly silenced her army.

"Today!" Sole shouted to the crowd. "The Holy Mother has blessed us with safe arrival of my sister Lola Sirena Porte of Mōsa, the last daughter of Porte House, survivor of the Darkness, yielder of life-bending magick, mighty Misa Warrior, sister to the High Queen of the Western Isles and…general to the mightiest fucking army in all of Transea!" Tears glistened in Lola's eyes as an emotional laugh escaped her throat. "General Lola," Sole said, turning to her sister. "Meet the first Misa battle mages in all of Transea. They wait for your command."

The battle mages began to chant the Karnothian battle cry, their voices low and steady like the rumble of distant thunder. The sound built gradually, each repetition of the phrase growing louder and more forceful than the last. The warriors around them took up the chant, voices blending together in a powerful, rhythmic cacophony.

"Kilthar, azenoth, arakor!"

The air around them seems to vibrate with the force of their voices. Lola swore that the very ground beneath their feet shook.

The words themselves seemed to invoke primal energy and strength. The language was guttural and rough, filled with hard consonants and sharp syllables. It was indigenous and raw, steeped in the traditions and beliefs of the warriors who spoke it.

The warriors' chant rose to a crescendo in a powerful display of strength and unity. The Misa were not just fighting for themselves, but for their people, their culture, and their way of life. Lola's tears fell at the sudden realization that she'd been wrong all along. She was never alone.

CHAPTER 29

Revelations and heirlooms

Eleven moonrises had come and gone since Lola's arrival in Grimerg Rise. Despite the passage of time, Luna remained asleep.

Sole sat cross-legged on the cushions in front of her comatose sister, her hands holding a tome and her eyes fixed on the symbols that lined it. She was completely absorbed in the ancient text, absentmindedly swirling her purple magick in dancing patterns around her fingers. The air charged with her energy, and the faint scent of lavender filled the tent.

Across from her, Lola had a pile of books stacked in front of her, but her attention strayed to the loose roots that she had unearthed with her magick. She twisted and twirled the slender tendrils between her fingers as she read, finding a strange sense of comfort in their texture. Every now and then, she held them up to her nose, deeply inhaling the wet scent of soil.

Sole looked up from her scroll and took in Lola's behavior with a small smile that quickly faded as she glanced back at the text.

"I think it's time we discuss the Champion's Choice," Sole said, gesturing to the tome. As she flipped the pages, Lola's attention snapped back to the task at hand. The sisters studied the drawing of the gleaming blade together, Sole tracing her fingers over the intricate details while Lola continued to fiddle with the roots.

Lola's eyes grew wide as she asked Sole, "What's wrong?" With brows furrowed, Sole asked, "When Kingsley gave you this did he tell you what the significance of this gift meant?"

"Yes. When I arrived at the Do'Ramos castle Kingsley was concerned that whomever held me captive would come again. I told him I could take care of myself. But he insisted I had something to protect myself."

Sole' amethyst eyes widened. "What?" Lola demanded to know what she was missing.

"Continue, Lola," Sole urged. "I need to know everything."

"I think he realized that I didn't need a protector. After that confrontation with the dire wolf, he knew I was a fighter and that I was capable of defending myself should I need to," Lola said, her mind drifting back to the serene space and time where she'd felt secure, radiant, and closest to

Kingsley.

"Lo," Sole muttered, bringing Lola back to the present. "He gave you this precious family heirloom for a reason."

"Yes, it's really not a big deal, Sole. I mean look at it. It's just an old weapon. He didn't know about the prophecy."

"Oh, Lo…" Sole smiled and shook her head in disbelief. "Leave it to my baby sister to not see what is right in front of her."

"What do you mean?"

"Do you not know that in Kingsguard Reef it is customary to give your love a small family heirloom as a way to say this is my betrothed."

Lola exhaled what felt like the last breath in her body. "No…" she said in disbelief. "That's not what he did. He wouldn't do that. Maybe he didn't know." But Sole's eyes told her everything. Kingsley hadn't told her the whole truth.

"I can't believe it," Lola whispered. "Kingsley gave me his family heirloom as a betrothal gift?"

Sole nodded, her expression serious. "It seems that way. This changes everything, Lola. You're going to be Queen of Kingsguard Reef."

"I agreed to no such fucking thing! I was meant to be a warrior, not a Queen," she sputtered, wringing her hands.

"By accepting this gift, you have already agreed, and as the Queen of the Western Isles I must honor your agreement."

"What?! I didn't know what I was agreeing to!" Lola was beyond pissed, but her heart skipped a beat at the thought of being Kingsley's queen. Never had she dared to entertain the dream that he could be hers.

"I don't want to be queen," Lola said, her voice trembling. "I'm not meant to be queen. I don't even know if I love Kingsley."

Sole squeezed her sister's shoulders gently. "Lo, take some time to think about it. But remember, if you accept his proposal, you'll be tying our kingdoms together and creating the strongest union the Western Isles has had in generations."

Lola nodded, her mind spinning with possibilities. She couldn't deny that she was attracted to Kingsley, but she didn't know if she was ready for the responsibility that came with being queen. His queen.

Sole could see the uncertainty in her sister's eyes. "Why don't you go for a walk, Lola? Clear your head. I'll stay here and look over the scrolls."

Lola nodded gratefully and quickly made for the exit of the tent.

"Lo, one more thing," Sole said, stopping her sister before she left. "Before you make yourself sick with worry, remember our mother was both a queen and a warrior. You can have it all if you choose."

As Lola walked out of the tent, her mind raced and her

stomach twisted like she was going to be sick.

Along came anger. She couldn't believe that Kingsley had not told her the conditions when she accepted the blade. How dare he put her in such a difficult situation without giving her any warning or explanation?

A wave of dizziness washed over her and she stumbled. She could barely breathe; the air was too thick and heavy. She tried to take deep breaths, but her lungs constricted.

Palms clammy, vision blurring, she couldn't focus on anything. She tried to call for help, but her voice was weak and barely audible.

Finally, after what felt like an eternity, her breath returned to her. She focused on the rhythm of her inhales and exhales and slowly, her vision cleared and the dizziness began to subside.

As she looked around, she realized that she was alone. The panic had caused her to wander far from the tent without even realizing it. She took another deep breath, and started to make her way to her own tent, her mind still consumed. She needed more time to think, to figure out what she truly wanted.

CHAPTER 30

Prideful journey

The tent flaps parted and Luce stepped inside, his black hair falling over his face. "Princess," Luce began, his voice carrying a hint of amusement. "You won't believe who has graced us with their royal presence."

Lola raised an eyebrow, her interest piqued. "You know I hate it when you call me that. I told you to call me Lola."

Luce rolled his eyes.

"Tell me then," she said. "Who dares venture into the heart of Grimerg Rise?"

"You mean other than us?" Luce quipped, eyes wild and full of debauchery.

"Yes! Other than us," she said, smirking.

Luce leaned closer with a mischievous glint in his eyes and whispered, "The boy prince himself, Kingsley Do'Ramos."

Lola's face flushed a deep shade of red as the realization washed over her. Her heart skipped a beat as excitement and anger surged through her veins. "Kingsley?" she exclaimed incredulously. "What madness possessed him to do such a thing?"

Luce chuckled, thoroughly enjoying Lola's reaction. "Ah, it is a peculiar thing," he said, grinning like a fool. "It drives even the most logical of minds to irrational acts. As I understand it, It seems he's quite furious about a certain woman who left him while he slumbered."

Lola's stomach dropped and her traitorous heart flipped in her chest. Her green eyes narrowed. "So he comes to Grimerg Rise, the forsaken mountain, in search of me? How dare he? I am no damsel in distress, waiting to be rescued!"

Luce leaned against the tent's wooden support beam, his expression both playful and wise. "Lola. You are far from helpless. But perhaps, just perhaps, he sees something in you worth fighting for. Worth defying the expectations placed upon him as the heir to the throne."

"Since when do you speak so highly of the prince?" she asked him.

"Since he scaled the most treacherous mountain, forsaking the king and the kingdom, to get to you."

"Where is he?"

"He is in prison."

Lola's eyes flashed.

"Take me to him at once!"

***

Entering the makeshift prison with Luce in her wake, Lola froze in place at the sight of Kingsley. Wrapped in a black cloak, he lay on the dirty ground surrounded by none other than his cousins and his sister. All of them were asleep, clearly exhausted from their arduous trek. They had all come for him? For her? Lola forced a hardened expression over her face before approaching the cell.

Luce raised an eyebrow, immediately seeing through Lola's facade. He recognized the guarded flicker of emotions in her eyes. "Hey, Lola," he whispered, teasing her. "You can try your hardest to hide your true feelings, but they're written all over your face. Love has a way of defying reason, my princess."

Lola tightened her jaw. "Love or not, it changes nothing," she replied firmly. "I won't let him or anyone else interfere with our mission. I won't be distracted by matters of the heart."

Lola turned away, her gaze fixed on the sleeping prince behind the bars. She struggled to hide the flicker of affection that danced within her. "Well," she said, her voice steady but her words vulnerable. "He will find no lovestruck princess awaiting him here. He has no claim to my heart."

Luce's smirk softened into a knowing smile. "Ah, Lola, your defiance is admirable. But remember, love always has a way of weaving its own story."

Lola clenched her fists. "I will speak to him through these bars, let him think what he may, for my heart is a fortress he will not breach."

Finally, Luce nodded in understanding, and Lola took a deep breath, steeling herself for the forthcoming encounter. She would face Kingsley with a mask of indifference, concealing the love that threatened to consume her. With a determined resolve, she withdrew Luce's sword from his side, stepped forward, and clanged it against the cell bars.

Kingsley and the others shot upright, blinking and gasping as they jolted from their slumber. Kingsley scrambled to his feet and stood face-to-face with Lola on the other side of the cell.

"Your Highness," Lola said in a stiff greeting, thrusting her arm back and handing Luce his sword without breaking her furious eye contact with Kingsley.

Fuck, he's perfect.

He tugged at her heart. She had been waiting for this moment longer than he could ever know, and she had never dreamed it would feel so sweet, so wonderful. His eyes smoldered, even in their half-awake state, with an emotion she refused to name. Her throat felt dry and when she tried to speak further, all that came out was a croak. She licked her lips and found them parched as well. Kingsley took a hesitant step forward.

"What are you doing here?" she demanded, controlling her voice and putting her warrior tone on full display. "I told you I needed to do this on my own."

"You could have told me to my fucking face, but you didn't," Kingsley said bitterly. "Because you, Princess Lola, are a fucking coward."

"Fuck you!" Lola scoffed as she turned to leave. Why she had even bothered to come see him, she didn't know.

Kingsley was not one to be deterred so easily.

"I know you did," he retorted.

Lola's eyes widened with silent fury, and Kingsley sighed. "I couldn't let you go alone," he said softly. "I won't stand by and watch my mate walk into danger without being by your side."

Lola's lips parted and a breath escaped from between them. His mate.

Lola's heart swelled as she saw love and determination shining in his eyes. She couldn't deny him, but she had to.

"You shouldn't have come here!" she yelled. "You are the future of Kingsguard Reef. Being here only jeopardizes that and—" she threw her hand out in a gesture to the oth-ers—"you brought Sirena with you! You abandoned your kingdom with no heirs for what?"

"I told you she would be pissed!" Melia snapped at King-sley. "Watch out for that magick, cousin."

"Melia stop! We came here to help her!" Sirena shut her

cousin down as she climbed up from the floor and stood beside Kingsley.

"We are here because we love you!" Sirena said to Lola. Lola softened at the sight of Sirena, but tensed right back up at the sound of another voice from the back corner of the cell.

"We are here because we owe you a debt."

Stepping into the light, Thad removed his hood. Lola's blood ran cold.

"Luce!" Lola bit out, and he immediately stepped to her side.

Facing the Sunguards, Lola issued her command with authority, "Set them free. Ensure they receive fresh clothing, a warm tent, and ample food."

"Yes, General," the shorter Sungard replied promptly, acknowledging her orders. Prince Do'Ramos is my betrothed, after all", she said, her tone laced with condescension.

A heavy silence fell over the prison. The Do'Ramos family couldn't believe their ears.

Kingsley wanted to say something—anything—but he knew this wasn't the place.

"What does she mean, King?" Sirena asked.

Not giving him the opportunity to speak, Lola said, "It appears your brother doesn't believe a woman can make her own mind up about who she wants to be her mate, or if she wants to be mated at all!" Her venomous words were not lost on King. Pointing to Thad and Mya, her green eyes flashed. "Those two are to remain right here until High Queen Sole decides what to do with them. Give them nothing to eat."

Before Kingsley was set free, Lola turned on her heel and walked swiftly away from the prison, heading towards the one person who knew her best and would tell her what to do—her sister.

CHAPTER 31

Emerging emotions

Lola burst into Sole's tent, her heart aflame with anger and pain. As she swept inside, her eyes fell upon Sole, who stood there with a look of deep concern etched across her face.

"Are you ok?" Sole asked. "I heard about our surprise visitor…"

Lola took a deep breath, trying to steady herself. She couldn't let her emotions get the best of her, not when Sole depended on her to be strong.

"I'm fine," Lola said, her voice sounding calmer than she felt. "I just…needed some air."

Sole studied her for a moment before nodding. "Okay, but if you need to talk, I'm here for you."

Lola felt a pang of guilt at her sister's words. Sole had always been there for her, no matter what, and she had let her anger get in the way of that. She took another deep breath.

"I'm sorry," Lola said weakly. "I don't mean to shut you

out."

Sole smiled softly. "I understand. Trust me, Rivian has done his share of shit to make me question everything."

"And still you give it all up to save him? A Sundonian? Forgive me, Sole, but I just don't get it. He's our fucking enemy."

They sat in silence for a moment, the tension she'd forced between them slowly dissipating.

"Falling for Rivian was unfathomable," Sole said with a sigh. "Even I struggle with how fast our love grew on that ship. But sometimes, love doesn't follow the rules of war. We can't always control who we fall for, but we can control how we choose to act on those feelings. Just remember, no matter what happens, I'll be here to support you."

Lola nodded, tears welling up in her eyes. "I feel like such a fool," she whispered. "How could I not have known that Kingsley made me his mate without my consent?"

Sole understood Lola's pain and gently placed a comforting hand on her sister's shoulder. "Lola, you're not a fool," she reassured. "Kingsley should have been honest with you from the beginning. But I am here for you and together, we can sort this out."

As the tears continued to fall, Lola felt a glimmer of hope and gratitude at her sister's words. She was beyond lucky to have Sole in her life, especially after all they'd been through. Together, they would face whatever challenges came their way, no matter what.

Desperate to change the subject, Lola asked, "Have you discovered anything else about the weapons?"

Their previous triumph quickly faded as Sole's expression revealed her frustration. "It appears that only someone possessing a specific kind of magick can retrieve the Ember's Edge from the lava at the base of the volcano."

Sole sighed and looked over at Luna's peaceful form in the center of the tent. "Luna's ashen magick is the only kind capable of such a feat."

Lola's heart sank. "So, without Luna, we can't get it," she said, her voice heavy with despair. "And without it, we stand no chance against Nasir."

The sisters sat in silence, Lola biting her lower lip and thinking hard. "What else does the scroll say?"

Sole proceeded to read aloud. "The Ember's Edge, born from the fusion of Ashen steel and midnight's essence, shall only be wielded by the one who possesses ashen magick. With its bolts infused with the power of bioluminescent fire, it will bring destruction to those who dare oppose its master. From the ashes of war, a new era shall rise, and the Ember's Edge shall be the harbinger of change, bringing chaos and order to the realm. Forged in darkness, it paves the way for a new dawn."

The sisters examined the image of the magnanimous crossbow, and Lola marveled at its details. The trigger and bolts were adorned with glowing teal and orange runes, and the attached quiver brimmed with golden razor-tipped bolts. However, what truly set the Ember's Edge crossbow apart was the intricate network of bioluminescent lava seemingly flowing within it, visible through its cracks. It appeared almost alive, pulsating with an otherworldly energy.

"It's no wonder this weapon requires someone with a specific kind of magick to retrieve it," Sole exclaimed.

"It is a weapon of both beauty and lethality," Lola said. "A fusion of darkness and light. It represents our only hope to defeat Nasir and restore peace to the land."

Sole nodded, her eyes filled with determination born from desperation. "We must find a way to wake Luna," she declared, her voice resolute. Just then, Luce burst into the tent.

"High Queen...urgent news," Luce panted.

Sole stood, her eyes narrowing. "What is it? Speak quickly."

Luce handed her a black parchment with the crimson Sundom crest upon it. It was a note from Rill, the High King of the Eastern Isles—Rivian's brother.

"Most importantly, we've received word that Zari arrived safely and they have news of Rivian's whereabouts. He's been spotted in Mōsa and he's expecting a ship from the Sanctum in four moonrises with captive mages and supplies from all over Transea," Luce shared.

Sole's heart skipped a beat. Rivian was in danger.

"We must leave at once. Gather the Misa!" she ordered, turning to Lola's with her eyes widened in fury.

"Are you serious?" Lola guffawed. "You're willing to stop everything to go save Rivian? This is the same man who tried to kill you? What about the kingdom? What about our people?"

Sole sighed. "I know it's difficult to understand, Lola. But Rivian is not my enemy. He's someone I care about deeply, and I cannot stand by while he's in danger."

Lola glared at her. "You're choosing him over our people?"

Sole shook her head. "I'm choosing to save someone I love. And in doing so, I hope to bring about a better future for our kingdom and all of Transea."

Luce stepped forward, his eyes flashing. "Your Highness, I suggest we move quickly. We cannot risk losing Rivian or the captive mages to the Sanctum."

Lola crossed her arms, scowling. "I can't believe this. You're willing to risk everything for your enemy."

Sole's tone hardened. "Regardless of my reasons, as your queen, I expect you to follow my commands without question. This is not up for debate, Lola."

Lola's anger faltered slightly under Sole's unwavering gaze. She knew better than to challenge her sister when she spoke with such authority.

Sole softened her expression, reaching out to grasp

Lola's hand. "I understand that you may not agree with my decision, but I need you to trust me. We will do everything in our power to protect our people, but Rivian's safety is also a priority."

Luce shifted uncomfortably in the background, sensing the tension between the sisters. "Your Highness…" He tapped his foot impatiently, reminding Sole that they had little time.

Sole nodded, releasing Lola's hand. "Thank you, Luce. Lola, prepare the Misa for departure. We leave at once." She turned to leave the tent, pausing for a moment to look back at her sister. "I hope you will come to understand my decision in time, sister."

Lola watched in frustrated resignation as Sole exited the tent. Pushing her magick down, she reminded herself that she couldn't disobey Sole's commands, but she couldn't shake the feeling that something was not right about this situation. With a heavy sigh, Lola followed Luce out of the tent to prepare for their journey.

CHAPTER 32

A volcanic embrace

Amidst the chaos of preparing the Misa mages for the mission to retrieve Rivian, Lola embraced the welcomed distraction. She firmly instructed the guards stationed near her tent to ensure that no one, particularly Kingsley, was to interrupt her.Though she was relieved not to have to confront her feelings, she knew that love had no place in the midst of war. She only had time to focus on the task at hand.

But sleep eluded her, as her dreams became consumed by the image of his captivating eyes. Determined to put an end to it, Lola shrouded herself in his dark cloak and took a stroll through the vibrant volcanic city, seeking solace and clarity.

As Lola wandered, her eyes took in the people who inhabited this fiery realm, their appearances reflecting the mesmerizing essence of their volcanic home.

Lola would never get over the cinematic views of Grimerg Rise, covered by ash, dark smoke, and teal, bioluminescent lava that ran through the land. Perching on the ash and teal rocks, Lola crossed her legs and took in a deep breath. She couldn't believe how comfortable she felt in Grimerg Rise. No one was worried about who was wearing last season's fashion. There were no conversations to be had about betrothals or politics. Here in this city, the people cherished every moment they had been given. They had honor and would rather die than betray their kingsmen.

The peoples' sun-kissed complexions radiated with the same warmth of the molten lava coursing beneath their feet. Lola admired their diverse range of skin tones, from the comforting hues of caramel to the deep, mossy shades that spoke of their close connection to the land. Their beautiful skin was embellished with the same bioluminescent tattoos she'd seen on Rayven, which seemed to pulse with an otherworldly light, as if drawing energy from the very heart of the volcano. Delicate lines and mesmerizing symbols were interwoven across their bodies, glowing vibrant shades of fiery teal and shimmering orange. The ever-shifting colors responded to the ebb and flow of the wearer's emotions and magick.

But Lola loved most about the people was the inherent grace and strength they resonated, wisdom and intensity in their piercing eyes.

Rayven had explained to her the transformative process in which they submerged their hands into the glowing lava in order to imprint their tattoos. Skilled artisans extracted the lava, infusing them with enchantments and sacred rituals, and then with delicate tools, they carefully applied the cooled lava as tattoos, ensuring that the bioluminescent essence merged seamlessly with the individual's being.

They were more than mere adornments; they were direct conduits for the wearer's magickal abilities and the deep power of the volcano. The radiant marks were symbols of honor and a testament to strength, resilience. Lola was sure of one thing.

Once this was all over, she would get those tattoos with her sisters.

Lost in her contemplation, she heard a rustling of the black ashen rocks stirring on the ground behind her. She immediately reached for the dagger Kingsley had given her and held it tightly in her hand.

"Show yourself!" she called out in an instant panic. Her magick rose. Were they here to take her again?

A figure stepped out from behind the bushes and Lola gasped when she recognized those glowing honey eyes staring back at her. Drinking her in.

Kingsley.

"What do you want?" Lola demanded, her voice shaking with fury. She still couldn't bear to look at him without reminding herself of his betrayal. How he'd tricked her and lied to her.

"I...I wanted to explain."

Lola refused to talk about it, so she set off in the opposite direction without another word.

Kingsley quickly caught up to her and put his hand on her shoulder. She whipped around and he was taken aback by the anger and hurt etched on her face.

How could he have kept something so important from her? She had trusted him with her life, and he had taken advantage of that trust. As he drew closer, she couldn't resist the urge to lash out.

Lola slid up to Kingsley as if to hug him, but instead, she balled her hand into a fist and delivered a sharp punch straight to his eye.

Kingsley stumbled back, stunned.

"I deserve that," he said, cupping his wounded eye and wincing. "How could you do that?" Lola shouted, her emotions giving way. "How could you not tell me what I was agreeing to? For making me look like a fool! Men have taken advantage of me. They have broken my bones and my spirit. But not you. You were different."

Kingsley's heart sank as he realized the gravity of his decision. He had taken Lola's trust for granted and was now paying the price.

"Tesoro..."

"Don't you fucking call me that!"

"I'm sorry. I should have told you," he said, his voice

heavy with regret.

But Lola was beyond his apologies. She stormed away, leaving Kingsley alone to contemplate the damage he had caused.

"This conversation is not over, Lola. FUCK!"

With just a couple of strides, he swiftly closed the distance between them once again, his hand firmly grasping her elbow as he turned her around. When his eyes met hers, her breath hitched, causing a flutter in her chest. Fuck he wanted to kiss her—to claim her—but he knew that she wouldn't allow him to come too close. Instead, he resolved to do the next best thing—reveal his true feelings.

"I never realized I needed rescuing until that day in the forest when I stumbled upon you! Since that very moment, I can't imagine any adventures without you by my side," he confessed, his voice laced with sincerity. "I should have expressed my feelings as soon as I recognized them, but I ended up messing things up. And for that, for everything, I am truly sorry."

Taking a deep breath, Kingsley's voice quivered with longing as he whispered, "I am and have been for quite some time, completely consumed by you. It defies reason and drives me fucking mad, but here we are. You talk of saving the world and I would burn it all down for you. In just a few heartbeats, I won't be able to resist any longer. I will kiss you. So, if you don't want this, if you don't feel the same burning intensity…"

His trembling voice stirred something deep within Lola, awakening both fear and desire. Her breaths came in quick succession as her heart pounded.

Was she ready for this? Was she ready to take the plunge into the unknown depths of love that Kingsley was offering? She was uncertain, but she couldn't deny the anticipation and fervor that coursed through her veins. She yearned to experience the passionate connection he spoke of, to explore the depths of his promises.

"Kingsley," she stammered. "I…I don't know what to say. This is all so overwhelming, but I can't deny how I feel about you. You have ruined me. You haunt my dreams, my thoughts are held captive by you."

A mischievous spark danced in Kingsley's eyes, his perfect dimple deepening as he leaned in even closer. She felt his breath on her lips. "Are you absolutely sure?" he asked with a mix of playful teasing and raw desire.

"If we do this? If we agree to this union, I need assurances. If you ever make a decision for me again, that will be the end of us. Never again!" Lola demanded. Kingsley's eyes flickered with deep understanding and unwavering devotion as he nodded in solemn agreement.

"Lola, today I vow to you that we will face this future together. As King and Queen of Kingsguard Reef, there will never be a decision that is made that we don't both vote on."

"I give you my word, Lola. I want you to know that I will earn your trust, moment to moment, and I will spend every day of my life proving to you that choosing me to love you is the right decision. Our love, as fierce and untamed as it may be, will always respect and honor the individual freedom we both possess. Together, we will build a bond that nurtures and cherishes the unique souls that we are."

His heartfelt words wrapped around her, igniting warmth and security within Lola's heart. In that moment, she knew that their love had the strength to withstand any challenge.

Their lips crashed together in a collision of desire, unleashing a fervent passion. In that electrifying kiss, they became consumed by an all-encompassing fire that burned through their veins. The urgency in their embrace forced them to pause, their eyes locked in a magnetic gaze.

Breaking free, Lola's voice was husky as she spoke with breathless anticipation.

"We have so much to discuss. But first, my king, it's time for you to meet my sisters."

The words hung in the air. Kingsley, as if emerging from a trance, blinks in confusion.

"What do you mean, your sisters?" he asked, bewildered. The spell of their passionate kiss momentarily lifted, leaving him yearning for answers.

"Your Highness." King bowed deeply before Sole.

"Please, rise," she said, settling behind her desk amid a clutter of books, scrolls, and tomes. "You can call me Sole. All my friends do." Her wink evoked memories of Kingsley's first encounter with Lola.

"So, you are Prince Kingsley Do'Ramos." Sole was intrigued but wary.

"Yes, my queen," Kingsley replied.

"You're the one who followed my little sister all the way to the volcanic city?" Sole's words dripped with playful sarcasm and she struggled to contain her smirk, yet she maintained her composure.

Kingsley shifted on his feet, searching for the right response. "Yes, my queen," he answered promptly.

Lola stood beside him, emanating unwavering confidence and love.

"Look at me, Prince Kingsley," the queen commanded. "Our world is in great despair. My sister and I feel called not only to save the people of Mōsa but all of Transea. It's not the path we would have chosen, but it's what the Holy Mother has bestowed upon us. My sister tells me you understand the weight of the crown." Sole's voice was firm, cutting through the tension like a blade. "My sister is not a prize to be claimed. She is Princess Lola Sirena Porte of Mōsa, third daughter of the Porte House, first of her name, survivor of the Darkness, wielder of life-bending magick, mighty Misa warrior, sister to the High Queen of the Western Isle, and future Queen of Kingsguard Reef."

At that moment, Kingsley knew that Sole knew all about the heirloom. She knew that he had broken tradition and bonded Lola to him without her consent. "Your Highness, I can explain."

"Listen well," the queen declared with authority. "My father instilled in his daughters the belief that we control our own minds, that we deserve to have our voices heard. Remember this always: never betray my sister's trust."

Lola's heart swelled at Sole's addition to her title. She couldn't deny him, not when they clearly loved each other. Simultaneously, Sole's heart ached with the absence of Rivian beside her. He couldn't console her, touch her, or let her know she wasn't alone in this dark world. But she would grant her sister this moment, a moment that might not come again once they went to war.

"Your Highness, if I may," Kingsley said. "My entourage and I would like to join you on a mission to Mōsa to retrieve Prince Rivian."

"By entourage, are you including your cousin Thad and your former betrothed, Mya Sarlee?" Her words landed like venom as her lavender eyes glowed.

"Yes."

Silence fell over them before Kingsley continued. "Thad was controlled by Nasir. We are sure that Nasir left him once he realized there was no use using him to gain access to Lola."

Wrapping his arms around Lola's waist while he faced the queen, he continued. "Thad owes Lola a debt. I will make sure he repays that debt. What better way to repay that debt than to defend her on the battlefield," Kingsley said confidently.

"Your cousin and Lady Sarlee are welcome to join our mission. However, let it be known that my sister requires no defense on the battlefield." The queen's plum gaze hardened. "Make no mistake, I will not hesitate to command the Misa warriors to strike down anyone who dares to cast even a glance of ill-intent towards Lola. Now, depart from me. We have preparations to attend to."

CHAPTER 33

Here, before, now and after

As Lola guided Kingsley through the volcanic city of Grimerg Rise, she pointed in awe at the ember crows forming a majestic crescent moon formation against the inky-black sky, their amber bellies glowing mesmerizingly over the landscape.

Lola, nervously avoiding prolonged eye contact with Kingsley, continued to lead the way, her steps quickening as they ventured deeper into the heart of the city. She had no idea why she was nervous to be alone with King, but she was.

"Look, Kingsley," she exclaimed, her voice slightly hurried, "Those are ember crows. They're believed to bring luck and protection to the villagers." Perched on rooftops and trailing them closely, the crows were indeed a sight to behold.

"Fascinating," Kingsley replied, his eyes following the

graceful flight of the birds.

"They remind me of the fireflies back home" Lola interjected, trying to steer the conversation. "How they represent the unity and resilience of the people." She glanced at Kingsley, hoping he would catch her drift.

"I have heard of them but never seen them up close," Kingsley added.

"For many moonrises I have stood right here, just watching as their bellies light up." Her voice softened to a whisper as she continued. "They reminded me of your annoyingly beautiful eyes." She quickly looked away, fidgeting with the hem of her cloak and avoiding prolonged eye contact with him.

Now that the truth was out—now that she was his—Lola felt out of sorts.

"The stars align in mysterious ways," Lola whispered to herself, her voice barely audible over the crackling of the volcanic rocks beneath their feet.

"And sometimes, they lead us to places we never thought we'd go."

Kingsley turned to her, his gaze like two pools of liquid amber filled with an intensity that mirrored her own overwhelming emotions.

"I don't know what the future holds," he said softly, his voice tinged with vulnerability, his eyes searching hers for understanding. "But I do know that I don't want to face it without you, Lola. I need you by my side, always." As he spoke, Kingsley's usually confident demeanor softened, revealing the depth of his emotions and the sincerity of his words.

As Kingsley bared his heart, Lola's green eyes softened with emotion, reflecting her acceptance of his words and the depth of her own feelings for him.

"Let's head to your tent," he suggested with a playful smile, his voice low and filled with anticipation. "I can't wait to be alone with you."

Feeling the intensity of their connection, they hurried towards Lola's tent, eager for the privacy it promised and the intimacy they craved.

As they arrived at Lola's tent, a charged silence enveloped them, anticipation hanging in the air like a veil.

Lola's heart swelled as she looked into his eyes and saw the love and determination shining back at her. She knew she couldn't deny him. Stepping back, she began to unfasten the clasps of her cloak, the fabric falling away with each deliberate movement, baring herself not just physically but emotionally, ready to fully embrace the connection they shared.

As Lola's cloak fell to the ground, revealing her petite yet toned frame, Kingsley's heart raced with awe and tenderness. Her caramel-colored skin glowed in the soft light, accentuating the curves of her body. Her short bob framed her face, adding to her aura of confidence and allure. In that moment, he couldn't help but marvel at the beauty and strength radiating from the woman before him.

He watched her, his gaze filled with admiration and a growing sense of reverence for the woman standing before him, vulnerable yet strong.

As Kingsley stepped back, his olive skin glowing in the dim light, Lola couldn't help but admire the defined lines of his six-pack and the tall, lean stature that exuded strength and grace.

As he undressed, revealing more of his sculpted physique, Lola's breath caught in her throat. She felt a rush of magick spread through her veins, her pulse quickening at the sight of him. There was a raw, primal energy emanating from Kingsley, a magnetism that drew her in despite her best efforts to resist. In that moment, she realized just how deeply she was captivated by him, body and soul.

"Fine, I guess we are doing this betrothal thing," she said, her voice softening with amusement, a shy smile gracing her full lips. "But on one condition: you have to promise to trust me and let me be who I am, a warrior, who can defend herself."

As Kingsley caught Lola's gaze, warmth spread across his features, his eyes reflecting desire and admiration. With a gentle smile, he closed the distance between them.

He reached out, hesitating for a moment before

intertwining his hand with hers, a silent promise conveyed through his touch. "I know no finer warrior than you, princess."

In that moment, Kingsley's heart swelled with a newfound sense of purpose, knowing that with Lola by his side, they could conquer anything ahead.

Lola couldn't help but marvel at how much her demeanor had changed since meeting Kingsley. He made her feel more confident and capable, and she couldn't imagine going through this without him.

Under the canopy of night, amidst the whispered secrets of the volcanic city, Lola and Kingsley stood, their bodies drawn together as if by an unseen force. In a hushed, intimate exchange, Kingsley's fingertips delicately caress Lola's growing curls, his touch lingering with unspoken tenderness

As Kingsley's fingers tenderly trace the contours of Lola's shortened curls, he murmurs softly, "Your beauty transcends any length of hair, tesoro. You are simply radiant."

Lola's fingers trailed the dire wolf's scar before caressing Kingsley's body, each touch reflecting their intense desire. His fervent kisses ignited a long-suppressed passion within her.

"Your touch," Kingsley breathed, his voice raw with emotion, "it ignites something in me I can't explain."

Lola's fingers traced patterns on his skin as she replied,

"It's the same for me. With you, I feel alive."

Their words hung in the air, mingling with the heat of their bodies, as they continued to lose themselves in the intimate embrace of the night.

As Kingsley's fingers found their way to her breasts, Lola's breath caught in her throat, anticipation coursing through her veins. His words hung heavy in the air, a declaration of possession that stirred something deep within her, a sense of belonging that she had never known before.

Kingsley whispered into Lola's lips, "Here, before, now, and after," punctuating each word with a tender kiss. His touch, like the flickering flames, caressed her face.

"Here," he murmured, his voice a caress against her skin, "in this sacred space, I see the echoes of our past, the whispers of our future."

Lola's heart fluttered at his words, feeling the weight of their shared history and the promise their tomorrows intertwined.

"Before," Kingsley continued, his tone rich with reverence, "before we found each other, before our paths converged I was lost."

Lola's eyes shimmered with unshed tears, her heart overflowing with gratitude which led them to this moment.

"And now," Kingsley whispered, his voice tinged with awe, "now, as we stand on the precipice of forever, I vow to cherish every moment, knowing that our love transcends the confines of time and magick."

In the hushed stillness of the night, with the world falling away around them, Lola and Kingsley surrendered to the timeless embrace of their love, their souls intertwined in a dance that spanned here, before, now, and after.

"I am yours," she whispered, the words a quiet confession in the stillness of the night. "There is no one else but you."

Lola stood on her toes and pressed her lips against his. For a moment, shock to hold him. Then a deep groan escaped him as he slipped his tongue into her mouth.

"Fuck," he muttered over lips as he grabbed her as brining her closer to him. Lola knew there was no turning back.

Running her fingers through his hair she could taste mango wine on his breath. More than the wine, Lola could taste him. For the first time she could kiss this man. Her man. Without reservations, or fear of the future. He was hers and she was his. Breathless, and shaking from his touch nothing else mattered anymore. Reaching up as high as she could on her tippy toes she refused to come up for air as they consumed each other. Their tongues collided in a desperate struggle for more.

King growled over her lips.

"If you have any intention of leaving me again, please tell me to leave right now. Because once I start, I don't plan to leave an inch of you unmarked."

"I am yours." Is all she could say.

He locked her arms behind her back.

"You have always belonged to me tesoro."

His kiss was no longer gentle. The heat on the back of her neck was making her crazy. Her entire body went limp.

"I need you now," he panted in her ear.

"I need to fuck you hard, please don't tell me to stop."

"I won't."

Her nipples stiffened.

"Don't stop, please."

He slid his hands up her sides.

They surrendered to the intoxicating rhythm of their union, their bodies becoming one in a symphony of desire and longing. As Kingsley's hands traced the curves of her flesh, claiming her as his own, Lola felt a sense of connection that transcended mere physicality, a bond that bound them together in ways she had never imagined possible.

He gripped her hips and began to caress her new bioluminescent tattoo on her right shoulder. Three fireflies claimed the caramel space, drawing him in. He gently began to kiss the fireflies adoring her back, gripping her hips and gently grazing it with his tongue.

She became incredibly wet with an urgent need to have him inside of her.

Suddenly she felt his two fingers slide into her folds. "You are so fucking wet, Princess."

"Every touch," Kingsley murmured, his voice husky with desire, "is a reminder of how much I need you."

Lola's heart swelled with emotion as she whispered back, "And I need you, more than words can say."

He gripped her waist tighter when he whispered, "I need to taste it."

Without warning Lola felt his hot lips between her legs. He devoured her. Kneeling he continued to take ownership of her body. It was like a symphony of movements. His tongue thrusting in and out of her with great precision while he worked his fingertips over her clit, hitting all the right notes. Lola knew she could never walk away from this. From him.

Gazing up at her that reflected hunger and desire. Returning his mouth to her swollen clit, he sucked on it with a renewed enthusiasm. His sexy moan vibrated between her legs. As her fingers raked through his hair, Lola knew she was about to lose control.

"I want to feel you cum all over my mouth but right now, I need to feel you come while I'm inside of you."

Placing his forhead against hers he said, "Remember the last time I fucked you like this. You were gone before I could devour you a second time. Tonight, I won't sleep."

When Lola looked down and saw his engorged cock, she couldn't help but place her palm against the heat of his erection. He hissed at the contact and removed her hand before holding her into a firm embrace. In the quiet intimacy of their embrace, Kingsley and Lola found solace from the world's chaos. Kingsley whispered tenderly, "With you, everything feels right."

Running her palm in a line through his chest down to the trail of his hair at the base of his abs lola whispered, "I love your body."

"You are all it needs right now, Lola."

His chest was rising and falling as he stared at her breast before he took one into his mouth and sucked it hard. He was sucking so hard Lola knew it would hurt tomorrow. She didn't care.

Lola pulled away from him.

"Am, I'm hurting you, Tesoro."

"No."

Without further explanation she rose from the bed and dropped to her knees.

He immediately understood what came next.

Wrapping both of her hands around him, Lola marveled at the hot veiny shaft as she slowly began to swirl her tongue along his crown. Tasting the salty arousal as he throbbed in her mouth. Circling her tongue faster around his tip before she lowered her mouth around the entire length. When he reached the back of her throat, she moaned so that he could feel it.

"Fuck, are you trying to kill me," he rasped.

Without hesitation she began to take him faster. Rubbing the pre-cum all over his dick with her hand. The sounds of pleasure coming from King made her want to suck him dry.

Leaning his head back, King took everything she had to give.

"You are amazing. This is the best head ever"—he pulled her hair back—"but you need to stop."

Grabbing her hand, he gently guided her to the white furs before he said, "The next time I cum, I have to be inside you. So please princess, lie back." She obeyed. He spread her legs apart wide.

"Let me know if I am hurting you," were the last words he said before he slowly pushed inside of her. The girth of his cock stretched her. What started as almost painful soon consumed her with pleasure.

"I love you." His words were soft in her ear, almost like an apology considering the intense way he was making love to her.

Lola couldn't get enough. At one point she bucked her hips as he groaned, "Fuck, that feels good." He wrapped her legs around his back so that he could go even deeper as he fucked her.

Lola didn't want it to end. As primal as this moment was, it was also the most tender moment.

As Lola dug her nails into his back, clinging to him desperately, she realized that no other man could ever fulfill her like King. He was her sole satisfaction.

His pace quickened, accompanied by deep, labored breaths. She sensed he was nearing his climax.

"Look at me Lola, Look at me and tell me when you want me to come inside of you. I want you to feel what you do to me."

Lola felt herself climaxing, but words escaped her. Her green eyes flickered as they rolled to the back of her head.

As his body descended with a series of powerful thrusts, his climax surged through them, his release flooding inside her. King exclaimed as he reached orgasm, "Fuuucck, princess, yes, yes, fuuuucck."

It continued for some time as his thrusts grew more strained, until he eventually collapsed on top of her.

"Fuck, yes," she panted and laughed as she tried to catch her breath.

When he slowly pulled out of her he kissed her gently as he whispered, "You are mine."

In the stillness of the night, Lola's green magick shimmered softly, casting an ethereal glow that illuminated the tent around them. The gentle light danced upon their entwined forms, a silent testament to Lola's power and the magick that pulsed in her veins.

Kingsley couldn't help but chuckle softly, breaking the serene moment. "Well, I always knew you had a knack for lighting up a room, Tesoro. But this? This is next level."

And with a tender kiss, they drifted into a peaceful slumber, wrapped in each other's arms a verdant wave of magick encircled them.

CHAPTER 34

Beyond redemption

In the glow of the pink-hued Sirena Sea, Sole and Lola set foot on their homeland. The whispers of the ocean breeze carried stories of love, loss and lineage.

This was their home.

The journey from Grimerg Rise to Mōsa was tense, every crashing wave echoing with the weight of their purpose, while the air seemed to hold its breath in anticipation of their long-awaited homecoming.

As Lola and Kingsley stood together on the Radiant, the ship where Sole and Rivian first fell in love, Lola's gaze fell upon Thad at the foredeck.

She hadn't seen him since they'd boarded. He took his place below deck until they reached land, and in the light of the day, exhaustion was evident in his eyes.

Lola subtly motioned to Kingsley and whispered, "How is he doing?"

"I don't give a fuck how he's doing. He's been warned that if he comes near you, I will strike him down myself, unless Luce beats me to it."

"That won't help us now. We're about to go to war, and I can't doubt his loyalty."

Lola broke away from Kingsley and closed the distance between herself and Thad.

Their eyes met briefly before Kingsley reached to grab Lola's arm, torn between concern and a desire to shield her.

"What are you doing, love?" he muttered.

"Do you trust me?" Her eyes bore into his. There was a moment of hesitation before Kingsley replied, "Yes, I do, but—"

"Then let me do this. It's the only way."

He couldn't help but smile at her determination.

"Fine. I will be right here, Tesoro."

Lola placed her small hand on Kingsley's cheek, whispering softly.

"I love you for always wanting to protect me. But I must face this alone. It's the only way."

She gently kissed her mate before approaching Thad alone.

Lola and Thad stood face-to-face, the surrounding onlookers silent. The Misa, forming a protective crescent behind Lola, understood the significance of this moment. She had become their general, and they loved and respected her. If Thad intended harm, nothing would stop the Misa mages from cutting him through.

"You look like shit," Lola said bluntly, her tone laced with bitterness. She didn't hold back her anger, unable to mask the hurt.

Thad's weary smile faltered under her piercing gaze. "I fucking feel like it too," he retorted, the exhaustion in his voice only fueling her anger.

"Princess, I wanted to thank you for your kindness."

As he expressed his gratitude for her support, Lola's anger began to waver, but was quickly replaced by a stubborn resolve. She wasn't ready to forgive. She didn't know if she could ever forgive Thad or Mya for the part they played in her kidnapping.

"Don't think a few words will make everything okay," she seethed, her hand clenching into a fist. "You've betrayed us. You betrayed me. Prove yourself, Thad. We have a war to face, and your apologies won't be enough to erase what you've done, but if anyone can find redemption in all of this, it's you."

Thad nodded, deep shame weighing down his eyes.

"I appreciate the opportunity to make this right, Lola," he said, seeming truly sincere. "I know I have much to prove, not just to others, but to myself as well."

The air crackled with magick, the tension a palpable barrier between them. Despite her willingness to fight for their common cause, Lola couldn't simply brush aside how he had drugged her and let them do those horrid things to her.

As she turned to return to Kingsley, Thad spoke up again.

"What about us?"

Lola met Thad's gaze, taking a moment to gather her thoughts before responding.

"Trusting you again may take me a lifetime, or it may never happen. You shattered our trust in the worst way imaginable. You left me to suffer. Forgiveness still eludes me. But, perhaps in this battle you can find redemption. Only then can any of the past start to heal."

Thad's honey gaze locked with Lola's, gratitude shining through his tired eyes.

"I will prove my loyalty and fight alongside you." He swallowed. "Here before, now and after," was all Lola could say before she walked away.

***

As the suns kissed the horizon and stretched warm hues across the sky, the sisters felt a surge of determination, ready to reclaim their land and rewrite the future. But on this day, their mission was smaller in scope. More urgent.

Sole had given an order to retrieve Rivian at all cost. Lola couldn't comprehend how her sister still harbored love for Rivian, their sworn enemy, but she would obey regardless. Her sister needed support, so she would do as she was told.

"Are the Misa ready?" Sole asked, eyeing Lola and Kings-ley's intertwined hands.

"Yes. They are ready," Lola proudly stated.

Sole had been mesmerized by Lola since their reunion. Her little sister was really beginning to resemble their mother in every way. Lola stood tall, adorned in her fitted, rose-gold armor. Her short hair had been braided intricately into cornrows, a testament to her heritage even after losing her long curls. As the sunlight caught the surface of her armor, she began to glow. Bioluminescent gold war paint was smeared across her face, accentuating her emerald eyes.

Gazing out at the vast expanse before her, Lola's heart beat in harmony with the rhythm of the sea. Turning to face her sister, Lola also saw Sole stepping into her new light.

Fearless. Relentless. A warrior queen.

In contrast to the Misa that stood before her, Sole was clad in sleek, black armor befitting of her regal stature. The armor hugged her form with precision. Dark war paint, meticulously applied in shades of deep indigo and charcoal, pulsated in the sunlight, turning the same shade of purple as her magick.

And her violet eyes were striking as they beat with enchanted energy. Her eyes bore the weight of the burden of leadership, and the immutable love she had for her people.

She was ready for war.

CHAPTER 35

Darkness descends

The island was dark and eerily quiet.

The sound of crashing waves was all Sole could hear as the moons rose, quite the contrary to the realm she left behind. The jungle was dense and foreign; it would be difficult for the Misa to move quickly. The warriors were on high alert.

"Shall we sister?" Lola eagerly asked.

"Yes. Tonight, we will make them bleed!" Sole whispered.

"I have to say I like the new you, Sole," Lola said, eyes smiling.

Standing on the Radiant, Sole raised her voice, watching over the warriors.

"Misa, hear me now!" she called. "Tonight, we stand on the precipice of battle, facing a formidable adversary. Nasir seeks to tear apart the very fabric of Transea and claim what is ours. But we shall not yield, we shall not falter!"

With a swift motion, Sole drew her sword from its sheath, holding it aloft as if wielding the very essence of their cause.

"In this hour, I invoke the ancient magick that courses through our veins, a gift from the Holy Mother, a legacy of valor and fidelity passed down through generations. Our strength lies not only in steel and armor, but in the unity of our magick!"

The Misa respond fervently, their agreement a chorus of unwavering support. Sole pressed on, her gaze alight with unwavering resolve. "The time has come to reclaim Rivian, a quest laden with the weight of our history and the promise of our destiny. Our adversaries may underestimate us, but we shall shatter their illusions. We are the Misa. Our heritage demands that we rise to this challenge!"

As if in response to her call, Sole raised her sword even higher, a beacon of hope in the encroaching shadows. The Misa mirrored her actions, a sea of determined faces illuminated by the flickering flames of defiance. "Here, before, now, and after! Let our war cries resound through the veins of our foes. Here, before, now, and after! Let our enemies tremble in the face of our unwavering might. Here, before, now, and after!"

The warriors chorused her chant in the language of Grimerg Rise. "Kilthar, azenoth, arakor!"

The air around them rippled with the force of their voices as their magick rose and the ground beneath their feet trembled.

Approaching the clearing where Prince Rivian was, the

battle grew louder. Swords clanged, bodies thudded, and magick crackled in the air. The Misa moved in formation, shielding their Queen. Surrounded by Nasir's soldiers, Prince Rivian stood before them, his blonde hair unkempt and his bright blue eyes wild with rage.

High Queen Sole stepped forward, her purple eyes glowing.

"Rivian," she said, her voice calm with resolve. "I've come to take you home."

Rivian's once familiar features were shrouded in darkness, as if the light within him had dimmed. His sandy blonde hair, now longer in the back, framed his face, but his eyes were weighed down by dark circles and fatigue. He'd grown a shaggy beard that showed just how much time had passed since Sole had last seen him.

Sole feels the walls he built around himself, the barriers that shielded him from further pain.

He said nothing. Sole spoke again, this time just to him.

"Rivian, please listen," she begged. "I know it's been a long and difficult journey for you, but we're here to help, to bring you back to where you truly belong. Our home awaits, filled with people who care for you."

At that very moment, Luce and Kia stepped forward and positioned themselves beside Lola and Sole. Zari would have been there too, had he not been summoned to Sundom, but his spirit fought alongside his fellow soldiers.

"Brother, it's good to see that you are still as confident as ever. Even if we will cut your men through," Kia quipped.

Rivian stepped closer to Sole, his armed men following suit. His words cut through the air like a blade, seething anger threatening to consume him.

"Home?" he scoffed, his nose wrinkling as though he smelled something putrid. "You dare to speak to me about home? The Queen of Nothing is offering me a place by her side."

He spat each word out so she was sure to hear him.

"Tell me, Queen Sole, was my mere presence in your bedchamber enough to cloud your judgment? Was my touch so intoxicating that you would sacrifice your people, your kingdom, to save me...a traitor?"

He turned to face his men.

"I guess the rumors are true, my cock is magickal!"

Luce wore the most disgusted expression as he tried to redirect Rivian's venom away from Sole and onto himself. He spoke as if trying to provoke Rivian. "I see you're still bragging about all the women you've bedded, brother."

Sole knew that bringing Rivian home was not going to be an easy task, but there was something in his eyes...a flicker of hope that he was still in there. It was enough to ignite her desire for reconciliation again.

"We will find a way, Rivian," she assured him. "Together, we will forge a new path and rebuild what was lost."

His icy gaze held no recognition of her. In his mind, she was just another enemy, someone who seeks to do him harm. To do Nasir harm. Without hesitation, he raised his hand, summoning a blast of golden magick.

Standing steadfast beside Sole, Lola's presence was a force of nature unto itself. With a swift and graceful motion, she called upon the ancient bond between herself and the natural world, tapping into the wellspring of green magick that flowed through her veins.

As her eyes flashed brightly, a symphony of leaves rustled in response, trees swaying in harmonious rhythm and the very earth beneath their feet stirring with vitality. With a flick of her wrist and a whispered incantation, Lola wove her magick into the fabric of the land itself.

The surrounding flora rose to her call, intertwining to form a protective barrier against Rivian's encroaching forces. Like a fortress of living green, the land rallied to their defense.

"So this is your lover, Sole? Remind me to have a discussion with you about dating the wrong men!"

Even amidst the chaos, Lola's quick tongue couldn't be contained.

Rivian's fury surged like wildfire. With each passing moment, his magick grew in ferocity, crackling like lightning across the battlefield. Despite his formidable power, he remained ensnared in the chains of his own inner turmoil, the weight of his conflicted soul evident in every strained movement beneath the burden of his black leather armor.

As he charged forward, his very presence igniting the air with tension, his eyes were ablaze with a primal hunger for dominance. The Misa warriors, undaunted by the tempest that approached them, swiftly positioned themselves against the impending onslaught. Their bodies became a shield.

As Rivian's magick crashed against their defenses, the Misa wove their own spells into the fabric of the battlefield, conjuring barriers of shimmering energy that crackled with raw power.

Rivian's enchanted soldiers surged forward to unleash a tide of darkness upon the battlefield, but the Misa warriors moved with unmatched grace and lethality. Their movements were a dance of death, each strike infused with the potent magick that coursed through their veins as they razed their way through the enemy forces like a scythe through a wheatfield.

Blades flashed and whirled through the air, which was thick with the scent of sweat and steel.

Rivian's soldiers pressed forward with unrelenting fervor, but the ethereal black mist that once comprised their formidable ranks swirled and dissipated, leaving naught but empty air in their wake.

The Misa radiated vibrant magick that swirled around

them, each member a living conduit for a spectrum of colors.

Fiery reds and sizzling golds streaked across the battlefield, leaving trails of scorching heat in their wake as the Misa wielded their powers with practiced precision. Verdant greens and azure blues dance in harmony, their movements mirroring the grace of nature itself, while the deeper, darker shade of purple pulsed ominously—a power held by Sole alone.

The Misa were not merely warriors; they were mages of unparalleled skill, masters of the long forgotten arts of magick. And as the last echoes of battle faded into the distance, the Misa stood victorious.

As they advanced across the sand, Sole feared that, if the battle continued, the Misa would have no choice but to kill Rivian. She couldn't have that.

Holding her tears at bay, she tried to weaken him with her magick, sending waves of her deep dark purple his way.

His magick had undeniably grown in power, as had hers; the only difference was Nasir's influence on Rivian.

The clash of enchanted swords echoed across the clearing with Lola watching from the sidelines.

Her emerald green eyes glowed as she channeled energy from the furthest depths of her magick. With each breath, she felt the raw power course through her veins. As her focus sharpened, the sand beneath her feet stirred, responding to her command. It swirled in intricate patterns, circling the remaining warriors that Rivian had unleashed.

With a gesture of her outstretched hand, Lola called upon the crystal pink sands of Mōsa. The sands gathered to form a massive, towering wall between the Misa and the malevolent forces opposing them.

With an outcry, Lola sent the wall collapsing down upon the enemy in a ferocious wave of mauve and moss glass shards, turning the barrier into a deadly weapon.

The shattering of the shards drowned out the cries of those they came down upon.

Jumping from the rubble of the glass, Rivian stumbled and looked down at the shards piercing his skin. With a squelch, he yanked the largest shard from his right thigh, crimson dripping down his leg. He roared in rage.

With one flick of her wrist, Lola commanded the vines from the jungle to meet her on the beach. It was taxing on her energy levels, but she pushed forward. Rescuing Rivian was her duty to Sole.

Slithering across the sands, the vines quickly entwined around the prince's body, attempting to tackle him. They crawled over his skin and coiled around his limbs like living ropes, but Lola could feel his resistance building.

The vines wove a cage—one that she prayed would immobilize him. She called on the strength of the roots and the steadfastness of the land to bolster her desire.

The prince's magick was formidable, and it fought against her with all his might, but Lola's cage was a work of art. Rivian looked both powerful and helpless at the same time, his muscles straining against the roots and vines. His chest heaved with exertion as he struggled against his restraints.

Slowly, the cage began to shrink, compressing around him until he was completely immobilized. Lola stood panting, sweat glistening on her forehead.

As Sole made her way through the dense jungle, the guttural screams of her beloved echoed across the beach, sending a pang of urgency through her heart. She knew Rivian was in pain.

He was a savage version of the man she used to love, but her heart ached for him nonetheless.

"Leave us!" Sole commanded her army as she laid eyes on Rivian. When the soldiers hesitated, she screamed,

"I said NOW!"

Reluctantly, the soldiers obeyed, dispersing from the area and leaving the two sisters beside the prince. Sole had to give her sister credit. She had managed to subdue him without outright ending his life.

With a heavy heart, Sole approached Rivian, her eyes filled with both love and sorrow.

"I know you are not yourself, but I believe the man I love is still in there somewhere, Rivian. If you can hear me, my love, I am here for you. I will protect you."

Sole gently reached out, her fingers trembling with hope, but her heart shattered as Rivian recoiled from her touch, his icy glare filled with disgust.

"Rivian," she continued. "All my memories of you feel like magick. We will be magick once more, together..." She pressed her forehead against his through the vines. In the vulnerable moment, she whispered, "I am the High Queen of the Western Isles, and I am here to fight for you, Rivian. No matter the trials we face, I will see you safe."

His eyes narrowed with bitterness.

"You talk of memories, of a love that feels like magick. But all I have now are scars. Nightmares that haunt me every damn night! Don't you dare speak to me of love, for you know nothing of the darkness I endured because of your love."

His words impaled Sole like daggers, each one piercing through her defenses and reopening wounds she thought had healed. The pain in his voice was twisted with resentment.

"You speak of safety and protection, but it was you who left Nisa unprotected, leaving me to suffer in the clutches of your enemy. She died because of you! I am here because of you! Your presence here means nothing to me! I am beyond your reach now, just as you are beyond redemption."

Sole's heart sank under the weight of his words, and she struggled to hold back tears.

But even with all the blows she'd taken, Sole was deter-mined to find a way back to the man she loved.

She was not going to give up.

CHAPTER 36

Into the darkness

Sole placed her mask back on her face, doing what she could to conceal herself and her shattered heart from her people. She summoned every ounce of bravery within her and turned away from Rivian, making her way towards Luce, Lola, and Rory. As she looked around the battlefield, she felt a growing sense of frustration. She had come to the island of Mōsa to rescue Prince Rivian and defeat Nasir's forces. The battle was over. They won. But it didn't feel like it was over. It wasn't enough. She needed revenge.

She wanted to kill Nasir.

Sole knew that Nasir was a cunning strategist, a truth that has her stomach sinking as she feared that he wasn't hiding from her, but waiting for her to come searching for him. Never mind his reasons. Hiding during the chaos of such a battle like a coward was all the more reason she needed to hunt him down. She turned to Rory, surrounded by the Misa as they tended to the wounded and fallen soldiers. They, too, looked weary from the battle. Weary,

Prince Nasir Asha

but determined to see the journey through.

"We need to find Nasir," Sole demanded. "He can't continue this reign of terror any longer." She waited for Rory to look her dead in the eye, then she spoke her next words with so much vigor it was as if the battleground quaked beneath her boots.

"I will make him pay for what he's stolen from me. For Nisa and my kingdom."

"Let's go get that fucker!" Lola exclaimed, her fiery spirit amusing and inspiring to her older sister. But Lola was needed for another matter.

"No," Sole said. "You will stay with Rivian and ensure his safe return to Grimerg Rise. -Lola's resolve wavered, emotions swirling within her, but ultimately she nodded in reluctant agreement. Fear and determination battled for dominance on her features as she made her decision.

"Yes, my queen."

Sole raised her mask over her face.

"Then it's settled. Kingsley, Thad, Luce, your task is to protect my sister and Rivian, and to stop for no one. Leave at once." Sole looked to the Misa nodding in agreement. Their armor glints in the moonlight, the sheen as unwavering as their loyalty; they would stand by their queen's side until the bitter end.

Unable to join them, Lola's heart sank. It didn't matter who was watching. She confronted her sister with a desperate plea.

"Don't ask me to do this, Sole! Don't ask me to leave you behind."

"Lola, you will do as I say," Sole asserted. She placed a soft hand on her sister's shoulder. "Only you can keep Rivian safe. Only you can protect the others from Nasir's wrath. And who will care for Luna if something were to happen to both of us? She is defenseless."

Lola's emotions intertwined with her powerful magick, as were her sister's. There was an unseen but ever-growing energy swirling between them in their eyes and in the air.

Lola exhaled sharply.

"Is this a fucking order?"

"Yes, it is an order," Sole confirmed without hesitation. With that, she turned to the Misa.

"I will embark on the search for Nasir. He must be brought to justice, and he must pay for his heinous acts. General Lola will be in charge in my absence. Now, go!"

With a heavy heart, Lola agreed to protect Rivian.

As the warriors dispersed, each accepting their role, Lola took a deep breath and prepared herself for the immense responsibility that lay ahead. A part of her wanted to defy her sister's wishes, but she pushed the immature impulse down. Sole had entrusted her with far too much for her to sacrifice it all to emotion now. The magick bubbling up in her chest began to flow down to her feet, and the frustration dissipated. With Kingsley, Sirena, Melia, Thad, and Luce by her side, she would do everything in her power to keep Rivian safe and uphold the trust placed upon her by Sole. It was about putting her troubles aside for the sake of the greater good.

Something her mother would do.

Sole adjusted her mask, readied her weapon, and prepared to shove off, but Lola grabbed her sister's wrist and looked into her eyes one last time.

"Here before, now and after," Lola whispered.

"Here, before, now and after," Sole replied with a gentle kiss on her little sister's forehead.

***

The longer they searched the island, the more Sole's agitation grew. Blood pulsed through her veins as she swiped at the sweat accumulating on her brow. Nasir was a master of deception; he could be hiding anywhere. A chameleon when pushed to survive, Nasir had learned through extensive training and experience how to turn any landscape into the snuggest of camouflages. If anyone was going to find him, it would have to be someone on his level. Someone relentless. Staunch.

Sole was not only capable of rising to the occasion, but she had the fate of her people resting on her shoulders as well. Their safety, their culture, and their lives were one hell of a motivator.

Hours into the search, Rory finally uncovered a shred of hope in the form of a clue; a swatch torn from Nasir's tunic clung to a branch. Sole recognized it immediately from Nasir's mating ceremony attire.

"Nasir's refuge?" Rory asked.

It was on part of the island Sole had only ever visited once.

With Nasir himself, she remembered.

Her eyes scanned the area. Anticipation sizzled in the air as her magick rose, radiating from her eyes, locs of her hair, and her fingertips.

Dammit.

Did Nasir simply vanish into thin air? Managing to slip away unnoticed would be quite the feat, but it wasn't impossible. Especially not for him.

"My Queen…" Rory hissed quickly, gesturing to a small rustling slithering from the bushes. Then…crack!

Swiftly, Sole signaled her army of five to take cover, all instincts honing in on the threat. Her magick was primed for action as she approached the bushes with measured caution. Her entire body buzzed as she drew her weapon.

A ripple of thunder sounded, and a concealed entrance materialized right before their eyes. A cave entrance—the beginning of a labyrinthine network of caves. She could see it; she could feel it now. Nasir was lurking within the dark recesses of the caves.

Her instincts compelled her forward.

"I'm going to venture forth alone," she told Rory.

Bracing herself, Sole stepped into the cave, casting a glow with her magick to vanquish the darkness. The dampness of the cavern would certainly envelop her if she didn't keep her wits about her. Faint echoes of lost souls sounded through the subterranean labyrinth, sending chills up and down her spine. There was far more to this cave than meets the eyes.

What was this place? And how had Nasir found it?

She delved deeper, her heart pounding in rhythm with the encroaching shadows. She couldn't stop moving.

The tight passages of the cave started to release, expanding and opening to a larger section that showed to be the very heart of the darkness. And there in front of her, standing alone with such a stillness, was Nasir—the ghost of the man that he used to be.

The glow of her magick captured the glint in his eyes. He didn't flinch. He had been waiting for her. The man she used to love. A dark smile played across his lips as he eyed her with a morbid curiosity. He was not the man she remembered, but neither was Sole the fragile woman he had once known.

"I must say, wife," Nasir snarled. "Black suits you." His

hands stretched out from behind his back, his eyes dark and fixed on her with an animalistic desire and rage ready to devour her whole. The look in his eyes...so devoid of love.

Her stomach felt repulsed, and her heart ached. "My Queen?"

Rory's panicked voice echoed from the far away entrance of the cave, faint as a whisper by the time it reached Sole's ear.

Sole kept her eyes on Nasir for a moment longer before crying out, "I am here! He is here!"

"Don't move, we're coming!" Rory yelled. Suddenly, a menacing growl erupted from the land beneath them and the walls of the cave. Magick surged from Sole's fingertips, but it was too late. Nasir sent a striking blast crashing through her defenses, propelling her forcefully to the ground. His sinister magick sealed the cave entrance, barring the valiant Misa warriors from intervening. Sole was trapped—alone with him.

Nasir sauntered over to her with long steps, gliding through the darkness like a ghoulish fiend. He bent down and yanked her up by her hair, pressing his lips to her face, his rancid breath hot on her skin.

"I was nauseated by all the gowns you wore while the rest of the world lay dying," he snickered. "This black armor demands attention. Even from a monster like me."

He forced her to look him in the eye, his own small windows into a bleak abyss. In a cruel power move, his tongue slithered out and swiped over her cheek.

Sole used to yearn for his touch—his lips. But she was utterly repulsed by him.

He tossed her back to the ground. She braced herself and rose to her feet, blasting him with a pulse of electric purple energy. Nasir faltered for only a moment before casting a lasso of energy forth.

She gritted her teeth and gasped, fighting against the grip of Nasir's oppressive magick. Every one of her muscles strained, unyielding. She did what she could to settle into a stance. With a flick of her wrist, Sole unleashed a new and powerful wave of purple magick, its vibrant hue pulsating as it surged forward, colliding with Nasir's dark magick in a tumultuous boom. The cave trembled as their forces wrestled for dominance, sparks of arcane energy spattering into the air.

Nasir grinned, almost aroused by Sole's resolve.

"You've grown stronger, wife. It's a shame your might isn't going to be enough."

He exhaled through his nose, a plume of black smoke escaping his nostrils as his stream of magick pulsed with more vigor.

"Enough of this, Nasir!" Sole snapped, refusing to yield to his taunts.

She continued her assault, unleashing a torrent of magick in swift, calculated movements. She needed to adapt if she was going to maintain her strength and withstand his brute force. Nasir countered Sole's onslaught with a strike of his own, breaking the chain between them. He rolled to the right to evade blast of hers, swirling dark magick around him. It coiled like a serpent ready to defend him to its final breath.

The eerie grace in which he fought enraged Sole. It was as if this was a game to him.

Sweat dripped down her brow and her breath came out in ragged gasps.

Nasir saw that she was tired. A stream of his magick flew forth like a tentacle, whipping her across the face. Sole cried out in pain.

"Feeble bitch. You were never meant to defeat me." His voice dripped with satisfaction. "This resistance is nothing more than a fleeting illusion."

This sick smile on his face faded into a dark frown as he glided closer toward her.

"I see now what that boy sees in you. Did he tell you about the nights he awoke only to remember what he had done to you…his mate? Can you believe that fucker tried to claim you, knowing you are mine?"

"I belong to no one who doesn't respect me!" Sole bellowed. "You've lost the privilege, Nasir."

She mustered all her remaining strength, calling upon the depths of her magick and spirit as more tentacles threatened to burst from Nasir's defensive coil.

"Have I really lost control?" he taunted.

"You have."

A wave of purple fire erupted from her palms. Nasir grunted in pain, casting his blasts in a frenzy in an effort to regain the upper hand. But Sole's lavender flames were too much. Finally, she gained traction and stepped closer. And closer.

"No!" Nasir screamed. A dark, thick cloud of smoke poured from his throat and extinguished the brilliant fire, sending Sole stumbling backward. Her breathing was shallow, her body battered and bruised, but still, the warrior queen locked eyes with the dark prince in abject defiance.

"You haven't won, Nasir," she exhaled loudly. "This war is far from over. We will never surrender. I will never surrender to you or the darkness."

Nasir smirked, his snide, premature sense of victory looming over her.

"Oh, my dear Sole, you can't resist forever. Look at you, you can barely stand."

He lunged toward her, pulling her in with his energy. A clammy hand gripped her face.

"I am going to extinguish that pesky little light from your eyes."

He raised his hand, delivering a final strike to her temple that sent her to her knees. She swore her head felt like it had split in two.

"You are a pathetic little girl, playing dress up in her mother's clothes," Nasir taunted. "Venturing here alone, forsaking the protection of your loyal sister and broken lover. You are still just a child."

Sole's indomitable spirit burned brighter than ever before. A fierce luminescence ignited her synapses, but even as her defiance blazed, Sole was met with the stark realization that he was right.

Her powers alone weren't enough to vanquish Nasir. She knew that. She needed her army, and she needed her sisters. Frustration coursed through her veins as she gritted her teeth against the numbing pains of Nasir's relentless assault. She wriggled out of his grip and shoved him back.

She was met with a sadistic smirk, his eyes ablaze with delight.

"I can see why he desires you, Sole. Oh, yes. The Nasir you loved...he wanted you, craved you. I, too, harbor a desire for you, however small it might be."

She reached up to smack him, but he grabbed her hand in midair. "After all, you are my wife, bound to me by a cruel fate."

The cavern shuddered in response to his venomous words, the air thickening with malevolence.

"Perhaps you didn't hear me the first time," Sole choked out, gaining spiteful strength with every word. "You have lost the privilege. I am no longer yours, and you hold no sway over me."

Nasir's eyes gleamed as he relished the moment. "How naive you are. You cannot escape what the Hoy Mother has bestowed upon us. You will learn, in due time, that resistance is futile."

Dark magick crept from his hand, ensnaring Sole in a suffocating hold. She fought against the tendrils of darkness for as long as she could, but as they snaked around her torso and her neck, the little resolve she had left began to seep away.

"I...will...not—" she gasped. "I will...see...you...dead." Nasir laughed in a chilling, booming symphony that was the last thing Sole heard before her vision blurred and the world went black. Nasir triumphantly scooped her into his arms, her motionless body cradled against him. He gripped her like an animal guarding its meal.

The protective veil that sealed the cave's entrance melted away. Just as the Misa warriors surged forward to confront him, Nasir vanished into thin air with the High Queen of the Western Isles in his arms. A collective gasp seized the group.

The High Queen, whisked away.

Rory stood with her jaw hanging open and tears in her

413

eyes, her outstretched hand grasping the space where Sole had just been. But she was gone, and the Misa warriors were left standing at the precipice of an uncertain future.

EPILOGUE

Her eyes flickered open.

Instead of the familiar sight of her bedroom, she was met with total darkness. Her heart raced, fear crawling through her body. How did she get here? She tried to move, but her body was heavy and unresponsive—as if she had been asleep for an eternity.

Where am I? What is happening?

"Help! Help! Heeeelp me—"

She attempted to call out only to have her cries stifled by the thick air—dank, musty, and cold. A small sliver of warm light peeked in from a crack ahead. It was dim, but as her eyes adjusted, she suddenly realized where she was.

She was in a crypt.

The scent of incense and burning oil was strong, but it wasn't not enough to choke out the putrid scent of decay.

A corpse was beside her.

She fought the urge to be sick and quickly writhed away, suddenly gaining control of her body again. She rose to her feet and found her legs aching and weak. The crypt was still and quiet. She started to shake.

Who had put her here?

The silence only amplified her fear. She carefully walked to the right, groping the wall and cautiously navigating in the dark. Her fingertips found caskets, and she prays she won't brush against another body. The walls of the crypt seemed as if they were closing in on her.

As she squinted at the light, she realized that it was flickering. A torch on the other side of a door. A hallway? So not just a crypt, but a mausoleum. Blinking to adjust her vision, she slowly began to make out symbols etched into the walls, stone shelves, and recesses.

Suddenly, she heard footsteps—boots on a stone floor. Someone was coming down the hall. The door slowly groaned open and a shadowy figure materialized in front of her. She couldn't see its face.

She dropped her arms to her side silently, realizing that she was naked. She hid in the corner, clinging to the wall and hoping she wouldn't be seen.

The figure dumped another body into the crypt, then left.

Counting the footsteps, then the seconds, she waited until she was well alone again before making her way to the door. Her whole body still felt hazy and numb. Had she been drugged? Or unconscious for a long time? She struggled but managed to pry open the door and slip out.

Feeling her way around the chamber, she eventually found a set of stairs leading upward. She crawled towards them, her movements slow and labored, as she tried to move as inconspicuously as possible.

Finally, she emerged out into the desert.

Her eyes burned. The harsh light of Sundom—the two suns—seared into her like a hot iron. The scorching, dry heat choked her as she tried to take in a breath.

It is a sensation she was all too familiar with, but it still made her skin prickle and her eyes hurt as she took in her surroundings. She stumbled forward, her feet sinking deep into the sand with each step.

"Halt!" A voice commanded.

She turned to see two Sunguards, their weapons drawn. Their golden armor glinted in the harsh light, polished to a high shine so bright they were practically glowing.

The shoulders and gauntlets were curved and sharp, ready for battle, but it was the swords that caught her attention. Long and slender, their handles were made of the same shining gold as the armor—deadly and beautiful at the same time. These Sunguards were not to be trifled with.

But she didn't flinch, nor did she show any sign of embarrassment for her appearance. Instead, she looked them straight in the eye and spoke with authority, her voice cracking from lack of use.

"Find me your king," she commanded. "And tell me what he has done with my queen."

The guards were taken aback, not by her nakedness but by her mere presence. One of them stepped forward in shock, offering her his crimson cloak.

"Lady Nisa," he said respectfully, "let us take you to the king."

Nisa set off with the guards, determined to find the answers she sought and to reclaim her rightful place in the world.

ACKNOWLEDGMENTS

Writing a book is a challenging endeavor that tests my strength and resilience. Writing a second book is even more challenging than the first. Yet, amidst the difficulties and sleepless nights, I find a deep sense of fulfillment. Often overlooked are the late nights, the moments when you feel like quitting, and the increasing difficulty of writing due to agonizig hand pain. This novel has enlightened me to the fact that I cannot accomplish it all by myself. Therefore, I heavily relied on my fellow indie authors and my family for support.

I would also like to express my appreciation to my son, Jaden, whose imaginative spirit has helped me visualize a world filled with science and magic. Being your mom fills me with gratitude every day.

This novel tells my family's story in many ways, navigating the challenges of entering a new world marked by prejudice and loss. It is also a testament to resilience, power, and profound love. The characters in Mōsa represent my deep connection to my Dominican heritage and its people.

I extend my eternal gratitude to my Mami Ligia, who

instilled in me the belief that I was destined to write. Her influence inspired the development of the character Queen Lygia, and she will always be a queen in my eyes.

Thanks to ABC Editorial for ensuring the novel was ready for readers to devour. Your editing skills are unmatched.

I extend my heartfelt gratitude to my incredible creative "team", my husband, Jade. Without his unwavering support, this achievement would not have been possible. His exceptional creativity, late-night conversations about characters, and invaluable assistance in shaping the world of "Magick" have been instrumental. I am deeply appreciative of his contribution in bringing our vision for the book cover to life. Jade, your boundless brilliance knows no limits, and I am truly grateful for your remarkable talent. Thank you for being my real-life Kingsley and for making this journey unforgettable.

To my readers. This book was made possible because of you. Thank you for loving Mōsa and its people. I hope this story inspires you.

xoxo,

Ligia

ABOUT THE AUTHOR

Ligia is a Dominican American writer. Born in New York City. She spent many summers falling in love with the warm sandy beaches and Mangú of the Dominican Republic. All while reading exquisite fantasy romance novels.

Those experiences inspire world-building in her novels. Graduating with two master's degrees in counseling and human services drives how she brings her characters to life. Ligia is located in Tampa, FL, where she enjoys brunch and travel with her husband, son, and their two Mini Aussies, Jake, and Ollie.

GRIMERG RISE

SANCTUM

THE
VENTANE
WOODS

HOUSE OF
DO'RAMOS

KINGGUARD'S REEF

GALAMEDA
BRIDGE

MENELIK
ATHENAEUM

HOUSE OF
PORTE

MŌSA

EX IRIS
EXPANSE

THE
SANCTUARY

THE GREAT LANDS OF
TRANSEA

THE SIRENA SEA
THE KENALI GARDENS
HOUSE OF ALACOR
SUNDOM
THE DARK WILDS
HOUSE OF AVIREL
AZURE COVE
THE AZURE MARKET

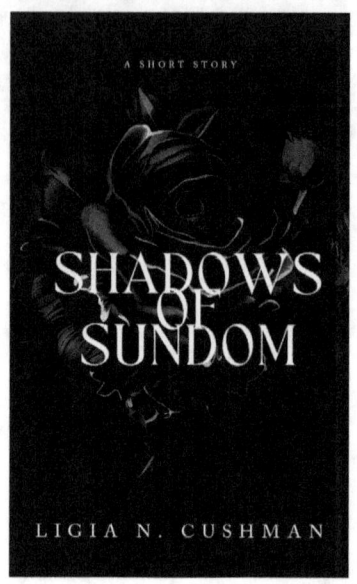

SHADOWS OF SUNDOM

In the heart-pounding prequel of The Mōsa Chronicles, two sisters with an unbreakable bond must navigate the treacherous world of Sundom, where one is betrothed to her ruthless enemy while the other faces unspeakable odds, setting the stage for an epic tale of survival, forbidden love and femme rage to defy the darkness threatening to consume them all.

Scan to read online.

RISE OF A DARK THRONE

When Sole Porte is healed from the darkness, a terrifying plague that killed her family, she awakens with the one thing she never wanted…magick. She soon discovers her unique powers can save Transea by curing the traitorous King of Sundom. Sole finds herself navigating a dark web of politics and betrayal in the land of her enemy.

www.ingramcontent.com/pod-product-compliance
Lightning Source LLC
Chambersburg PA
CBHW050915030726
47503CB00007BB/2310